⅄ Reviews and Personal R... ...... t. ....

(Your book) is I think a remarkable and very valuable achievement. A modern parable, allegory, myth or whatever one might call it, that has the potentiality of making the essence of Christianity accessible to the average 21st century inhabitant of the UK - something which we theologians and preachers try to do, but we don't seem to get very far!... I do think you and I would be in very large measure of agreement. Inevitably there would be some differences at some points, but it would take hours to discuss all the topics about which you have written.

John Macquarrie, author of 'Principles of Christian Theology.' *etc., personal communication.*

(Your book) is a powerful way of presenting some very interesting insights in a coherent and vivid way… I enjoyed the liberal theological reflections on the views of God and Jesus particularly. The sections drawing from science and the parallels in mystical experience are fascinating.

Ian Barbour, author of 'Religion in an Age of Science.' *etc., personal communication.*

I have been interested by your book *'What is Happening?'* though I take a more quizzical view than you do of Whiteheadian and Jungian thinking and I think that there is rather more to say about Yeshua than you express. I do agree that myth, properly understood, is an important avenue of approach to truth ('a raft to float on seas too deep for knowledge'), someone once said.

John Polkinghorne, author of 'Science & Religion in Quest of Truth' *etc., personal communication.*

What's the meaning of it all? We all ask ourselves 'big' questions like this at times. This pseudonymous book… offers a series of visionary dialogues between the narrator… and a supernatural 'Mediator', with whom he tackles a huge range of these 'big' questions. The nature of the physical universe; the nature of time; human psychology; biblical criticism; the future of human kind; the nature of God; all are grist to their conversational mill… The author is clearly very well-read, although his take on some of the matters discussed is a little eccentric (and) the theological viewpoint of the book is sometimes unortho-dox... it is no less stimulating for that... A way of looking at this book might be to see it as a response to its own plea for a re-introduction of stories and myths into our understanding of reality...

Michael Fuller, reviewed in 'Inspires' *Feb 2006.*

I found the discussion of human psychology and of the nature of Jesus helpful. The relationship of the Trinity and the ongoing purpose of creation were also very meaningful. The emphasis on *Now*, the Present Moment, resonates with De Caussade's *Sacrament of the Present Moment*. But I think the whole system... hangs together without the support of metempsychosis. I my opinion, this is a myth too far.

John Howard, reviewed in 'The Edge' November 2005.

Your book is admirable in its clarity, faith and scope. It is easy for specialists to ignore the big questions posed by modern cosmology, especially as they are so troublesome. I recently suggested at a sym-posium that we may still be living in the age of the early church. If it is still around in 100K years time, then probably we will be regarded by our successors as quite primitive in various respects. So it is bracing to read of your reflections and the scale in which they are set... (Your book) may trigger some further thoughts as I prepare the Gifford Lectures for delivery in Glasgow next spring.

David Fergusson, personal communication.

This (is a) very special book: and thank you for writing it. I have read it with great interest. (I) have found much that is stimulating, a great many new insights, and of course some things I would want to challenge. I greatly enjoyed your method, in which I found strong echoes of Plato, Socrates, John Bunyan, CS Lewis and JK Rowling! I found it especially interesting because of my own interest in the escha-tology of the interfaith dialogue, and because of your informed and serious discussion of interplanetary migration... I found much that was helpful and penetrating in your discussion of the Trinity and the various triads of (values and virtues)... I have found similar interest in some Indian triads like *sat, chit, ananda* and the three *margas* of *jnana, bhakti and karma.*

Robin Boyd, author of 'The Witness of the Student Christian Movement.' *personal communication.*

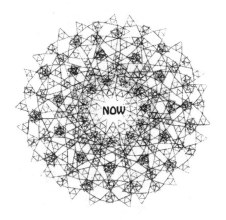

NOW

What is Happening?

A Mystical Dialogue

by

N. E. Boddy

Order this book online at www.trafford.com
or email orders@trafford.com

Most Trafford titles are also available at major online book retailers.

Note for Librarians: A cataloguing record for this book is available from Library
and Archives Canada at www.collectionscanada.ca/amicus/index-e.html

Printed in the United States of America.

ISBN: 978-1-4120-4526-1 (sc)

Trafford rev. 04/19/2012

www.trafford.com

North America & international
toll-free: 1 888 232 4444 (USA & Canada)
phone: 250 383 6864 fax: 812 355 4082

We shall not cease from exploration
And the end of all our exploring
Will be to arrive where we started
And know the place for the first time.
Through the unknown, remembered gate
When the last of earth left to discover
Is that which was the beginning;
At the source of the longest river
The voice of the hidden waterfall…

Little Gidding. T.S. Eliot.

שְׁמַע יִשְׂרָאֵל יְהוָה אֱלֹהֵינוּ יְהוָה | אֶחָד:

Deuteronomy 6.4

Αγαπήσεις κύριον τὸν θεόν σου
Εξ 'ολης τῆς καρδίας σου
Κὰι εν 'ολη τῇ ψυχῇ σου
Καὶ εν 'ολη τῇ διανοία σου
Καὶ τὸν πλησίον σου 'ως σεαυτόν

Luke 10.27

Contents

Contents ...

Acknowledgements

This book covers so many diverse interests in my life that it is not possible for me to acknowledge and thank everyone who has helped and guided me. At the bookish level I have tried to indicate influences by an annotated bibliography.

Of particular significance for me, however, in recent times have been the many member of the Scottish Episcopal Church who 'took me in' when my family and I came here from Africa, and tolerated and allowed me to explore my crazy ideas in so many ways.

I want to mention particularly Bishop Alastair Haggart who encouraged me by reading and appreciating some of my early writings which eventually combined and emerged as this one. Latterly I have been greatly helped by Bishop Richard Holloway who, by appointing my wife and me as lay chaplains to Edinburgh University for a few years, encouraged me to think that my ideas may be worth publishing more widely. He also inspired my rebelliousness with his own open-minded writings.

Then there is the group of scientists and others who have been meeting regularly here in Edinburgh for many years to discuss matters at the interface between religious faith and science who have latterly called themselves 'The Caledonian Place Group'. There have been too many members over the years for me to list them all here, but I'm particularly indebted to Lisbet Rutter who founded the group and who often read and criticized constructively my own contributions; Rev. Canon Philip Crosfield who has led the group discussions and who latterly read earlier drafts of this work and allowed us to discuss some of their contents for an extended period. I must therefore also mention gratefully the names of recent members: (in addition to the above), Professor Brian Kilbey, Rev. Dr. Robert Gould, Beth Cumming, Brian Flemming, and Eion Rutter.

Above all, however, I must thank the rectors and congregation of St. Columba-by-the-Castle with whom I have worshipped for many decades. Significant for their encouragement were the rectors: Rev. Alex Black, Rev. Canon Brian Hardy and Rev. Alison Fuller. Especially important for me has been 'The Wednesday Morning Group' which has been meeting before dawn for many years for midweek eucharist and to discuss a series of more than one hundred books. This has given me the chance to learn much and 'try out' and clarify many of the notions which I have developed in this book. I would like to mention especially, Brian and Sarah Kilbey, who founded the group, and Elizabeth and Iain Thompson who have hosted most of our meetings. Also especially important to me has been the encouragement of the Rev. Canon Professor John Richardson with whom I have had many discussions and who read an earlier draft of this work and urged me to persist.

Lastly I must thank my family, who over many years have had to endure my mental and physical absences as I wrestled with these issues. I have not always been the husband and father that I should have been and, in effect, demanded a 'sacrifice' from them to which I was not entitled. My wife Helen, especially has had to endure much, but without her love this work would never have seen the light of day, and I can only hope and pray that she and they will come to see that it was all worth it – for the sake of others.

Faber & Faber: *Little Gidding, Four Quartets.* T.S. Eliot.

Oxford University Press and Cambridge University Press: The Revised English Bible. Excerpts from, *I Corinthians* chapter *13. Romans* chapter *8; John* chapters *14-17*

Oxford University Press: New Revised Standard Version. *Colossians 1.15-23a*

This text and cover were produced using Techwriter and Photodesk on a RISCOS computer and then converted to MSWord for the purpose of publishing.

Introduction

Have you ever wondered about *What is Happening*? What is happening *ultimately*, I mean. After all, none of us can recall having been asked to come into this mysterious existence, especially as this individual person in these particular circumstances! Furthermore, we are all aware that there is for us a terminus–that this life of ours will come to an end somehow, and so far as we can honestly see, that will be that. What can possibly be the point of it all?

Of course, these have been the great questions of philosophy and religion from time immemorial, but many of us (in the West at least) seem to have ceased asking them. Why is this? I can think of two main reasons. First, those of us who have been influenced, however indirectly, by the views and achievements of modern science, tend to think these sorts of questions to be either unanswerable or meaningless. And second, we have all become much more aware than previous generations of the sheer variety of human opinions about such things. Even within one religion there can be apparently radically different denominational claims to possess the absolute truth of these matters. So, unless one is content arbitrarily to adhere to one such view, how is one to choose between them? It is not enough, anymore, just to go along with one's 'tribe'.

Now of course, I am not going to claim to have found personally the true answers to these ancient questions! But I believe, that in our modern global, pluralistic and highly conductive society, it is important that we all make the effort to discuss these matters openly, especially since we now have good evidence that secular humanism, while providing some much-needed corrections and perspectives, is no better at providing ultimate 'world-views' than any of the ancient religions. However, instead of trying to construct our mythologies (for that is what they are) on the basis of some putative claim to divine revelation, ratified by say, some Council or other, we need, I believe, to have an *open, ongoing, continuous, dynamic dialogue* across all cultures and religions. Priestly authorities, and the like, belong to the childhood of our species: they had a central rôle to play in the past, but today (when there are more people alive now than the sum-total of those who have ever lived) they can no longer claim a monopoly on the truth. In Christian terminology, we need to learn to give space to God the Holy Spirit: we should be happy to be playfully creative with our myths–to see them not as divinely authenticated absolute truths–but rather, imaginative explorations that hopefully point in the right direction.

So what is this book about? I have used an imaginary, dialogue form to tell the Story of a fictitious event which allows me to explore a wide range of *speculative possibilities* about what might be going on, without having to try to be academically pure about them: the subject-matter is too vast for me (or any other individual) to do that. I'm trying to express visions of truth that are beyond my words and probably beyond my comprehension.

I have lived through the vicissitudes of about two-thirds of the Twentieth Century; been a school teacher in emergent Africa, and have worked for the last quarter of the century as a research scientist. The particular circumstances of my 'placement' in the world have meant that I have tried to be a faithful Christian with a deep interest in the relationship between scientific 'truth' and my religious belief. The views expressed here, are just from the perspective of one individual who has wrestled long and hard with these matters, and who now wishes to throw them into the pool of serious current concern. I, like everyone else, can only write from my perspective: if anything I have written gives offence to those who think or believe differently may I say that that is not my intention–let's dialogue together and then we can all learn. Plato defined Myth as 'a likely story': I hope you will like mine and be encouraged to express your own. We are all in this together.

"Love will never come to an end. Prophecies will cease; tongues of ecstasy will fall silent; knowledge will vanish. For our knowledge and our prophecy alike are partial, and the partial vanishes when wholeness comes. When I was a child I spoke like a child, thought like a child, reasoned like a child; but when I grew up I finished with childish things.

At present we see only puzzling reflections in a mirror, but one day we shall see face to face. My knowledge now is partial; then it will be whole, like God's knowledge of me. There are three things that last for ever: faith, hope and love; and the greatest of the three is love."

From the 13th chapter of St. Paul's first letter to the church in Corinth, circa 50 C.E.

Ten years on since my original draft, I have taken the opportunity to make some corrections and additions. I would also like to thank the many people who have commented on the book, both critically and appreciatively.

Nicholas Edwin Boddy.

Cycle One:

The Mediator

I'm in hospital. I have been prepared by the jocular nurse who has shaved the critical places and has a fine line in practised patter, "There Enni–smooth as a baby's bottom." I think, "Who gave you the right to be on nick-name terms with me?" But decide it is a generational thing and keep quiet.

Now I have been changed into a flimsy, cotton night-dress and, feeling slightly ridiculous, am being wheeled, lying on my back, along apparently endless corridors and up and down lifts. The two nurses involved are mutually absorbed by the weekend sports results. I watch the ceiling lights passing, and wonder vaguely how often they get dusted up there.

I arrive at an operations ante-room. The young nurse sent to attend me, and presumably to see that I don't make off, says brightly, "You're next." I have a vision of gowned figures scurrying about, cleaning up the blood, covering stainless steel surfaces with temporary sterilised paper, and snapping open packets of new, disposable instruments– especially for me. The nurse complains about the hours and the wages, apparently unable to think of anything else to say by way of cheering up this elderly person. I'm relieved when the doors open and I'm wheeled into the theatre. There I'm moved expertly across onto the operating table.

Now there are masked faces everywhere. I hear the clank of instruments being put out. Can I recognise the face of the surgeon I met a few weeks ago in the office? "Ah, yes", she said then, looking at some read-out or other, "another of those". I'm not sure that the masked face leaning inquiringly over me belongs to the same person, and wonder, in a moment of panic, if they have perhaps got the wrong patient, and I'm going to wake up to find that I've had my appendix removed–or worse. But she speaks and I'm reassured–before I have had time to make a fool of myself. "This will only be a small prick" she says, "just relax and breathe normally." I feel a needle in my arm and a seemingly hot liquid speeds into my blood.

Then suddenly, an enormous weight crashes down on my chest. I just have time to wonder if the ceiling has fallen in. Shooting pains spread down my arms, and I hear someone shout "Emergency!" Then darkness overcomes me. [It was explained to me later that I had chosen just that moment to have a heart-attack, and the surgical team had to suspend the operation and switch instead to resuscitation.]

The next thing I remember was seeing an outline of my body described in fire in front of me, and a strange feeling of shimmering and tingling all over and a pulsating roar in my ears. The rapidly undulating, fiery form began to rotate: slowly at first and then ever more quickly as it started to rush away from me. This merged into a sensation of sliding down a long, dark, smooth and winding tube, getting faster and faster as I went. Then I began to panic as I recalled that I was supposed to be in hospital for an operation. What on earth was happening?

Quite suddenly, the roaring and the tobogganing stopped, and I was shot out into a field of almost silent, brilliant light. I tried to look around but could see nothing except whiteness in all directions. It was not possible, in fact, to see properly, since there didn't seem to be anything on which to focus. Then I began to notice other sensations. There was a sweet smell, as though I were in a garden of flowers, and the air was filled with faint, swishing, tinkling sounds, like little bells–or were they children's voices? Then I heard a sonorous, multiple voice. I could not really tell where male or female, or whether it was one or many. It/they said firmly but gently,

"Don't be afraid, you'll soon get used to it!"

Startled, I began looking around for the source but could not see anyone. I started to panic again and cried out "What is happening? Where am I? Who are you? Where are you?" I say 'cried out', but to my alarm I found that I was unable to make

6

a sound, but could only shout 'in my head', so to speak! I raised my hands to my face and found that I didn't have any hands! Horrified I looked down at my feet and discovered that I didn't have a body at all! Now I was really terrified, and the thought came to me that I was probably dead. "Oh no", I shouted inside, "I don't want to die yet. I have much left to do. In any case I want to say goodbye to everyone, and there are those to whom I need to say 'sorry'."

The voices spoke again, more warmly this time,

"Don't be afraid, you are not dead–only near-death, and We are here to look after you, until it is decided what's to be done with you."

Then I thought I caught a glimpse of some shapes in the otherwise uniform field of brilliant light. When I looked directly anywhere I could see nothing in particular, but slightly to the side of my field of vision, in fact everywhere around me, I could just make out what seemed to be a sea of flickering faces. Each time it or they spoke, the forms became more clearly focussed directly in front of me.

"I/We are *'The Mediator'*. You will soon learn to see Us better. We are here to support you while they work on your body."

Gradually I began to see more distinctly and found myself before a strange, multiple Being, whose many and rapidly changing features were both stern and infinitely compassionate at the same time. As I was wondering what sort of being this *'Mediator'* could be, whether male or female, He/She read my thoughts and said,

"None of those notions apply to Us. I am, as you can see, both singular and plural, beyond gender and your space and time. You may call me *'HeeShT'*, if that makes you comfortable; since I am neither *'He, She nor It'*–but a Being in advance of such categories." [Looking back, I know that sounds slightly ridiculous, but it seemed perfectly plausible at the time–just like that joke that seemed so funny in the dream but appeared utterly banal in the morning.]

Feeling somewhat reassured, I now found the courage to ask hesitantly, "Well, er– *HeShT*, what am I doing? Where am I, in fact? And who are you? *Don't I actually know you from some-where?*" [This last question surprised even me; it just seemed to slip out. The very moment before I formulated it, the thought came to me that *HeShT* was somehow familiar.] Then the features before me softened further and clarified and we began to talk freely. Slowly, slowly a remarkable calmness began to come over me.

Mediator (HeShT): "You will have many questions, and not all of them will be answerable now: some because they are the wrong questions and others because it is too soon for you bear the answers, and some because the replies would be beyond your finite understanding. Now that you have calmed down somewhat, perhaps you would like to start asking again–one question at a time, please!" Then a wave of gentle laughter wafted around me on all sides.

Me: "Very well, what is happening to me now?"

Mediator: "Would you like to see?"

Me: "Yes."

Mediator: "Look down then."

I did so and saw, as though through a parting in a curtain of light, myself lying on the operating table with four or five figures bending over me with anxious looks on their faces. I was staring upwards with my mouth open inside a mask of some kind, and one gowned figure was applying something to my chest. However, they all appeared to be rooted helplessly to the spot and doing nothing. I cried out, "Why don't they *do* something, instead of just standing there."

Mediator: "Oh they are, I assure you, it is just that you are now outside their time, and in ours. It will seem to you that they are not doing anything at all. We happen in many dimensions beyond the ones you are aware of, and for a short time, in this state of near-death, you are privileged to share them with us. In the time you have been assigned to be with us you will experience brief, alternating periods of waking and sleeping. These correspond to the cycles of your brain-waves. So you should be ready for this to happen and not be worried."

I looked away from the scene of my body and returned to the *Mediator*, who was there before me, moving in and out of focus, apparently awaiting my next question.

Me: "Can you tell me who you are?"

Mediator: "I will try, but there is much you will not be able to understand yet. We are, as you see, both single and multiple. Think of Us, for the moment, as your travelling companion in life: the most you will be able to comprehend of the 'beyond' towards which you are developing and evolving. You have just a tiny capacity to be with Us at the present, which is the means by which we are able to share this experience now."

Me: "But how is it that I thought I recognised you just a moment ago?"

Mediator: "That is because I have always been with you, and from time to time you have caught glimpses of Us–in moments of crisis or ecstasy or proper achievement."

Me: "Proper achievement?"

Mediator: "Yes, those occasional moments when you felt the satisfaction of believing that you were moving with the grain of things and in conformity with the ultimate destination of us all."

Me: "Oh, and what is that?"

Then before *HeShT* could answer, a wave of profound darkness began to spread over me, and I screamed out "Stop, stop, don't leave me now. I am too frightened to be left alone and there is much I still want to know!"

Mediator: "Don't worry. We will have plenty of time for that. You need to rest now. Remember what I told you about your cycles of waking and sleeping? Just relax. We are with you always–whatever happens."

Then I plunged into a deep sleep.

9

Cycle Two:

The Cosmos

I awoke feeling as though I was in the most comfortable bed imaginable, rather as I suppose a fish might feel in a warm, tropical sea. It took me a moment to recall where I was, and what had been happening.

Then I heard a calm reassuring voice declaring, "So, you're back. Feeling any better now?"

Instead of being alarmed, as might be expected, I started looking around and found that I was in a beautiful garden, filled with exotic, aromatic plants of a kind I had never seen before.

The voice continued, "We thought you would be more comfortable like this, so I made it and put it in your mind."

I replied, "Thank you, it is truly splendid", and went on looking about me, wondering what was going to happen next. All the while I felt the presence of the *Mediator*, perhaps a little more distinct than 'yesterday', as it were, but still alarmingly here, there and everywhere simultaneously.

HeShT said, "We are sorry, you find Us disturbing, but I can only be what We are. We have accommodated Ourself as far as possible to your current state and limitations. Are you ready to resume?"

By now I was fully awake, and immediately wanted to know what was happening to me 'down there'.

HeShT said, "Take a look" and so I did.

There I was, my position unchanged, with the doctors apparently still frozen impotently over me.

"It's all right," said the *Mediator* before I could complain, "remember what I told you last cycle. We are outside their time. I assure you they are doing their best. Meanwhile we have 'all the time in the world' as your idiom has it. Let's make good use of it." It took a moment for my disappointment to subside, and then I acquiesced.

"Good" *He/She/It* said.

Me: "You were about to tell me HeShT, what was the ultimate destination of everything, if I remember rightly."

Mediator: "Correction: you had just asked that question, but fell asleep before We could reply. But consider for a moment: do you think it very likely that I would be able to give you a simple answer to such a large question, and that if We did, your tiny human mind could be able to take it in?"

Me: "Well, if you put it like that, I suppose not. So where do we go from here?"

Mediator: "Don't despair. We will eventually work around to a kind of an answer, which will point you in the right direction and satisfy you for the time being. We have a lot of preliminary work to do first though, because you have many inherited misapprehensions about the nature of Reality."

Me: "Now you have me mentally paralysed again, and don't know what to ask in case it's 'the wrong question'. Why don't you suggest something?"

Mediator: "Very well. You like big ideas, don't you? And you were once a scientist?"

Me: "Ye-es."

Mediator: "So why don't you begin by asking Us something about the Universe, or what some of your religions call 'The Creation'?"

Me: "Yes, why not. Good idea."

Mediator: "Well, go on then. Ask something!"

Me: "Oh, Ah, let's see… I could ask you how it all began or something like that. But let's start with, 'How big, in fact, is the Universe?' Will that do? Our cosmologists are always arguing about it."

Mediator: "Yes, that will do to start us off. You should prepare yourself for some surprises though! You will know already that what you call 'Our Universe' is a vast collection of galaxies: hundreds of billions of them each comprised of hundreds of billions of stars. One of those myriads of stars is your sun; it just looks different to you from the rest of them because it is relatively close–the one which your planet revolves around. Moreover, all that is only the humanly visible matter of your universe; 99% of it is not visible to your eyes at all. Furthermore, even the densest parts, like the interior of stars, are mostly empty space."

Me: "I find that difficult to believe. How can even a solid lump of lead or gold be mostly empty space?"

Mediator: "Let Me assure you it is. It is just that the forces inside it make it impenetrable by other lumps of matter under your normal pressures. But consider the fact that all of the substance of your universe, visible and invisible, emerged from a volume much less than that of an atom about fourteen billion of your years ago, in what your scientists have called 'the Big Bang.'"

Me: "I feel arising in me all those questions which my teenage children used to ask, and to which I was unable to give a good answer, like: What happened before the Big Bang? Is there an edge to the Universe, or does it go on for ever? Are there perhaps other inhabited planets–some of them perhaps with higher life-forms like, or even beyond us, on them? And then, what has God got to do with all this?"

Mediator: "Well well, you do seem to have found your tongue! Good. And as you discovered with your children, it is often easier to ask these sorts of questions than it is to answer them: particularly when the replies are possibly beyond what they can understand. However, We shall endeavour to give you some pointers, but I warn you, you will find some of them difficult to comprehend, and even more difficult to believe."

Me: "Please go on. I would like to try."

12

Mediator: "Very well, to questions like 'What happened "before" the Big Bang which gave rise to your Universe?' or 'What lies outside the space of your Universe?' it is necessary to answer on two levels. Firstly, that your space and time are both aspects of your universe and that from this perspective, there is no meaning to the notion of space and time 'outside' or 'before' your universe. (It would be rather like asking 'What time is it on the sun?') Then secondly, one would have to reply, that there are higher dimensions of both space and time which are beyond and include your space and time, and these 'contain' the nearly infinite number of universes which comprise 'the Cosmos' or 'Creation.'"

Me: "Hey, hold it there: 'the nearly infinite number of universes'? Did I hear you correctly?"

Mediator: "You did. From the perspective of your universe, there is only one of its kind, with its own space and time, matter and energy. But 'beyond' your universe, and quite inaccessible to you at present, there is a huge number of universes which have existed for an infinite length of time, and there always will be. Moreover they, like yours, are all evolving and giving birth in their turn to new universes which grow, develop and die. It is a never ending Creation."

Me: "Now you are beginning to blow my mind. There are now so many questions arising in me, that I don't know where to begin."

Mediator: "We appreciate that, and I'm sorry if you feel overwhelmed. Perhaps you should let yourself be guided by Us for the moment. Let's get back to your first set of 'child-like' questions."

"You asked 'Are there other inhabited planets in your universe' (and now by implication, in all the other universes)? The answer is 'Yes, certainly, many of them'. It is in the nature of some kinds of more evolved universes, including yours, to teem with <u>living</u> matter, some of which has developed to the point of being able to ask the kinds of questions you are asking, and even of discovering some of the answers. We find it very pleasing and satisfying–except that it so often goes wrong."

Me: "What do you mean–'goes wrong'? And how do you know all this anyway?"

Mediator: "Perhaps We had better leave the answer to the first of those questions for another cycle. As to your second one: 'How do We know about these matters?' The answer is, We are there also."

At this point the *Mediator* seemed to explode and to fill all visible space. Every direction in which I looked *HeShT* was there, as far as my eyes could see. Completely overcome and awestruck, I cried, "Is this something to do with God?"

Mediator: "Think about it."

And at that point, the comforting darkness descended upon me once again, and I fell 'asleep'.

Cycle Three:

Do we All fail?

I came around, feeling refreshed, and there was *HeShT*, watching me gravely.

Me: "How are they getting on down there?

Mediator: "Just fine, don't worry. You can look of you wish."

Me: "Don't bother: I'll look when there is something to see."

Mediator: "Good. Are you ready to learn some more about what is really happening in the world?"

Me: "Oh please go on, then I may have some more questions to ask."

Mediator: "Very well, how about this then?"

Suddenly, the field of light and the garden around me disappeared and everything went completely black. It was as though I was suspended in empty space. I instinctively tried to put my hand down to stop myself falling (although I had no hand to put down). I looked anxiously around for the *Mediator,* and there *HeShT* was, looking at the scene with deeply concerned expressions on their faces. Turning back, I saw that the blackness was no longer absolute, but was studded with myriads of clusters of multicoloured lights, like a night sky in the tropics.

I gasped with awe and amazement.

Me: "What are we looking at?"

Mediator: "We are showing you your universe from Our perspective; or part of it anyway. Those are the galaxies of stars nearest you which your astronomers call 'The Local Cluster.'"

Me: "Aren't they magnificent: all those countless numbers of suns burning away in their splendour!"

As I spoke I noticed that one of the tiny dots in the whole vast host was winking slightly, while the rest shone steadily.

Me: "Why is that one different?"

Mediator: "It is not. We have just caused it to appear so in order that you would notice it."

Me: "Well, why should I do that, it doesn't look special in any way."

Mediator: "It is and it isn't. Astronomically it is just one of many of its kind. But it is special to you, because it is your sun!"

I cried out in amazement and suddenly felt very frightened again, and began to shout:

"How did I get out here? How can I possibly get back?–Were they not able to save my life after all?"

Mediator: "Calm down. We have not 'gone' anywhere. I am merely giving you an impression of a tiny part of what We can see all the time. And no, nothing new has happened to you 'down there' as you put it. They are still hard at work."

Feeling greatly relieved and, filled with increased respect for the powers of my 'companion', I composed myself and went on.

Me: "Thank you, *HeShT* for that reassurance. I really thought that I must have died. Now I can enjoy this marvellous sight in peace: a view, I suppose, no other living person has ever had!"

Mediator: "Good. You recovered from that shock very quickly. Let Us now show you another aspect of all those stars."

Then as I watched, I saw that large numbers of them had appeared to turn green and to begin pulsating gently.

Me: "So what are these? In what way are they different from the rest?"

Mediator: "We have distinguished them for you because they are stars which have given birth to planets with living matter on them."

Me: "What, all those? Are you telling me that there is all that life out there?"

Mediator: "Yes, and remember that this is only a tiny portion of your whole universe I'm showing you. The rest is much the same. Also, many as they are, they are only a small proportion of all the stellar objects, because only some very special stars support life."

Me: "Now you are making me feel very insignificant again. Up to now, I have never really faced the possibility that we could be sharing this universe with other kinds of living things, and here you are showing me that there are huge numbers of them. If it is true, as you say, that You are there with them in the same way as You are here with me, can you also let me see some of them up close?"

Mediator: "No. While there is still a possibility that you may recover from your present crisis, and make some sort of report of what you have experienced here; and while it is also possible that some people might actually take seriously what you write, there are certain kinds of knowledge about your companion life-forms which your species should not acquire until you are ready for it. Not until you are capable of encountering them yourself, in fact."

Me: "Do you mean that we will eventually meet some of these other intelligent beings, by space-travel perhaps? Or will they come to us?"

Mediator: "We do not know precisely what will happen in the future, since that has yet to be determined by many free choices, including yours. But what you anticipate is highly probable and ultimately a necessary one–but only when you are ready for it."

Me: "I would certainly like to be amongst those who first made such exciting encounters."

Mediator: "That is not very likely–not in this life, anyway."

Me: "What do you mean 'Not in this life anyway'?"

Mediator: "That is a question which I shall try to answer for you later–if our time together in these dimensions lasts long enough, that is. Meanwhile let me show you something else– something which concerns Us greatly and which you should know about."

Looking once again at the galaxies of stars with the winking, green ones highlighted, I saw that some of them were getting steadily brighter.

Me: "What is happening now?"

Mediator: "I have speeded up their time for you, so that what you see is a representation of the evolution of higher life forms on some of their planets. Their developments proceed at different rates, and we watch-over them all with great love, faith and hope."

Then, as I watched, some of the signals began to increase in intensity exponentially, becoming almost blindingly bright, and then suddenly they went out and disappeared. All around, amongst the steadily pulsating green stars, there were star systems whose illuminations increased mightily in this manner, and then were extinguished.

Me: "What does this mean? Why are those beautiful lights going out?"

Mediator: "Those star-systems have given birth to life-forms that have attained to advanced civilisations and have developed an understanding of many of the laws of nature."

Me: "But why then are they disappearing?"

It was then that I became aware of a keening noise around me, like the sound of many mourners. In astonishment I looked for the *Mediator* and found *HeShT* was gazing at the scene and

18

weeping! I cried out. "What is happening? Why are you crying? I can't bear to see you like this!"

Mediator: "These are beautiful cultures that have attained to high possibilities for future development, but have not been able to deal properly with the powers of nature which they have unleashed and in consequence are destroying themselves. As you can see, it is happening all the time. It is a perpetual cause of much sorrow and disappointment to Us and it hurts greatly every time."

"Oh *HeShT, HeShT*," I cried, "I am so sorry. I had no idea you would have such cares. What can I say?"

Mediator: "Thank you, my friend, for your sympathy. It is one of the good and promising things about you human beings at your best, and one of the reasons why we still have high hopes of you. If only you would always show these sentiments to one another, then a great deal of sorrow and suffering in your world, and Us, would be avoided."

We fell into silence for a time while I watched all those civilisations flaring up and disappearing, and a great wave of horror and disappointment swept over me, and I wept too. Eventually I spoke up again.

Me: "Are you telling me that extinction like that is bound to be our fate also?"

Mediator: "As We have explained already, I do not know the exact answers to questions of that sort. I can know the probabilities of how the present moment may develop, even a long way further into the future than you could ever know, and can influence it to a degree. But the outcomes are still subject to the free choices of all the parties involved, and what those will be, not even We can know–they would not be free choices if We could. Certainly the dangers increase as your knowledge increases, but so do the possibilities for advancement and greater communion. As for humanity, however, you and We will doubtless suffer many great tragedies as the ages pass, both on your planet and off it. Some of them will be of your own making, while others will be due to chance accidents or the machinations of other, bad wills. However, We have taken steps to ensure that all will be well for you *in the End*: but that is still a very long way off."

I opened my mouth to ask another question but was stopped by sleep rushing upon me again. I had a brief glimpse of *HeShT*'s grave and kindly faces regarding me, and then I was gone.

Cycle Four:

The Story of Planet Earth

I become aware of a splendid brightness and the gorgeous scent of many kinds of flowers, and woke up eagerly to be greeted by *HeShT*.

Mediator: "Hello. Welcome back. You are getting used to Us, I see. Before you ask, your treatment is going as well as can be expected."

Me: "Hello and thank you. I have just realised that I haven't eaten and I could kill some breakfast!"

Mediator: "There is no need for that here. You are hungry from your operation-fast. The pangs will soon pass. Shall we get on?"

Me: "Very well. What do you suggest we begin with this time?"

Mediator: "You've just said it! We have had a preliminary look at space. Now let's look at time."

Me: "That sounds a splendid idea. I have always been puzzled and fascinated by the subject."

Mediator: "You are in good company! Where would you like to begin?"

Me: "Well, while we are considering the universe as a whole, can you show me something about the age of our universe and, in particular, how much longer we can expect it to last?"

Mediator: "That is well-covered ground, but once again, we can usefully begin there, since few of your contemporaries have really come to terms with it. We have already said that your universe began about fourteen billion years ago (that is fourteen thousand million years) with what you call 'The Big

Bang'. We have indicated that it emerged from the demise of a previous universe whose achievements were the bases for the starting properties of this one, and very promising they were. We had been overseeing this sort of thing for aeons and aeons of other time dimensions already, and we get great joy from the challenge of it."

Me: "I must say that sounds pretty awesome. It is quite different from the sort of thing which was generally believed only a few centuries ago. You already indicated also that there are other universes in the Cosmos, with their own times and spaces."

Mediator: "You learn quickly. Yes there are, but you need not concern yourself with them–leave that to Us. There is more than enough for you to cope with here! So to begin:

At the beginning of your time, this universe was projected with great force from the collapse of its 'parent' universe, as a single, simple, almost infinitesimal and slightly asymmetrical <u>entity</u> of enormous mass and energy. This immediately began to inflate and evolve. Because of its tiny asymmetry it was unbalanced, as it were, and began to fall forward into new patterns (which is partly why you have your time).

As it expanded at an enormous rate, it began to cool, and a series of new re-arrangements began to emerge, just as ice crystals do from freezing water; only this was occurring at highly energetic temperatures of trillions of degrees. The details need not concern us here (though there are important things which you should know about time, which we will return to later). For now, I will outline for you the main story."

Me: "Please do, I was beginning to get lost in all that."

Mediator: "Here is the main sequence of events as they transpired, most of which We will arrange for you to experience as a sort of panorama in time. Let us show you the story of your universe so far, as though it took place in one 'day' of 24 hours, just to get the sense of how long the various phases lasted. I won't go into too much detail-after all, a lot happened in 13.7 billion years!

In real time first of all, much complicated evolution occurred in the first brief moments after your universe's emergence, which your physicists don't understand yet, and with which We will not trouble you now.

Ten seconds (again in real time) after what you popularly call 'the Big Bang', and after a huge amount of energetic behaviour, your universe had expanded from being less than an atom in diameter, to being thousands of times larger than your Solar System, and was quite simple and utterly different from what it is today. It was made throughout of an extremely hot gas composed of X-ray light, with a density 200 times that of lead, and a thin wisp of turbulent matter, including protons, neutrons and electrons, nearly completely evenly distributed throughout. Its temperature had fallen from trillions of trillions of degrees to a mere thousand billion degrees.

Then over the next two to four million years (that is 12 seconds after midnight on our model) the universe continued to expand its space and cool down until it became very cold and dark. Meanwhile the matter (mostly hydrogen and helium) had begun to collect under its own gravity until suddenly the whole universe became ablaze with new light as the matter clumped to become stars. Their cores had become as hot again as the whole universe had been at about one second old.

These first stars were very large and short-lived. They 'died' by exploding and forming new kinds of elements as they did so. All the carbon, oxygen, nitrogen, sodium, chlorine, phosphorus, iron etc. which go to make up your body were formed in this way. Generations of stars 'lived' and 'died' like this, making it possible for you to live!.

Over the next three hours or so in the model, the stars began to gather into huge fuzzy collections called galaxies, all buzzing about furiously colliding and swirling through each other. You would not have survived then!

Things eventually began to calm down somewhat, as space continued to expand, so that by two o'clock in the afternoon (after many billions more years) the beautiful spiral galaxies emerged from the melee – hundreds of billions of them, each composed of hundreds of billions of stars!

HeShT then concentrated upon just one of these galaxies the one we call 'The Milky Way'. It was in a relatively quiet spot, well away from large galaxy clusters. Then, within it, somewhere out towards the edge of its disc, in another quiet spot, one of the huge numbers of stars was singled out as it developed its own array of circulating planets. This was our solar System with its own central star the Sun. The model time was now 4.00 pm.

It wasn't until 5.15pm, however, that things had calmed down enough on planet earth (the third one out) for water to have accumulated in the hollows between the primitive continents, and within them the miracle of life soon began. This took the form of myriads of different microscopic forms, populating water wherever they could, and swapping their genetic materials so easily that no single kind emerged for a very long time. They suffered huge planetary catastrophes. For instance, the surface of the earth was covered completely by ice more than once during this period. They did, however, learn to use sunlight to get energy and to fill the atmosphere with a lot of oxygen. But it wasn't until about 10.00pm that advanced, stable, life forms evolved, though still microscopic. And then at about 11.00pm some larger and advanced forms of plants and animals evolved to populate the seas and eventually to emerge onto the hitherto naked land. This was a huge and adventurous step.

Then I witnessed the spectacle of spreading forests and numerous kinds of animals such as spiders, scorpions, insects etc. all scampering about in the undergrowth. There followed the amphibians, then reptiles and birds and some primitive mammals. These all appeared before my fascinated eyes.

Between 26 – 7 minutes before midnight the kind of reptiles we call 'dinosaurs' evolved to rule the land, seas and air. Their reign was abruptly ended by the catastrophic impact of a huge asteroid (one of the last, hopefully), which cleared the way for mammals and birds to rule the roost on the land and in the air instead.

Amongst the mammals of special interest to us, were the apes who evolved at about 6 minutes to midnight. The first ape-like human beings appeared in Africa at about 44 seconds before 12.00am, some of whom spread a little way over the earth. Our kind, the self-styled 'Homo sapiens', evolved shortly before one second to midnight. Then, half a second before midnight, some of our species left East Africa and spread over the face of the earth, absorbing or eliminating previous kinds of man-like beings.

It wasn't until 6/100ths of a second that our ancestors dis-covered how to domesticate some plants and animals in the form of crops and herds, thus removing the need for a nomadic existence. Civilization and writing appeared in some great river valleys with only 3/100ths of a second to go.

Jesus of Nazareth lived, died and rose from the dead 12/1000ths of a second before midnight, so inaugurating the 'New Creation'.

For a while I was struck dumb with awe and amazement and could find nothing to say. *HeShT* waited patiently for me to recover. When at last I found my voice I asked: "How much longer will all this go on?"

Mediator: "We expect your sun to last another five-billion years, or 8 model hours, before it too burns out, swells up and engulfs your planet. Before that, your galaxy and the Andromeda galaxy will collide with upsetting consequences. However, your universe, as a whole, still has some way to go in the form its has.

All this left me terribly shaken and alarmed. Eventually I man-aged to say: "That is a terrifying way of presenting the story and it makes me and the entire human race seem merely transient and irrelevant. We have been here for only such a tiny fraction of the time our universe has existed, and it doesn't seem likely that we will be around for much longer – certainly not another 10 hours of model-time. So what can be the point of it all for us–or anything else? I also find myself wondering what my descendents will be like in, say, another' seconds' time!"

Mediator: "It is perfectly understandable that you should feel like that. The magnitudes of the Great Creation are on a different scale from human concerns. In fact, many of your contemporaries are unable to believe any of this story at all. It amounts to a major re-contextualising of the big questions which your species has been asking since you first entered the world of abstract thought. Your ancient mythologies did not have to face it, which is why so many of them can't 'work' for you any more. However, since you human beings are one part of the universe which has reconstructed much of all this for itself, that says something about you which you should consider before you write yourselves off. After all, no star or dinosaur could have done it.

As for your question about what will be happening in another 'second' (not to mention another hour or twenty four hours) of model-time, you will appreciate by now that there is no way in which we can tell you any of the details of that. Only one thing is certain: there is much evolving still to be done, and *the future will be as different from the present, as it is from the past.* Nobody–not even Us–could have foreseen for certain that the one-celled animals of your planet's primeval seas would have evolved into beings quite like you, although we did have a gentle hand in the process. Likewise, no-one can know exactly what the future holds for your species. It will not, in fact, involve extinction–that has been seen to–but it could involve changes to your form and ways of living which are utterly beyond your comprehension now, and would probably horrify you if you were to witness them. Things could be at least as different from now as the present universe is from the time of the 'quark soup', as it has been called. This is one of the reasons why I cannot show you other, advanced, civilized beings living in other parts of the universe today. You probably would not like, or be able even to comprehend, what you saw."

Me: "O dear, I can feel the next sleep session coming on. There is a huge number of questions arising in my mind which I suppose will have to be postponed until next time. I hope I will be able to remember them. In particular I am anxious to know what all this future you talk about, could mean to me, personally? And then, what sense are we to make of the apparently meaningless death of our universe as a whole, which our cosmologists are predicting?"

Mediator: "Yes indeed. We know that these matters exercise you greatly. But there is still much preliminary work to be done before…"

And *HeShT's* voice faded out as I fell, exhausted, into unconsciousness.

Cycle Five:

The Mysteries that are Space and Time

"It's time to wake up, lazy bones", a voice penetrated my light sleep.

"Oh, good", said I, pretending sarcasm, though in truth I had been nearly awake for some time, puzzling over what we had been considering previously.

"They are about the shock you", said *HeShT*, "and that may reach to your present level of consciousness, and We wouldn't like you to be too alarmed."

Me: "Thank you, that's very considerate of you. I'm rearing to go, really. Now let's see where were we? Oh yes, you were frightening me about time."

Mediator: "You didn't seem particularly frightened; in fact I think you took it very well, even if you were already familiar with the general ideas."

Me: "Yes, but it is possible to live with unthinkable notions without actually taking them on board, and your presentation opened up all my generally unspoken anxieties. I'm especially worried about how all this future time could be relevant to me personally–which you seem to imply was the case, or else why were you telling me?"

Mediator: "Yes, well, but you are not yet ready to go into all that. We must take a much more careful look at what you call 'reality' before you are ready to take that one 'on board', as you put it."

Me: "Very well, as usual I will be guided by you."

Mediator: "I'm going to frighten you once more, so get ready! You have to learn that both space and time are illusions!"

Me: "Oh no! Here we go again!"

Mediator: "Only a moment's thought should show you that space is nothing? Is that not so? Is that not what 'space' means?"

Me: "Well yes, if you put it that way, but somehow that doesn't seem to do it justice."

Mediator: "Quite right, there is more to it than such a negative characterization. Space is simply the possibility that things could be differently arranged, and it is a basic source of the energy of such possibilities. But the re-arrangements on offer are not infinite in number, and moreover, the current pattern of things puts some constraint upon what can be arranged next. The limitation is due to the finite amount of 'energy' which is available at any moment to the universe. This also accounts for the fact that the velocity of light (or of any other information) is finite. And that brings us back onto time."

Me: "Now hang on a minute, all that was a bit too fast for me. Let me try to play it back and see if I have got it. You say that 'space' is nothing in itself but only the possibility that things could be differently arranged. Yes, I think I have got something of that. You say that the amount of energy available to the universe at any moment is limited, so that it can only change slightly from one moment to the next, and that includes how fast even the fastest events can succeed one another. Yes, I think I have now got something of that too, although I find myself wondering about the source of this finite amount of energy."

Mediator: "Well done. You have grasped that admirably. We will come back to the Ultimate Source of the energy later. I think we should return to the subject of time. You will remember that We said that it, like space, was an illusion. I'm speaking particularly, at this moment, of the one-dimensional time which you experience in your universe. We cannot enter here into the multiple temporal dimensions in which We happen. Your mind would not be able to cope with them, even though your mathematicians will eventually model them. You experience reality as a sequence of moments and you picture time as a continuous entity through, or by means of which, you 'travel'. Your physics commonly envisages time as a dimension, partly analogous to the three dimensions of your space, so that you can specify an event as occurring at exactly this or that point in space and time with respect to some chosen reference point. (Of course, you cannot specify this exactly, since you have no single origin to which to refer everything else– hence relativity.) Are you still with me?"

Me: "Struggling, but go on."

Mediator: "Time, like space, is just one of the conditions necessary for things to be differently arranged, and arises directly from the fact of the finite amount of energy available to your universe at any given moment. It is not possible for any current situation to change instantaneously into any other one–however desirable–it is usually necessary to go through a process, that is a sequence of ordered steps in order to arrive at the desired pattern. The rate at which this can occur is determined by the total amount of energy available."

Me: "Yes, I think I can see what you are getting at now, but what about the source of this energy? You said you would get back to that."

Mediator: "Yes, well the Ultimate Source of all energy is The Holy One, without whom there would not be anything at all, but we should not get into those matters yet. It is sufficient for you to recognise that the total amount of energy that is available for what you call 'Creation' is very large, though finite. But since the number of universes in the Cosmos approaches infinity, each individual universe can only have a finite slice of the cake, so to speak."

Me: "Gracious, what a truly awesome and stunning idea. This 'Holy One' of yours must be something else."

Mediator: "You have a fetching way of putting things. Hardly respectful enough though. But that can wait too. Now let us get back to time."

Me: "You mean we haven't finished!?"

Mediator: "No, we must still spend more time on it."

Me: "Oh very funny!"

Mediator: "I'm glad you are enjoying it. The problem for your current world-views is your insistence that time is continuous. Even though you experience Reality as a sequence of detached moments of attention, you persist in the illusion that time is continuous, that is, infinitely divisible.

You may recollect how some of your ancient philosophers wrestled with the question of whether or not <u>matter</u> was infinitely divisible (We remember watching them at it, fascinated to see what they would conclude). They found themselves impaled on the horns of an intellectual dilemma: either, they said, one should be able (in principle) to go on chopping up a bit of stuff into smaller and smaller pieces for ever and ever (which seemed inconceivable); or one would come to a point in one's chopping when one arrived at the smallest possible piece of the substance, at which point further chopping was impossible 'in principle' (and this also seemed nonsense–why couldn't one just make a further cut?). So they had to leave it in the air. Your science has lived for some time with a preference for a version of the second option, calling the supposed indivisible ultimate entities 'atoms' or 'fundamental particles'. However, that has also been abandoned, because entities like atoms don't seem to behave like chunks of stuff at all, and everyone is in a bit of a quandary about it. Your mathematicians have come up with good working models, but these cannot be pictured by human minds. They are half way there, as the name given to the phenomena in the atomic world indicates: 'quanta', which denotes discrete entities. This approach postulates that, in terms of space, substances–even the most solid of them–are not continuous, but granular. (You will remember that I told you earlier that everything 'is' mostly empty space: many possibilities of being differently arranged.) However, the reason why your cultures have been hung up on this question on the divisibility of matter is that you haven't appreciated that at the heart of your reality there isn't some being–little chunks of inert matter, continuous in time– rather there is something continuously re-happening. *Experiencing event*, not substance, is the basis of your Reality. The ultimate events are a sequence of stills–rather like a motion picture which seems to be a smooth sequence of continuous actions but is in reality a rapid succession of still pictures. In other words, you have to recognise that time is also quantised."

Me: "Wow, wait until I tell them about that."

Mediator: "Oh, some of you are playing around with the idea already. The problem is that the integrals of time are infinitesimal on your scale of happening, and so you still have the difficulty of how seeing how to get from there to the macroscopic world as you experience it."

Me: "But didn't you say that one has only to examine one's own experience of time to see this for oneself?"

Mediator: "Yes, We did. But the specious present of your experience is hardly the basic integral of time of which We have been speaking. Your momentary present lasts from about a hundredth to a tenth of a second. The basic quantum of time is less than a billionth of a billionth of a billionth of a billionth of a second! Much evolving has gone on since your reality was at this level only. The question is, how was the gap closed?"

Me: "Yes, I see. Well then, how was it?"

Mediator: "We will have to leave that matter for another cycle."

Me: "All this sounds rather mathematical: tell me, is the whole of mathematics relevant to our understanding of the world?"

Mediator: "No, mathematics is the science of all possible relationships, and your universe is an implementation of just one of them."

Me: "Do you mean that other universes are formed on the basis of other sets?"

Mediator: "Yes. Every universe is an expression of a sub-set of all possible mathematical relationships, and you should try to identify your sub-set."

Me: "Would that mean that we could then answer all our questions 'about Life, the Universe and Everything'?"

Mediator: "No it would not. Every mathematical system has its crop of unanswerable questions, and this one is no exception."

Me: "Have we come across some of those kinds of questions already?"

Mediator: "Yes."

Me: "O do tell."

Mediator: "No, it is important that they remain for you a perpetual spur."

Me: "Will we ever know which these unanswerable questions are?"

Mediator: "'Ever' is a very long time."

Me: "Yes, but you know what I mean!"

Mediator: "In practical, historical terms, No you will not 'ever' know for certain."

Me: "Is the problem of the relationship between the real Self and the Ego, one of them?"

Mediator: "That is a good question."

Me: "Yes, but is it one of them?"

Mediator: "It is a good question."

   At that moment I experienced a sharp flash of light, a loud roaring sound, and a searing pain shot through my whole being.

HeShT appeared to surround and close in on me on all sides and I screamed out, "What are you doing? What have I done to deserve this?" *HeShT* replied in a calm, commanding voice, "It's all right, do not fear, it will soon pass. I'm not doing it, your doctors are applying electrodes to your chest–as I warned you they would be doing."

And with that I passed out again.

Cycle Six:

The TriUnity of Time Present

I awoke feeling heavier than usual. *HeShT* spoke immediately:

"Don't worry. You have slept through many cycles. The combination of electric shocks, and a pulse of anaesthetic kept you under deeply. Which is perhaps just as well or it might have been very unpleasant for you. Anyway, if you are up to it, we can resume."

Me: "Does this mean that I can soon go back?"

Mediator: "That depends. Several factors are involved. The success or otherwise of the treatment you are having; whether or not you really want to go back–or will want to when you have finished here; and finally, whether or not We deem it appropriate for you to return: that depends partly upon how you respond to your experiences here."

Me: "That sounds rather ominously like examinations."

Mediator: "It is nothing like that. I assure you, whether you go back or go on, each will be the best possible outcome, taking everything into consideration. That is something you cannot decide alone. We can."

Me: "What to you mean by 'go on'?"

Mediator: "All in good time, all in good time. We have looked briefly at space and time, now we need to look a bit more closely at time in your natural Reality."

Me: "Very well, I'm all ears."

Mediator: "You have had some experience of meditation, and will remember one of the main points emphasised, is the need to learn to be truly present. Most people waste a good deal of their time day-dreaming about possible futures or reminiscing nostalgically about the past and so fail actually to live in the present at all! (Of course there are proper times for making one's present concern the past or the future, but that is different from wasting time.) Now I want to ask you to try to remember what you observed about your experience of the present moment at those times when you were truly present, which your meditation techniques facilitated."

Me: "That is rather difficult to do in these very peculiar circumstances."

Mediator: "We appreciate that it might seem so to you, but it should not really be difficult–in fact it could be easier since you don't have the distraction of your body. Just try, for a moment to put all thoughts out of your mind, and just observe the apparent passage of moments of time."

Me: "I can't make anything of that suggestion. You will have to help me."

Mediator: "Very well. If you pay careful attention you will notice that the present moments of your experience are not, in fact, continuous, but come in a series of detached instances. Each one will probably be much like the last, although it will also be utterly unique–the only time, in fact, that you will have that moment. Then it is gone for ever!

Now in normal life, such moments of free observation are rarely possible for you: each moment runs into the next one, apparently continuously. But you can learn a little of the skill that is necessary to carry over into them some of the detachment which you have acquired during meditation. You can steadfastly refuse to 'waste time' dreaming about past or future and concentrate upon living now. If you do this you will make some interesting discoveries. First, you will come to see that neither the past nor the future actually exists: '*All is always NOW*', as some of your poets and mystics realised. What you call 'the past' is the pattern the present *once had*, and 'the future' is the pattern the present *could have* later: <u>Reality, however, is only NOW</u>."

Me: "Just a minute, let me try to get this clear. You say that there is no past: then what do we mean when we say that historians 'study the past'?"

Mediator: "That is acceptable as shorthand for what is happening. But if you think about it, an historian would need a 'time-machine' to study the past (and time-machines are merely entertaining nonsense). No, historians have to study the present very carefully, in order to try to reconstruct what the present once was. There is no 'past' to study! Or, perhaps more usefully, one aspect of every present moment is its 'memory' of past moments. That is to say, your past is present in the form which it bequeaths to the present. The present moment, right across your universe, is the moment of your Reality and it is a sort of memory of all past presents–of how things got to be the way they are."

Me: "Just a moment again. Some of our physicists claim that the notion of a universal present is meaningless–all is relative, or something."

Mediator: "Yes and they are partly right: although there is a bit of a positivist paddy in that position. They are saying that they, as finite observers, can only witness the world from their single vantage point, subject also to the finite velocity of information. They are therefore not able to know what is happening everywhere at this moment. So, for their practical purposes anyway, the notion of a universal Now IS meaningless. But We who are everywhere in your time simultaneously, and are not subject to a finite velocity of information–We do know what is happening throughout your universe now. For instance, while you cannot know what is going on at this moment in your distant galaxies, but only something of what was happening there billions of years ago, We are not subject to that limitation - as you have seen."

Me: "Oh, do tell what is happening there now!"

Mediator: "Yes wouldn't you like to know! But it would serve no useful purpose. So you will have to wait until you eventually join Us permanently.

Me: "Really!?"

Mediator: "Yes, but to get back to our consideration of the nature of your Reality now. I have shown you how all the past presents are still present in a sense, as a sort of memory in the present moment. You, with your technology, are familiar with the way in which you are able to encode the sounds and appearance of some particular event in a material form such as a video recording. So in an analogous, but much more extended way, is every present moment of material reality a sort of recording of the significant aspects of all past present moments. What you call 'the past' therefore is a perpetual aspect of the pattern of the present.

Me: "That is certainly a different way of seeing things."

Mediator: "Yes, and similarly the future does not exist and could not therefore be 'visited' in some sort of time machine or be foretold by some kind of mental technique (there are experiences that look like that, and are often mistaken for it, and we may come back to those later, if we have the time). No, the future, like the past, is an aspect of every present. But the relationship is asymmetrical. Whereas the 'past' is given and unchangeable, the 'future' takes the form of a range of potential future-presents, amongst which either 'chance' or deliberate choice has the power to select. Every present moment of Reality, therefore, has three 'faces': it is a TriUnity. There is the present face in its sheer experienced presentness, the past face in its unchanging facticity of what was once present, and the future face with its offered potentials for what could be present. Every present moment falls forward, so to speak, into the next present moment taking the form chosen (within the limits of possible change) and bringing the achievements of past moments with it. This is happening right across your whole universe NOW, and your own personal experience of it is a tiny, and very human–and, yes, 'relative'–aspect of the whole. It therefore represents your opportunity to contribute something to developing Reality."

Me: "That is fascinating. I had never thought of time in that way before. You seem to be working around to saying that the nature of every present is such that it allows us freedom to choose what the next present will be. But doesn't this contradict the 'scientific world view' which maintains that every sequence of events is governed by cast-iron laws of nature?"

Mediator: "Ah, yes, you Westerners and your 'laws of nature'. The whole model of the world you refer to, the one which sees it as a sort of gigantic machine, whose running depends entirely upon its structure, is only a first approximation: a 'myth', in fact. It is true, that in the course of its evolution nature has acquired many habits of behaviour which you call 'laws of nature'. These do indeed govern the pattern of the sequence of real momentary moments: everything would be chaotic if it were not so, and you would not be able to make simple mathematical models of it. However, the actual sequence of events is rather more subtle than that. Much of the apparent rigidity of the behaviour of large objects in your world is due to the sheer numbers of constituent entities whose free behaviour is swamped by the masses, in much the same way as human crowds have an effect as a whole, not necessarily intended by the individuals that make it up. However, many world processes fall forward into their 'futures' in a very unstable manner, so that a tiny decision at a critical point in time can result in an entirely different outcome from the one which would have followed from another decision at that time. You will remember that in your own life there have been moments of recognisably momentous decision, when whole alternative futures lay before you and you had to choose amongst them. Much of the time, your lives run on a pretty regular basis, but from time to time, critical moments of decision occur. So it is with the rest of nature, and has been from the very beginning. What has changed, is that at the start, when the entities comprising Reality were all very small and simple, only very little 'decisions' could be made. However, as they evolved to become more and more complex, so they became capable of deciding bigger things. You human, living organisms are amongst the most complex entities currently in your universe, and you are consequently capable of deciding to make changes of enormous proportions–relatively. That is partly what evolution is all about."

Me: "I'm beginning to feel rather tired. You have given me much to digest.

- I take away the notion that Reality is always and only NOW.
- That I experience it as a sequence of separate moments, each of which has three 'faces': the past face, the present face, and the future face, and that I have some power and responsibility for making choices about what pattern the next moment should have.

It seems to me that there is still a huge gap between this experience of mine, and what you say is happening, at base, in nature. In what way does my experience of the threefold nature of the present moment of reality relate to that of say an electron–or is that a silly question?"

Mediator: "No, it is not silly at all. In fact, it shows that you are on the ball. Let me leave you with this observation. Why is it that you human beings always seek to detach yourselves from nature? As though you were not a part and product of it? Can you not see, that your investigations of nature are nature investigating itself–now that it has become, in you, capable of it? You seem to think that the only reliable knowledge you can have of reality is obtainable by so-called 'objective' observation, with careful measurement and then mathematical modelling. But you, in your personal experience, have an 'inside' view of Reality, limited it is true, but still a real source of knowledge, and not to be downgraded in the name of objectivity. *Reality IS a self-experiencing Experience!* It was, perhaps necessary, that your culture should go through a phase where it attempted to obtain objective, intellectual understanding of everything, if only to discover the strengths and limitations of this approach. Now it is time to recognise that such a way of seeing things, powerful as it is, is only part of the story. You must be much more confident of the value of knowledge that you can obtain by introspection, and by the direct experience of Reality experiencing, which you can then compare with the experiences of others–even if you cannot mathematise it! You need to learn again the skill of expressing these insights by Story or Myth."

With some relief I felt myself drifting off again into sleep, and I didn't resist.

Cycle Seven:

The Evolution of Things and Persons

I opened my eyes and was immediately awake, and found myself no longer concerned to look at what was happening to me 'below'.

"Quite right," said *HeShT*, "are you ready to resume then?"

Me: "Yes."

Mediator: "Right, let's get on.

You remember we were considering how to close the gap between your experience of the present moment, and what might actually be the ultimate present moment of experience at an infinitesimal integral of time?"

Me: "Yes, that's right. There seemed to be an enormous leap from the sub-quantum level to my present moment."

Mediator: "That's correct: there is–and filling that gap is what has been happening in the various phases of the evolution of your universe. Entities like yourselves, all over this universe, are the end-product, for the moment, of a process of complexification, whereby the tiny freedom to be different in the next moment, of the initial and fundamental entities, has been magnified into the kind of freedoms to make much larger choices of the scope which you enjoy. You will learn later how this is an invitation to the Cosmos to co-create the future with the Holy One.

For the moment, though, let's get back to the question of the nature of matter, since that is one of the foundations of your kind of reality. The details of how the initial, simple, asymmetric entity from which your universe sprang are somewhat complicated. This is not the place for Us to spell them out: you would not understand or remember them anyway. However, We can give you a sort of qualitative feel for what happencd."

Me: "I'm relieved to hear it. I had rather feared you were about to give me a lecture in higher physics."

Mediator: "Now now, you can have nothing to fear from Us."

Me: "Only joking."

Mediator: "Right. The essential idea is that, at bottom–and that is a long way down–the world-process is a succession of discrete events that alternate between being an unconscious experience of a relatively precise state (the way things ARE at that moment) and another state, comprised of a superposition of a tiny range of different possible future states, amongst which the fundamental entities have an extremely limited capacity to choose, unconsciously. We are there for them, down at that fundamental level, just as We are for you at your advanced level, urging and encouraging you all to make the kinds of choices which will lead to a good outcome. Of course, they, too, will sometimes go their own way, with possibly unpleasant consequences for all. In this manner, the universe moves forward from one ultimate experience to the next, permitting a change of pattern which is hopefully for the better."

Me: "That reminds me of one of the ancient paradoxes. Somebody once said something like 'A flying arrow cannot move, since before it can advance any amount at all, it has to move somewhere closer first."

Mediator: "Exactly. That is what the situation would be if time were continuous–infinitely divisible, so to speak. But as We have shown you, it actually proceeds in minute experiential jumps, rather like the sequence of stills in the cinema. Those ancients of yours had a marvellous knack of knowing the right questions to ask, even if they could not possibly arrive at the answers. It is a capacity which some of your subsequent cultures abandoned, losing their nerve and becoming engrossed by what they thought were 'absolute revealed truths' requiring no more investigation."

Me: "So, if the world-process does proceed in jerks, as you say, I'm still interested to see how you are going to explain how we evolved from these infinitesimal, unconscious experiences to the sequence of Nows experienced by me consciously: I certainly don't encounter reality at that fundamental level."

Mediator: "Of course you do not. What happened in the course of the evolution of the universe, and as a direct result of the very limited choices made by the ultimate material entities, is that the sequences of possible patterns crystallised into larger, nearly repeating, cycles of habits. Each of these larger cycles of events then experienced itself as a particulate entity, which itself had a range of options to break out of the repetitive cycle. The range of options at this level was somewhat wider than those of the 'parent' entity. Thus there began a process of forming nested cycles upon cycles of increasingly large, complex, and apparently continuous entities, rather like those Russian dolls which are dolls within dolls within dolls, if you know what We mean. Physical reality is a fractal: one possibility amongst many possible ones."

Me: "Yes, I've seen them. Are you saying that the sequence of entities each made up of, and containing the other, such as quarks, electrons, protons, atoms, molecules and so on, are actually cycles upon cycles of behaviour patterns, ultimately built upon a foundation of discrete series of experiences."

Mediator: "Yes indeed. Or at least, that is the most you could hope to understand about it.

Me: "I have just remembered something else about what we were covering earlier. Remember you were talking about the reality of the universal NOW?"

Mediator: "Yes, go on."

Me: "Well what about the so-called 'twins-effect'? Doesn't that contradict it?"

Mediator: "Very well–you outline it for us."

Me: "As I understand it, there are these twins, Jack and Jill. Jill is an astronaut who sets off in, say the year 3000, on a round trip to the nearest star and back, reaching velocities near to that of light. When she returns, Jack has aged ten years and says the date is 3010, but she has aged only one year and says the date is 3001. This is in accordance with Einstein's Theory of Relativity and shows that the idea of a simultaneous now is meaningless."

Mediator: "Not at all. You shouldn't be worried by the names they give to the time: the moment they shake hands is still the same moment NOW, whatever they call it. Both experienced the same number of fundamental moments of time, but Jill 'used up' many of her's in changing her position greatly in relation to everything else, so that there were fewer available for her higher cycles - including her biological ones which were therefore reduced in number and so she aged less."

Me; "How fascinating. Now I begin to see how your insistance that time is a series of discrete moments begins to make sense. Can we get back to the evolution of the series of nested cycles of behaviour patterns that look like particles?"

Mediator: "Certainly. This series continued in two fundamentally different directions: one towards Thinghood and the other towards Personhood. The level of entities you described just now, are all what your scientists call 'quantal entities' that is, they show experimentally the peculiar properties We referred to as alternating between particle and possibility. You have discovered by experiment, that entities of this size all show a measurable tendency to proceed from one particular state or pattern to another state or pattern by passing 'through' a state that cannot be described precisely, but can only be modelled mathematically by what are called 'wave equations'. These equations imply that entities change by adopting just one out of a range of possible outcomes on offer, and although experiments have shown that one can put a safe bet upon what are the most likely outcomes in a particular transition from one state to another, one cannot be absolutely certain which will happen. This is what you call the principle of indeterminacy."

Me: "This is getting rather heavy for me. Why are you going into all this detail?"

Mediator: "I'm sorry you are finding it difficult. I assure you I'm trying to simplify it as much as possible–enough to stretch your capacities usefully! If you want to understand more, you will have to go and study physics when and if you get back. The secret is in the Primes.

The reason for the detail is simply to show you why the world-process is not a cast-iron sequence of events. That is a partially true and useful, but older, oversimplified scientific-world view, which, however, most of your educated people still assume to be absolutely true. Because of the indeterminacy at the ground of the material world, many of the hierarchical levels constructed upon it have their own freedoms of choice, within specific limits, together with a built-in, 'genetic' tendency to proceed in a regular manner. This is where the constancies of your 'laws of nature' come from: the apparent dialogue between chance and necessity. This is also the ultimate ground of <u>your</u> freedom of will."

Me: "Yes, I see now–I think. Thank you. You said a moment ago that the evolution of entities above the level of molecules proceeded in two different directions: what were they?"

Mediator: "I'm glad to see you are alert! Yes, the two directions can be described as 'inorganic' and 'organic'. Most of your universe has proceeded in the inorganic direction. That is to say, by the formation of huge conglomerates of quantum entities to form solids, liquids or gases, and so on, which sometimes assemble into arrays forming crystals and larger lumps of 'Thinghood'. On this path of development, the quantum 'freedom' to which We referred just now, tends to become swamped by the contrary actions of the sheer numbers of individually acting quantum entities. As a consequence you have things whose limited freedoms average-out as properties like hardness, wetness, chemical affinity etc. Think of rocks, oceans, atmospheres, fire, planets, stars and galaxies. These are the relatively simple objects whose aggregate behaviour your physical sciences have made such marvellous progress in modelling. This kind of apparent entity does not have experiences.

The second line of development applies to only a small proportion of the larger entities of the universe. It is only found in some very special environments because it is very sensitive to extremes of energy flow. This is the organic or living line of development. This can be characterised as a form of matter that is so constituted that it continues, and projects some of the features of the quantum levels into much higher levels, reaching right up into the macroscopic strata of the world. Organic forms of matter eventually evolve to 'Personhood'. *This is where the true future of the Cosmos lies.* It is an aspect of experiencing Reality, of which your science has so far been largely unaware, or has ignored, which is ironic since it is where you are! This macroscopic branch of development has 'experiences and partially free behaviours' rather than 'properties'."

Me: "You are full of surprises. No sooner do I begin to think that all this is rather old hat when you come up with something like that. Let me try to put it in my own words to be sure I've got the point. You say that living protoplasm is a another state of matter, which by the way it is organised, projects quantum properties into the macroscopic world."

Mediator: "Correct."

Me: "Now that I come to think of it, your hierarchy of structures continues within living things too, doesn't it?"

Mediator: "Yes, go on."

Me: "Ordinary molecules give rise to super-molecules like DNA, these are organised into organelles (like mitochondria, chloroplasts, etc.), organelles of many kinds are assembled to form cells, cells into tissues, tissues into organs, organs into organisms and organisms into communities. Are you saying that quantum indeterminacy continues to operate at all these levels?"

Mediator: "Yes and no."

Me: "That's helpful, I must say."

Mediator: "Be patient. In your excitement you are tending to rush things."

Me: "I'm sorry."

Mediator: "Much of protoplasmic and organismic activity is still conducted in the inorganic manner, as your physiologists have discovered. It may be very wonderful and complicated, but there maybe nothing particularly 'quantal' about it. However, certain parts and arrangements of protoplasmic materials form arrays of quantum entities that can get into a state of what is called 'quantum coherence', rather as happens to the photons of light in a laser beam. It is this quantum coherence which is the basis of your mental life and is the physical basis of the correlation of your brain activity with your mentation, moment by moment."

Me: "There you go again: another bombshell. You are saying that thinking is a quantum phenomenon?"

Mediator: "Yes, in fact it can be said that your ancient conundrum of the relation between mind and matter should now be reformulated in terms of the wave and particle duality of quantum reality. This does not 'solve' the problem for you exactly, since you are still some way from understanding quantum reality. However, it does allow you to see why you really had no hope of approaching answers to problems about the relation between mind and matter in the past, and it gives you a direction in which you can now press your investigations. It is not a matter of Either-Or, but rather of Both-And. You can safely say that minds and matter are 'complementary' aspects of the same reality–just as waves and particles are 'complementary' aspects of tiny physical entities. Remember, however, that nothing IS continuously: at bottom, the world-process is a succession of temporary 'happenings' (experiences even) that alternate between precise 'particulate being' and a superposed 'wave of possibilities' of becoming. Above that level, it is a hierarchy of habitual, repeating cycles upon cycles of experience, which don't necessarily repeat exactly all the time because of their quantum base, but do so often enough to seem to be continuous entities that just ARE. What you call 'matter' is an interpretation of the past-face of the present; while 'mind' is the experiencing and choosing components of the present and future faces of Reality Now.

Me: "That reminds me of some other ancient thinker who said, 'One cannot step into the same river twice, because the water is always moving on.'"

Mediator: "There you are: open-minded, flexible thinking again. Your ancient Greeks really had something. That is brother Heraclitus."

Me: "Ah yes, I remember now. Hello, '<u>Is</u> brother Heraclitus'? No, on second thoughts, don't answer that, I think I have probably had enough for one session. I hope I'm going to be able to remember all this."

Mediator: "Don't worry, you have been chosen for the task and will do it well enough."

    With that somewhat comforting comment I drifted into another sleep.

Cycle Eight:

Beauty and Time Present

As the 'day' of my new cycle dawned I became aware again of a lovely scent of flowers and the swish of wind in foliage, reminding me of the gum trees of my youth. Slightly surprised, I opened my eyes to find that the garden was much more extensive than it had been previously. *HeShT* said, "Enjoy." So I wandered around gladly, looking with amazement at the assemblage of beautiful plants, most of which I had never seen the like of before.

Me: "What are all these?"

Mediator: "We are giving you a view of some of the plant-like beings which exist in other worlds of your universe. You had asked to see something of other living forms, and it is safe to show you these. How do you find them?"

Me: "They are so beautiful. I'm reminded a little of our garden at home–greatly extended of course. Every plant is so marvellous in itself, and in their arrangement, with just that right mixture of symmetry and asymmetry to keep it endlessly interesting. O what a wonderful sight! Thank you so much for showing it to me. I don't think I shall ever want to leave!"

Mediator: "Go on, take your time, there is no rush." So I continued looking for what seemed like hours that passed in no time. Every corner I turned revealed another marvellous vista and I became quite intoxicated with wonder.

Me: "It's all so beautiful, so lovely. Why can't things always be like this? But why are you showing me this now?"

Mediator: "We want you to think a bit about the experience of beauty and what it means ultimately. Let Us give you one further happening and then we can begin considering the matter."

Before I could say anything, the great garden disappeared, and I began to experience a sort of amalgam of all the beautiful things and events I had had in my own life. It is quite impossible to explain exactly what it felt like. Presumably because I was living temporarily in a higher time dimension, I was able to enjoy <u>simultaneously</u>, events which in my own time had been encountered singly and separately. Just try to imagine a dynamic panorama of every marvellous experience you ever had–both personal and impersonal, including the ones which you had forgotten. It was quite astonishing and even rather frightening. It invoked in me a sense of having wasted at lot of opportunities and of abusing the beautiful things and persons I had encountered. Also I felt a surge of thankfulness for the privilege of having had these experiences and I resolved to respond to such things more appropriately in the future. I heard myself crying out, "'O, thank you, thank you', and, 'O I'm sorry, I'm sorry'" over and over again.

Then gradually and gently the vision faded.

Mediator: "Come with Us now to a quiet place where you can calm down. Then let us consider together what has just happened to you." The scene cleared, and we were back in my small comfortable garden again. HeShT continued, "You have just had, in a purified form, one of the fundamental kinds of experience of which your human life is composed. Although you will not always have been aware of it, beauty is there to be found in every moment of your life. Sometimes it is obvious and to the fore, but in others it has to be sought out diligently in amongst the ugly and even the horrifying. What do you suppose is the meaning of this kind of experience?"

Me: "I don't know, I've never really thought about it. One tends either to just accept it when it happens, or to seek it out when it doesn't. For me, music has been the principle source of beauty that I have sought out in my life, and also I suppose, beautiful looking people."

Mediator: "How do you feel when experiencing beauty?"

Me: "Joyful; ecstatic; really alive. Wishing that things were always like this. A desire to prolong the experience–indefinitely if possible."

Mediator: "And do you find that you can do that?"

Me: "O no, rather the contrary. Beauty never seems to last, and attempts to prolong the experience of it seem often to bring it to an end. It is most frustrating."

Mediator: "What happens to your sense of time when absorbed by beauty?"

Me: "Time disappears–even when listening to music, which is odd because, after all music 'takes time'. Yes, when I am transported by beauty I lose track of time."

Mediator: "Good. These thoughts of yours about your experience are a good starting point for us to take matters further. Would you agree that the beautiful could be described as a vision of how things ought to be?"

Me: "Yes, I suppose: especially if there was some hope that things could turn out that way."

Mediator: "Indeed. Can you see any problems with such a description?"

Me: "Well, yes I can. One is that there appears to be no universal agreement about what it is. Even people who are considered 'expert' in aesthetic matters often disagree with one other: one declaring 'ugly' what another finds 'beautiful'."

Mediator: "You are quite right, although there is often a lot of fashionable posturing in such arguments. However, you will agree that everyone has their own sense of what is beautiful, irrespective of the opinions of others, even if it would often be better for them to be honest with themselves about their own values?"

Me: "Yes."

Mediator: "In fact, everybody, without exception, has probably had this experience."

Me: "Yes, probably–as far as I can know what 'everybody' experiences."

Mediator: "Yes, quite. We can assure you that all human beings do. Do you think that they are any better for experiencing beauty?"

Me: "Well now, this is difficult. Speaking for myself, I sometimes find the experience uplifting and go away from it feeling great and motivated to do good things. But at other times I'm afraid, the beautiful arouses in me the desire to possess and to hoard."

Mediator: "Very well. Would you say that beauty should inspire the highest ideals, but can be subverted by self-centredness?"

Me: "Yes, that seems a good way of putting it."

Mediator: "What is the purest emotion that you can think of that the beautiful inspires in you?"

Me: "Oh love. Yes, love: pure, contemplative love."

Mediator: "Would you agree that love is the greatest thing in life?"

Me: "Yes, yes. Hasn't it been said that 'God is love'?"

Mediator: "Indeed. Would you say that ideally the experience of the beautiful should invoke a loving response?"

Me: "Yes, but…"

Mediator: "But what?"

Me: "But there are all kinds of love, aren't there: some more admirable than others? After all, the urge to grasp the beautiful for oneself, which I have just confessed to, could be seen as a form of love, couldn't it?"

Mediator: "Yes, but it's a pretty primitive one. When beings like you get a glimpse of perfection–which is what the beautiful is–they feel an enormous attraction, recognising that something of great value is here, and, quite naturally, they want it for themselves. This urge is a primitive form of love. But as you yourself remarked a moment ago, the beautiful never lasts, so such responses are ultimately frustrated. It is important to refine love so that its response to the beautiful is appropriate. We will come back to that later."

Me: "You just introduced another big word: 'perfection'. What should we make of that? You said 'beauty is a glimpse of perfection'."

Mediator: "Well spotted. What do you think 'perfection' means?"

Me: "I suppose it means the state of being just as things ought to be; 'just perfect' in fact. I'm going round in circles aren't I?"

Mediator: "That's right. Perfection is an idea you can have, but not being perfect, you cannot yet have more than an imperfect vision of it. For you, 'perfection' is a direction of thought, rather than a state-of-affairs. (As a matter of fact, it is not useful to think of it as a 'state' at all, but we will come back to that, too, later.) You can think of perfection as the highest ideal you can imagine. It would be a situation in which everything was beautiful. But already you will find this to be something of which you cannot form a clear image. All attempts at this sort of utopian vision, though useful if not taken too seriously, turn out to be grotesque. It is better to think of perfection as a direction of thought (rather than a state) and of beauty as a sort of pointer in the right direction. Beauty is also a provoker of that longing for perfection which we call love."

Me: "But it is not just a matter of longing, is it? I mean, longing is so passive. While it is a component of love, is it not also true that love includes a resolution to do something appropriate in response?"

Mediator: "Well done, just so. Now let's press on further. You will remember that when we were considering the nature of your experience of Reality, we saw that every, ongoing present moment of it has a three-fold structure?"

Me: "Yes I do: three 'faces' I think you called them: the past-face, the present-face and the future-face; every moment falling forward through this sequence."

Mediator: "That's right. Now with which of these faces would you associate the experience of beauty?"

Me: "With all of them, really."

Mediator: "Yes, but with which one in particular?"

Me: "O with the present. It is now, in the immediate moment of experience, that I know beauty."

Mediator: "Right. Could you say that you experience beauty as a kind of beckoning in every moment, an encouragement to go on, a direction in which to strive? And if the moment is one in which the absence of beauty predominates, to seek it out, or, if necessary, create it?"

Me: "Goodness, there is rather a lot in that last sentence."

Mediator: "I'm sorry. We tend to forget that you can only think of one thing at a time. Let's tease it out. What do you recall?"

Me: "Firstly, that the experience of beauty in every moment is a kind of beckoning forward towards perfection. (I find myself wondering, from whence comes, this 'beckoning')."

Mediator: "Good, but let's leave that for now and go on with the other points We made."

Me: "Secondly that the experience of beauty is an encouragement to go on when things are getting bad. I suppose this is the idea behind re-creation?"

Mediator: "Yes, partly."

Me: "Thirdly, the absence of beauty, or more positively, the presence of its opposite–sheer ugliness, is a challenge to do something about it; in particular to try to create something beautiful out of the mess."

Mediator: "Well done."

Me: "Yes, but that is all very idealistic, isn't it? Most of the time in fact, I find things neither beautiful nor ugly: just rather neutral or boring. Moreover, when I do find something exceptionally beautiful, the last thing I usually want to do, is to see it as 'a call to perfection'; rather, I want to grab and keep it for myself."

Mediator: "True. And We are glad to see that you are ready to admit that much about yourself: without it you would not be able to continue maturing. As to finding life 'boring', that is simply a matter of not knowing how to be truly present in every moment. This is a skill which you can acquire with the proper effort. If you learn to do it, you will find that every present moment is just that: a 'present' in which there is a gift of beauty to be discerned–if you look carefully enough–accompanied by a challenge to do something to encourage it to grow, and/or fight what is stifling it. That is what 'spiritual development' is all about: a perpetual attempt to be truly creative with what life 'throws at you'–however, 'boring'!"

Me: "It sounds awfully strenuous."

Mediator: "Think of it as exciting. Remember, I am always there to help you, if you ask."

I suddenly felt very tired but strangely relaxed and comforted. There was a bit of a niggle over the recognition that I hadn't been able to live up to this sort of thing, and probably wouldn't do so in the future. But I also felt a strong reassurance that all would turn out for the best in the end: *beauty would eventually prevail over the ugly*, even if this seemed a long way off in life as I and others usually experienced it.

With that I fell asleep again.

Cycle Nine:

Goodness and Time Present

This time I awoke to the sound of splendid music. But it was music such as I had never heard before. It was like all the harmonious sounds of nature joined with those of myriads of human voices: great waves of beautiful, infinitely rich, harmony. I opened my eyes and there was *HeShT* on every side, singing ecstatically like a great chorus. I cried out in amazement, "Oh *HeShT*, how wonderful. I've never heard anything so beautiful." After a while the singing subsided and I was left feeling greatly elevated.

Mediator: "You have just heard a little of our perpetual song, snatches of which were discerned by some of your ancestors who called it 'the music of the spheres'. It lies behind all your experiences of the call to the beautiful about which we were talking in your last cycle."

Me: "I would like to hear it always."

Mediator: "You are not ready for that yet; but one day you will contribute to it."

Me: "Never! I could never do anything like that!"

Mediator: "You'd be surprised. There is no limit to what you will eventually be able to do–if you are willing, and with our help. But that is enough of this speculation. Let's get back to work."

Me: "O it's 'work' is it: you never used that word before."

Mediator: "Well you are personally far from 'finished'. You and I have much labouring to do before you will be ready for your current assignment, let alone your ultimate destiny."

Me: "O dear, now you alarm me. However, let's get on with it."

Mediator: "Good. Now what can you remember about what we were discussing in your last cycle?"

Me: "We were contemplating the notion of beauty, weren't we?"

Mediator: "Yes, would you like to try to summarise where we had got to?"

Me: "No, but I will try. When we are truly present at any moment in time, we experience Reality as being more-or-less beautiful, that is, it approaches what we can envisage as more-or-less perfect. Further, this comes to us as a sort of mysterious gift from 'beyond' (whatever that means), and is both an encouragement to stick with it, and a challenge to be creative in response."

Mediator: "Excellent. Now we should consider what is meant by making this appropriate response to the experience of the 'more-or-less beautiful' in the NOW of every moment. Would you like to reflect upon the differences of your responses to beautiful as compared with ugly experiences?"

Me: "I'm not sure what you are getting at, but I suppose that beautiful experiences come as a sort of gift to be enjoyed, and the only challenge in them is how one should appropriate them. On the other hand the experience of ugliness, awfulness, or even boringness, is a challenge to do something positive about it: to try to remove it or convert it into something beautiful."

Mediator: "Very well. We have been considering the great human value of beauty; what further great value would you properly pursue when challenged by beauty or its absence?"

Me: "Oh, I suppose goodness."

Mediator: "Correct. You find yourself asking what is the morally right thing to do in the current circumstances. If you are truly present and awake, that is. And how do you know what is the right thing to do–what is goodness?"

Me: "O come now, how could I be expected to answer that sort of question?"

Mediator: "There you go, underestimating what We can achieve together! Let's examine the problem a little more closely. When confronted by moral dilemmas where can one usually hope to get some help?"

Me: "From traditional rules of behaviour, I suppose: like commandments, or even social mores."

Mediator: "And what is the status of these, in your estimation?"

Me: "Well, I know that many people think that things like the 'ten commandments' of Jewish tradition come straight from God, and I suppose that most ancient systems of thought consider something like this to be true. I'm told that they often have much in common."

Mediator: "So, do you think that any of these 'come straight from God', as you put it?"

Me: "I don't really know how I could establish that such a claim was true–and I'm not willing to assume that something is correct simply because it is part of my tribal tradition. I suppose, since you press me, I believe that such moral traditions are best thought of as deposits of human wisdom accumulated in the light of experience–an examination of the consequences of human actions in the past?"

Mediator: "That is part of the truth, certainly. But would you allow that the urge to goodness, like the perception of beauty, has something of 'the call from the beyond' about it? After all, all human beings have to make moral decisions, whether you want to or not, and even if you come to different conclusions about what sorts of behaviours count as good in different cultures. So we can say that the urge to goodness is a universal human experience."

Me: "That sounds all right to me, but I'm not sure that everybody has a moral sense."

Mediator: "O but they do, even when it is not apparent. The possession of it cannot be denied consistently, for to say that it is 'better' to behave without regard to the question of what is good, is itself a moral assertion, and assumes what it is at pains to deny."

Me: "Are you suggesting therefore, on an analogy of what has gone before on the question of beauty, that if someone is 'truly present' that they will obtain guidance in making moral decisions 'from beyond'? That sounds dangerous to me."

Mediator: "You are quite right, and your history is full of the most horrendous acts performed by persons who claimed, and truly thought, that they were 'obeying God' or whatever equivalent language they chose to use. No, while it is the case that help in making moral choices is indeed available to individuals, they usually also need the help of a committed community of persons with whom to engage corporately in their contemporary problems. To operate properly they need to be communities that are open-minded enough to recognise new approaches to novel problems or to ones which have hitherto been resistant to traditional solutions. Proposed moral responses, especially if they are new, usually need to be submitted to corporate examination before they should be adopted. Only rarely are exceptional individuals required to plough a moral furrow by themselves. Moral judgements, moreover, are sui generis, and cannot be reduced to anything else."

Me: "Does this mean that ancient traditions are worthless, and it would be better to dispense with them?"

Mediator: "Goodness me, no. Why should you think that your generation is all that much wiser than those in the past? Traditional codes of conduct were the product of generations of insightful wrestling with the human condition, and often represent very <u>creative</u> responses to it; they should be respected as such. However, the human situation changes–often radically–and new creative responses become necessary. Look at the new situation produced by the techniques of reliable contraception, and the challenges which that produces about proper and improper human behaviours: the simple application of traditional mores is inappropriate in such conditions."

Me: "Does that mean that we cannot have any absolute standards of human behaviour?"

Mediator: "No you cannot. There are no 'absolutes' available to you in this realm any more than there are in aesthetic judgements. However, human nature being as frail as it is, it is also important that attempts be made to formulate useful guidelines for behaviour, accompanied by some acceptable justifications for them. Both the act of discovering new kinds of moral behaviour and the construction of clear statements of these are creative acts. One of the genuine fruits of your so-called 'modern' knowledge is that there are no 'absolutes' available to human beings, in this or any other sphere."

Me: "Does this mean, then, that 'all is relative'? That it is up to everyone, or every group, to make up its own mind about how it should behave?"

Mediator: "Again, you put things too starkly. While it is true that every individual situation is unique and therefore ideally requires a unique response, it is not open to finite, sinful human beings to respond *de novo* to every situation in which they find themselves; the potentials for self-deception and 'enlightened' self-interest are too strong for that. However, in every situation there is the best response possible, and sometimes a whole range of adequate though less desirable ones–together usually, with some thoroughly undesirable ones–but only The Holy One knows exactly what the range is. We have to judge how far to try to influence your choices in the matter, without in anyway detracting from your creative freedom. We can only act out of Love, and that is incompatible with coercion of any kind."

Me: "But what about reason? Is it not possible to judge what would be the best thing to do by trying to compare the possible consequences of the different choices before us?"

Mediator: "Ah, now that is another subject, and we will have to get onto it in detail later. Your Western societies attempted, for a few centuries, to substitute reason for every other kind of judgement, serving the useful historical purpose of showing the strengths and weaknesses of trying to do things this way. But reason certainly has something to contribute, as we shall see.

Can we get back to the relationship between moral judgements and <u>time</u>? We have seen that the experience of <u>beauty</u> is especially associated with engagement with the very present of every present moment; what do you suppose is the temporal association of <u>moral judgements</u>?"

Me: "After leading me up the garden path like that how else can I answer except to say that moral judgements are clearly associated with the futures-present: they are concerned with what we should do in the future to try to improve on what we find in the present-present."

Mediator: "Right. However, you appear to be talking again about the 'future' as though it is already 'out there' waiting for you 'to come upon it', as it were."

Me: "I wasn't, as I suspect you know very well. I have taken on board what you have taught about reality being only NOW, though I acknowledge that it is very easy to forget it and relapse into old habits of thought–thank you for reminding me. I assume you are leading up to asking me to summarise in my own words the relationship between the futures-present and goodness."

Mediator: "Got it in one."

Me: "Very well. Just as the value of beauty can be experienced as a sort of 'lure' in every present moment–holding out a vision that points in the direction of a distant perfection–so the experience of the need to make the proper moral choice in the light of the present, is a 'lure' that challenges us to be creative with regard to the range of future-presents before us. Both the judgement about what is 'beautiful' (that is pointing towards perfection) and that about what is 'good' (that is working towards perfection) are <u>creative</u> acts for which we can expect some kind of help from You. Though, at the moment I'm in a bit of a fog about just how that is supposed to work."

Mediator: "We think you are doing very well. Yes, there are numerous 'loose-ends' all over the place, and we shall try to tidy them up in good time. Meanwhile I think you have done enough work for one session, so just relax back into the present and listen to some more 'music of the spheres'–and rest assured, you are not required to do anything about the future-presents at this time: just enjoy."

I leaned back and turned my attention to the perpetual music. I was immediately carried away into realms of beauty quite beyond my powers to describe or reproduce. Then I drifted blissfully into sleep.

Cycle Ten:

Truth and Time Present

I woke up with a question for *HeShT* already formulated: "Why isn't <u>reason</u> a sufficient basis for morality?"

Mediator: "Goodness, you're quick off the mark today? Don't you want to know how they are getting on below?"

Me: "That can wait. I am more anxious that there will not be enough time for you to answer all my questions."

Mediator: "I can tell you now that there will not be time enough for that! Besides, We must leave you something to work out for yourselves! However, there is no need for you to worry."

Me: "Very well. What then about the question that is exercising my thoughts at the present: Surely the more we know about how the world works, the better able we will be to decide what to do about the things we find wrong with it?"

Mediator: "Yes, that was the great dream of what you call your 'Enlightenment' –the programme to replace the superstitions of religion with the certainties of reason. There was just one major snag."

Me: "Oh, and what was that?"

Mediator: "Rational judgements and moral judgements (and incidentally, aesthetic judgements) are quite distinct from each other. While it is true that rational thought might often give one insight into the possible consequences of pursuing different courses of action, it will not, of itself, tell you which outcome is the right one."

Me: "I don't see why not. If one course of action will lead to, say, the saving of lives and another to the loss of them, then surely it is obvious which of them one should choose."

Mediator: "Sometimes it is true, the alternatives can seem pretty obvious, with the right choice being the one with which most human beings would agree. In such cases, the rational prediction would certainly be a help. But once again, it is not a matter of a simple either/or. Even you presumably, can recognise that there have been situations when a group of people have felt it better to die for what they thought were noble ideals, than to live only to fall into the hands of a savage enemy."

Me: "True."

Mediator: "Sometimes, even when the alternative logical outcomes are very certain, there may still remain a very difficult moral choice to be made: as for instance, when a doctor has to choose between the life of a mother and the life of her child in a difficult childbirth. It is here that most human societies prefer to resort to traditional mores or laws as a guide, since most individuals baulk at trying to make momentous decisions of this sort on their own. Even then, there is not necessarily any protection against a terrible sense of guilt, which ever choice is made."

Me: "Yes, I see it is more complicated than I had realised. What then is rationality for?"

Mediator: "Well it arose in your animal ancestors because of the survival value of knowing something about how the world proceeds. It has burgeoned in you human beings into an insatiable curiosity about just about everything. Although, of course, the dominant motive is more often the practical one of trying to get what you want done.

Can you suggest what great <u>value</u> rational thought is principally concerned with?"

Me: "I wondered when you were going to ask me that. I suppose, following on from what we have done so far, Truth is what you are after. Thought is the pursuit of truth."

Mediator: "Quite right and there are many kinds of truth. Furthermore, nature, through the great amount of thinking which you human beings have done over the ages, especially in recent times, has certainly unearthed many truths about herself."

Me: "I would not have put it that way myself, but that is an interesting slant on the matter."

Mediator: "Yes, as we have noted already, you tend to think of yourselves as over-against nature (which your men set out to 'conquer') instead of recognising that you are simply nature studying herself. Rational thought is an attempt by nature to understand itself. It can usefully be divided into the pursuit of general truths and the search for forensic truths. General truths are those patterns of behaviour of nature from moment to moment, which include what your scientists have called 'the Laws of Nature': an understanding of these regularities to date is the bases for predicting the future–think of weather forecasts. Much more subtle, are the general truths of human nature which all mature cultures develop and explore by their literatures, drama, and so forth. Forensic truth, on the other hand, while it might involve notions of general truth, is much more concerned with what actually happened in a particular instance. These are the truths pursued by detectives, historians and journalists, for instance. So what is truth?"

Me: "Just when I was settling down to enjoy today's 'lecture', you have to come up with a brainteaser like that."

Mediator: "Yes I noticed you were falling asleep. Well, go on have a try–What is truth?"

Me: "O dear, let me think. I suppose it is just what is the case–absolutely?"

Mediator: "Very good; that will do to start. Truth is 'what is the case'. Do you think you can ever know that?"

Me: "Yes, why not? But I suspect that you are going to say that I, or we, can't."

Mediator: "Give me an instance where you think you know the truth about something."

Me: "Very well, and just to show you that I haven't been asleep, I'll give you a general truth and a forensic one."

Mediator: "Bravo! Well go on–have a try."

Me: "As an example of a general truth, I could say that the disease malaria is caused by a microscopic organism (whose name I've forgotten for the moment); and as a forensic truth, I give the recent case in the news, of a wife convicted of stabbing her husband to death: one can safely say that it was 'true' that she killed her husband. How about those?"

Mediator: "They are indeed good examples for us to examine. (By the way the name of the malarial parasite you were looking for is Plasmodium–a Protozoan.)"

Me: "Thanks, now I remember. It must be age, or the anaesthetic."

Mediator: "Both! Now let us take your example of a general truth first. You say the truth is that Plasmodium is the cause of malaria. That is certainly a humanly useful way of putting it, and it is clearly part of the truth, since it enables you to get some control over the disease. But a moment's thought should show that the whole truth about 'the cause' would also have to include at least, the mosquito that carries the parasite from person to person; the marshes in which the mosquito breeds; the weakness of the public health system which fails to drain the marshes; the non-delivery of anti-malarial drugs due to the diversion of funds into military adventures; the genetic susceptibility of the host, and so on. These are all also part of the truth of the situation, because without any of them there would not be any malaria. In fact, one can say that the human hosts themselves are also 'part of the cause of malaria'.

Your second, example, the proposed forensic truth, that this particular wife killed her husband by stabbing him to death with a kitchen knife: this is also only <u>part</u> of the truth–sufficient indeed, to invoke the laws which put her in prison for life. However, We can tell you that her deed was an act of desperation, after year upon year of psychological abuse from her husband, who was able to put on a very plausible front of normality in public. He in his turn was terribly scarred by the ways his step-parents had treated him. Also, she had not been taught to stand up for herself early in a relationship, and had let it fester to breaking point. So it could be said that both the husband and the respective parents were also 'part–cause of his death'–not just the act of stabbing. Of course, the law, no matter how subtle, can never take every such level into account. There are human limits to how far one can probe."

Me: "I suppose it is the aim of liberal laws to extend these limits as far as possible?"

Mediator: "Certainly, but they can never take into account the whole truth."

Me: "Oh, and why is that?"

Mediator: "Can't you see the implications of what I have just outlined?"

Me: "Well no–my mind has gone numb again."

Mediator: "That the absolute truth about absolutely anything, entails the absolute truth about absolutely everything else: which is something that no finite being can know!"

Me: "Does this mean that there is no Absolute Truth?"

Mediator: "No, of course not. It means that only The Holy One can know the Absolute Truth about anything–you have to put up with constructed, partial truths–creative, open-ended attempts to approach the Truth."

Me: "Very well. Where does today's discussion take us?"

Mediator: "Let me ask you, with which aspect of the present moment of reality do you associate truth?"

Me: "Oh I see what you are getting at. By extension from our contemplations of the values of beauty and goodness and their relation to the three-faced present, you are asking me to associate truth with the past-present face of the present."

Mediator: "Well, isn't it so?"

Me: "It is not immediately obvious to me–after all we often speak of the truth about the present and the future as well as the past."

Mediator: "You have lapsed once again into normal human habits of thinking of time as a continuum from the past through the present and into the future. Remember, reality only happens in the present–there is no separate past or future to be truthful about. I realise that you will have difficulty in holding this in the mind, but you must persist in trying.

Just think: 'the past' is simply *the memory in the present* of what the present once was. What one calls 'the truth of the past' is simply a reconstruction of either what the present once was on a particular or sequence of separate occasions (forensic truth), or it is the discernment of a typical pattern of behaviour of successive past presents (laws of nature or general truths). There is no absolute guarantee that such patterns of events will continue into future presents–if there were, then nothing would ever change in a significant way. 'The truth about the future' is simply informed guesswork, based upon 'the truth about the past'.

As for the truth about 'the present': this ultimately means how nearly it approaches perfection, and this cannot be known to you as an imperfect being: you have, in fact, only your aesthetic judgement of how beautiful it is.

Can you see a pattern emerging in all this?"

Me: "Well I can see that there is a correlation between three important human values and the three 'faces', as you have called them, of reality NOW. But so what?"

Mediator: "These are not just any values. Beauty, Goodness and Truth are the three classical cardinal values. Between them, properly generalised, they include all human values. The pursuit of them is what human life is about. They are obviously closely related, and your philosophers (and poets) have often wrestled long and hard to try to reduce them to each other: truth is beauty etc. But while there is a commonality between them they remain stubbornly distinct, and now I hope you can see why."

Me: "Vaguely, yes."

Mediator: "Don't you see? Your experience of Reality is irredeemably temporal: you know it as a succession of three-faced present moments, and each member of the great triad of human values is associated primarily with just one of the faces. So: experience of the lure of the Beautiful is associated with the sheer presentness of every given present; the lure of the Good comes in the form of the range of futures-present felt to be on offer in every present moment; and the lure of the Truth is the challenge to try to unearth the past presents still present in the actual form which the present moment inherits.

This then, is the pattern of the strategy of human life: you experience the mystery of each moment of Reality as more-or-less as it ought to be (so far as you can judge), you know yourselves to be challenged concerning just what to do about the situation; and you recognise that only a good understanding of how things got to be the way they are, will help you to make an informed moral choice about what to do next."

Me: "Yes, now I see how all these things fit together. Very impressive; but it all seems rather abstract."

Mediator: "Of course it is. Every individual person happens in a unique situation, and the beautiful, the good and the true are specific to them. We have just been trying to give you the picture at its most generalised. There is much more still to come."

Me: "I look forward to exploring it with you. You have given me much to think about, but I can't take any more just now."

Mediator: "Of course: use this present to rest.

Cycle Eleven:

Temperaments, Triune Virtues and Reality

"What you were saying last cycle, reminds me a bit about a way of classifying persons as head-, heart- or hand-people", I said immediately I came around.

Mediator: "Hello. Welcome back! Yes, that can be a useful way of dividing people by temperament, which was discovered by brother Galen–one of your ancients, though it requires four groups in fact."

Me: "Really? How is that?"

Mediator: "Since you have brought up the matter, we might as well start with it. We can relate it to where we have reached in our exploration of Reality.

The first thing to notice is that temperaments are <u>biases</u> in the personality–rather like handedness. A properly balanced person would always act appropriately with either the head or the heart or the hand. However, most of you human beings are disposed by your genes to emphasise one or other and then neglect the remainder progressively."

Me: "Oh it is a matter of genes, is it? Perhaps you would enlighten me.

Mediator: "Gladly. But first you should try to see where the fourth temperament comes in.

There are two kinds of temperament in what you have called the 'hand' group. Let me characterise them. 'Hand-people' are the *activists*: they comprise rather more than half your populations and are concerned primarily with <u>doing</u> things, not so much with thinking about them or evaluating them (although they may do these too). However, there are two kinds of activists, about equal in numbers: those who like to do things <u>by the</u>

71

book; these value traditions, rules, mores, timetables, schedules and so on–they run your institutions. The second kind of activists prefer to act <u>spontaneously</u> and get easily bored by rules and regulations; they like to put off decisions until the last moment and then act on impulse–you will find them in dangerous sports and jobs, and in spur-of-the-moment activities, like fire-fighting or stand-up comedy. Teachers know these two groups very well, as the earnest, co-operative kids, on the one hand, and the easily bored, uncooperative ones on the other.

The remaining, smaller half of your populations is composed of about equal proportions of the remaining two of your three temperaments: the head- and heart- people. The head-people react to any situation by wanting <u>first</u> to <u>think</u> about it: to ana-lyse it or classify it, or attempt to anticipate the consequences of it (do you recognise the type?). The heart-people on the other hand, react immediately to a situation by wanting to <u>evaluate</u> it in terms of whether or not it is good for people; they tend to be the carers in society. These last two temperamental types may not be much good at practical action, and tend to be looked down on by the majority activists as hopeless dreamers or idealists, but when they manage to inspire activists they can change the world."

Me: "That is very interesting, but how do you make it out to be 'in the genes'?"

Mediator: "You have long been a social species, with co-operative behaviour (at least at the level of the small troop) being one of the secrets of your biological success. We watched the evolution of it amongst the various hominid species which came and went on your planet. Now you should appreciate that the 'organ' of human societies is the institution–a set of mutually agreed pro-cedures which has been found to work. Institutions are run with enthusiasm by the hand-type which likes traditions. However, to maintain their usefulness (that is survival value in biologi-cal terms), institutions must change in a perpetually changing world and not become fossilized–which is certainly what they would do if they were left in the hands of traditionalists only.

So the spontaneous activists were evolved, by your successful kind of human being, to ensure that your institutions are kept fluid and moving.

But the spontaneous activists tend not be much concerned with the direction of movement so long as there is some. This is where the two minority temperaments come in. By themselves, they would be hopeless at running things, but they perform the vital task of analysing and evaluating them–why they fail (which they all do eventually since they are finite creations of a finite being) and in what directions they could and should change. The head-type evaluates by analysing structures intellectually and by looking for rational possibilities for improvement, while the heart-type evaluates in terms of how they could be more as they 'should' be in human terms: that is more beautiful. The latter are upset, both by the inevitable victims of imperfect institutions, and also by the wounds inflicted on one another, especially by the two majority hand-types, who find each other maddeningly incomprehensible."

Me: "I find that very helpful, but perhaps a bit oversimplified?"

Mediator: "All good classifications tend to be both useful to a degree and oversimplified. Not only do individuals sometimes show the characteristics of more than one temperament, as growth and maturation round off the personality, but also, no classification covers all aspects of a reality–especially of a being as complicated as you are (it may say nothing about a sense of humour, for instance). The broader significance of this type of classification (and there are other, more subtle ones) is that it draws attention to your individual limitations, and how you should learn to rely upon one another in order to make properly balanced and socially valid responses to things."

Me: "Thank you. That clears up that bother for me. Now where do we go from here?"

Mediator: "Well, 'head-person', to get back to where we were last time: if you agree that human values can be classified under

Beauty, Truth and Goodness, as the lures of Reality in every single, triune moment of experience, can you suggest three human <u>virtues</u> which may correspond to them: that would be the proper responses to these three lures?"

Me: "I might have known that you were going to start challenging me with questions like that. You should realise by now that I am no good at these comprehensive kinds of answers."

Mediator: "Just relax and let something come into you mind. We can wait."

Me: "O dear, you are not going to let me off the hook, are you? Let's think … virtues associated with beauty, truth and goodness. Ah yes, I can think of a threesome of virtues, but whether it is relevant I don't know. What about faith, love and hope?"

Mediator: "There you are: spot on first time. You really should have more confidence in yourself. Yes, these are the three 'theological' virtues singled out by that remarkable early Jewish Christian, Paul of Tarsus, in a letter he wrote to the newly formed church in Corinth. Like the three classical values we have been examining, they are related but distinct, and cover comprehensively all human virtues. Can you now pair them off with the values?"

Me: "At first sight they all seem to apply to all three."

Mediator: "Indeed they do, but each has a special relevance to one of them."

Me: "Let's see: Love would seem to be especially associated with beauty. I suppose one can say that beauty evokes love–Oh yes, we have been here before, haven't we? While Hope seems more appropriate to Goodness than Truth. For if the opinion of what is right is always somewhat tentative, then one needs Hope to persist with it. That leaves Faith which would therefore have to be paired with Truth, but I don't see quite how."

Mediator: "You have paired them off correctly. See, once again, you've got it right, though we need to consolidate your tentative identifications.

Love is indeed the natural virtue that is evoked by beauty. Of course, as we remarked previously, there are lower and higher forms of love. The kind of 'love', for instance, which at the biological level is for the attraction of mates, might lead to the betrayal of beauty at certain higher levels of social interaction. Expressions of higher love often call for the restraint of lower love.

Then, as you rightly recognised, Hope is the virtue most strongly associated with goodness. One might have thought that virtues like fortitude, consistency, moral fibre etc, were more appropriate, but they are all contained in the broadest meaning of Hope. As we saw when considering goodness, there is no absolutely sure-fire way of knowing what is the morally correct thing to do in any circumstances. Moral-judgements are *sui generis*–they stand by themselves–and are a measure of *the moral maturity and insight* of the being who exercises them. This means that having made one's moral choice, *one has to proceed in hope that it is the correct one*, since there can be no complete going back to try again, once a choice has been launched. A morally active person is always a hopeful person. Part of this hopefulness comes from a positive attitude to life itself; but we will have to come back to that later.

Finally, there is Faith. It is commonly thought that faith is the opposite of doubt. Certain types of religious persons are always urging others 'to have faith', by which they mean 'know for certain'. In fact, *faith is the opposite of certainty*. Your human knowledge of truth is always partial and incomplete, and this means that your beliefs about things will always be shadowed by doubts. Many people have been made to feel guilty about this, which is very cruel. Doubts are an inevitable part of honest thought. But intellectual integrity requires you to work continually towards a better understanding of the truth, in the faith that there is truth to be found, and that what you have already is an approximation to it. Faith in persons is sometimes contrasted with faith in your knowledge of things and processes, but this is really only a matter of degree. Faith is trust and understanding in the face of finitude.

Would you like to try now to sum up where we have got to?"

Me: "I'll try:

- We human beings experience Reality as an ongoing present moment which has three faces: the past-presents still present, the present-present in its sheer presentness and the range of future-presents on offer at this moment.
- Each of these is experienced as a kind of mysterious 'lure': the present-pure as <u>beauty</u>, the future as the call to <u>goodness</u>, and the past as an invitation to unearth the <u>truth</u>.
- The appropriate human responses to these lures are the virtues of <u>love</u>, <u>hope</u> and <u>faith</u>, respectively.

This presumably applies to <u>all</u> human beings, irrespective of culture or religious allegiance?"

Mediator: "Very good. Yes, it applies to everybody, though not everybody would want to put it in this way. We have accommodated our presentations to you personally, considering your particular temperament and limitations: we do it very differently with others."

Me: "Once again we seem to have covered a lot of ground in a concentrated way, and I feel exhausted."

Mediator: "Of course. Have a well-earned rest."

Cycle Twelve:

My Parents - Real Now

"Wake up Enni, wake up child...!"
I came around hearing these repeated phrases. At first I thought it was *HeShT*, but was puzzled by the words. Then I awoke with a start, for I had recognised the voice, or rather the voices: I opened my eyes and there, surrounded and supported by the myriad faces of the *Mediator*, were my mother and father–long since dead and half forgotten!

"Mother!" I cried, "Father, what are you doing here?" There they were, in front of me, a sort of composite duo: first my mother was to the fore and then my father. They were facing my direction but seemed to be looking right through me, almost as if sleepwalking. Then they spoke together.

"We are glad to meet you again and to see that you have done so well. How is your sister?" "She is very well", I stammered, hardly knowing what to say, "And how are you?" "We are progressing", they replied rather oddly.

And we went on for some time in this way, exchanging platitudes, since I was too startled and overwhelmed to think of anything really appropriate to say.

Then the encounter terminated suddenly.

They said, "We are glad to see that you have met the Great Friend - listen to *HeShT*...listen to *HeShT*...listen to *HeShT*..." and they began to fade back into the crowd again.

I was panic stricken and cried out "Don't go, Oh please don't go, I haven't begun to tell you all the things I have done; and about our children whom you never met and your great grandchildren... Mummy, Daddy, stop, stop, don't go away. Please don't go away!" And I began to flail about and sob helplessly. But they merged back into the huge mass of faces.

Then *HeShT* began to sing and embrace me warmly, rocking me like a baby. I was racked with disappointment and frustration, and a sense of great personal inadequacy. It was a long time before I recovered. Eventually I asked angrily and petulantly, "What was all that about; why did you do that to me? It was cruel, and probably hurt them too. Or am I talking nonsense, as usual?"

Mediator: "I'm sorry to distress you so, but it was necessary to ensure that you took this cycle's matter seriously and not just as an interesting idea to be entertained in your head. The meeting was reassuring for them also."

Me: "You mean that all that was just a put-up job, a sort of charade to get me into a proper state of mind?"

Mediator: "No, not exactly. They were certainly your mother and father, or a part of them, which We awoke temporarily from their unconsciousness to meet you here…"

Me: "What do you mean, 'part of them', and 'awoke from unconsciousness'"?

Mediator: "Patience, patience, we are here to understand all that– but all in good time. I want to assure you that your parents were genuinely glad to meet you again and to be reassured about your life after their death. But they have now returned to their long sleep, until the time of their re-integration and awakening."

Me: "All this is too fast for me. What had they to be reassured about? What is this 'long sleep'…?"

Mediator: "All good parents have some lingering regrets about what they did or did not do for their children–none of you are perfect, and by now they will have been exposed to their naked selves–never a very comfortable experience. But you are trying to rush Us again. Let's take this matter step by step."

Me: "Very well, but I'm still very upset and puzzled: 'naked selves?'"

Mediator: "I know that, so let's begin. We are going to consider what has happened to your ancestors–all of them."

Me: "All of them?"

Mediator: "In principle, yes. Where do you suppose they are now?"

Me: "That sounds a very silly question. How on earth should I know? I'm not even sure I know what it means, 'Where are they now?'"

Mediator: "Just think back to what we were considering earlier. When is Reality?"

Me: "Well NOW, of course."

Mediator: "So when are your ancestors?"

Me: "You don't mean to say … No you can't mean it … you don't mean to say that they are here and now? … You do, don't you!"

Mediator: "Yes indeed I do. Remember that the present is a record of past-presents. It is all there is of Reality for you. All that ever happened NOW–or all that could be preserved of it, is here and now, always."

Me: "I can't get my head around that idea: you will have to help me."

Mediator: "Of course. Let Us lead you into some sort of an understanding. Your present life is a succession of moments of experiencing Reality in which you are given the opportunity to do the best you can to leave things better than you found them– however awful. This can be seen as a process of stamping your imprint upon that part of Reality which is within your reach– including, of course, other people. Every single, morally free agent, in this way makes their own characteristic mark upon the way things are. As you go through life, you become surrounded, as it were, by a halo of patterns that are a sort of extension of yourself. Just as you may leave your unique finger-print upon a cup, so, in the course of your life, you leave a characteristic mark upon the face of Reality. It is the humanly recoverable parts of this unique finger-print that historians and biographers use to reconstruct what they think once happened in a life. Of course, their powers of recovery of past-presents in the present are very limited, but it is all there still and visible to Us. A good analogy is the way in which the coded information about the appearance of an object is dispersed all over a hologram, so that illuminating even only a tiny piece of it with a laser beam recovers a slightly degraded image of the whole. You may only be able to discern a very small portion of the traces of another person still active in the present, but We can decode it all."

Me: "You said something about my parents 'relapsing into unconsciousness'; does this mean that beings in this extended state of yours are all unconscious?"

Mediator: "Yes and no."

Me: "Here we go again!"

Mediator: "You are asking the questions–and their limited assumptions circumscribe my answers. To continue: Let us go back to your parents. In the course of their lives both of them, like everyone else, made an impact upon and a difference to Reality. Since they lived together meaningfully for much of their time, a large proportion of their extended Selves became entangled with each other's extended Self–this is the reason why you saw the composite image of both of them just now; part of each of them will remain so enmeshed for always. When they died, and the matter of their temporary bodies went back to nature for recycling, all that remained of them was this, ongoing and developing, pattern of their extended Selves: the multiple ways in which the world was characteristically different because they had operated in it. This includes you, of course, since much of you is one of the ways in which the world is characteristically different because of them!

Me: "So my parents are in me?! What a strange idea."

Mediator: "Yes, and in many other persons besides. Now, while they were alive and awake, they were conscious. Consciousness is a form of mental activity which is possible to creatures like you because your brains have evolved to a level which maximises your capacity to respond in a considered fashion to what happens around you. Your conscious 'simulator' of anticipated events is fast enough to keep up with the changes in your immediate vicinity so that you can react swiftly and appropriately according to your will. The frisson between what you anticipate and what actually transpires (which is almost always minimally different) is the immediate cause of your 'consciousness'. It all depends, however, upon having an intact and properly functioning, complex structure like the brain. You lose consciousness if the brain is injured, or it goes 'off line' in deep sleep–and when it decomposes in death. (Incidentally, this gap between what your stimulator anticipates and what actually transpires when you catch up is the basis of your human sense of humour–especially when the disparity is surprising and delightful.)

Now, to get back to where we were: Your lifetime memories are encoded, in the first instance, in the material of your brain, and as such are more-or-less immediately available to aid in your conscious responses to Reality as it happens moment by moment: they are the basis of good habits. However, after your death, when your extended Self is dispersed widely in the world, it is no longer closely integrated and therefore is incapable of conscious thought. *However, it still functions unconsciously*–this is the physical basis of 'the climate of the times', or 'the soul of a nation' etc. For these are the combined influences of all previous lives in your culture. You will remember what We indicated to you about the mental, being a complementary aspect of the material? That all Reality is *Experiencing Reality*? Well, your consciousness is a wave aspect of certain material functions in your <u>brain</u>, while your post-mortem unconscious mentation is the wave aspect of your <u>dispersed Self</u>. In consequence, when you die you will survive <u>initially</u> as only your unconscious extended Self but will still influence the world

81

process in your acquired, characteristic way. (This Self is what is what is really meant by 'the Soul'.)"

Me: "You say 'initially', what do you imply by that? And what is this 'acquired, characteristic way?'"

Mediator: "Patience. There is certainly more to 'life after death' than an unconscious influence! Your biological bodily organism gives you a spurious sense of being an integrated whole person–its very integrity chains you down, so to speak. But in reality, the real you is much wider than your body and your little consciousness. (It is also a bundle of contradictions, with both good and bad habits.) When your body disintegrates at death and ceases to function, then these deficiencies will stand exposed to you. When this happens you will, mercifully, not be given quite as comprehensive a view of them as We have all the time, but you will see enough to be humbled. But for now We want to be sure that you have grasped the full significance of what We have said so far. So if I ask you again 'Where and when are you ancestors?' how will you answer now?"

Me: "Pity I have to let all that lot go until later, but let's see if I can get this right. Since the present moment is the only Reality, then the past–including all the people in it (if it is to have any reality at all)–must also be here and now. The present is a record of the past and the only 'where and when' in which dead persons can still be happening. They continue to happen in the ongoing present moment as the form (both physical and mental) of the characteristic pattern which they imprinted on the present in their lifetimes. However, since they are no longer happening in an integrated, higher organism, but in a dispersed pattern, they are no longer conscious, but operate unconsciously. How is that?"

Mediator: "That is a fair summary of where we have got to. Corrections can come later. Good. I wonder if you have noticed the relevance of all this for another phenomenon which has puzzled human beings for a long time?"

Me: "Oh, and what is that?"

Mediator: "Hauntings."

Me: Ah yes, of course. Hauntings are a sort of visualisation of parts of past Selves, still dispersed in the present."

Mediator: "Yes, and you may also recognise that hauntings often seem to happen when they relate to incidences of considerable emotional weight. Characteristically they are found where a group of people have been living together under great emotional tension for a long time, and the whole thing comes to a climax of some sort–often involving the violent death of some or all of the parties concerned. These are the kinds of life-experiences which leave behind in the ongoing present, a very vivid and more than usually coherent record. Moreover, the persons who experience the resulting hauntings are often themselves a prominent part of that imprint, whether they know it or not. Their experience of the ongoing unconscious reality is a sort of internal echo–a resonance which they externalize through their simulators. Others, similarly related to the events in question may witness the same haunting experiences–even simultaneously. Your encounter with your parents earlier was of this nature–We just facilitated it."

Me: "But if that is all there is to life after death, it sounds pretty dull and what is the point of it?"

Mediator: "Yes, of course, and we will get around to that, but We think you have had enough to consider for the time being. Rest assured that We have a much more interesting story to tell later."

Me: "I still miss my parents, you know, and wish that I had taken the trouble to know them better."

Mediator: "We know you do, We know you do. But you will be able to rectify that eventually."

Me: "Really?"

And with that I gladly relapsed again into unconsciousness myself.

Cycle Thirteen:

Body and Mind, Ego and Self

I awoke and demanded right away, "I want to know more about where my parents are now."

Mediator: "Not so fast; and that tone, though understandable, is not appropriate here. We will tell you as much as you can understand and is profitable for you to know, when you are ready to hear it, which is not quite yet."

Me: "I'm sorry, I'm sorry. It's just that you have revived so many guilty feelings in me. I didn't always treat my parents as well as I should, and I want to know that they are not suffering still in consequence."

Mediator: "Of course, I understand, and you will be properly assured, and in good time will be able to make amends. But first we have a few other matters to clarify. We want you to get a better understanding of who you are first, then you will be better able to appreciate the position that others, including your immediate parents, are in."

Me: "'Immediate parents!'?"

Mediator: "Good, you are awake. Let's get on.

By now, you should have begun to see yourself as a sort of mind-body composite, related to what your physicists describe as a wave-particle duality in atom-sized entities. You cannot have one without the other. Currently, your personality is focussed upon a particular body–the one 'down there'–and will remain so until it finally ceases to function. (Oh, and by the way, before you ask, you are coming on just fine.) You also have the now common knowledge that your mind can be divided into a 'small' conscious part, and a 'large' unconscious part–often likened to the proportions of an iceberg above and below the water line. Some of your psychologists have also recognised that the unconscious part is itself 'layered' in some way. I will now tell you more about that.

A useful analogy to keep in mind, is that of an archipelago of islands in an ocean. Each island represents an individual person and has a portion which is more-or-less permanently above water–this corresponds to the <u>conscious mind</u> of each separate individual. (I suppose you could envisage it is being flooded at night when you are asleep.) Then there is the littoral zone–that area on the beaches which lies between low and high tide: this is equivalent to what has been called your <u>'personal unconscious'.</u> This 'contains' all those memories which you have temporarily half forgotten, but which still influence your conscious behaviour without you recognising it. Then there is that part of the island which is permanently underwater. This corresponds to an aspect of your personal unconscious which has deeper roots than simply forgotten memories. It is this layer which We want to elucidate for you just now. Then, finally, there is the seabed, upon which <u>all</u> the islands stand, and which joins them all together, so-to-speak. We will have a look at that too. Are you still with Me?"

Me: "So far, yes–I think."

Mediator: "A word about your superficial, personal unconscious–the one corresponding to the littoral zone in the model. There are many reasons why you have forgotten memories. Some, simply because the events did not have sufficient emotional strength to be recorded in a way which would make them readily recoverable, and others, which had so much negative emotion attached to them that they were buried because too painful to recall. The details need not concern us here–it is sufficient to point out two things: firstly, such memories continue to influence your behaviour unconsciously (think of phobias, for instance) and, secondly (which is implied by the first), that you are much more than your conscious 'self'.

It is this last point that We wish to emphasise for you since it is such a common source of misapprehension in you human beings.

All human persons have a sort of centre-of-gravity of their waking consciousness which is often referred to as 'the ego'. This, in common language, is what most of you call 'myself'. Each of you has a conscious self-image, which is a composite <u>memory</u> of the kinds of ways you have behaved in the past. You commonly think of this as your 'self'. You also have an image of each of your friends and acquaintances, and you construe this as their 'self'. In both cases you are only partially right. The 'selves' which you normally consider yourselves to be, are simply the centre of that *temporary mental complex* called the conscious mind. You Westerners have spent several centuries building up a very strong sense of this kind of 'self', which is the basis of your individualism. But just think for a moment how precarious this consciousness with its 'ego' is: you lose it every night when you go to sleep; you can lose it if you have a blow to the head; it vanishes under anaesthetic (as a general rule!); and, particularly relevant to our concerns here–it disappears when you die; permanently this time."

Me: "Well, if I am not who I am, who am I? That sounds very confused doesn't it?"

Mediator: "That is because you are confused, and it illustrates Our point admirably. The conscious mind is an important product of your biological evolution, it allows you to be effectively present in the everyday, and to bring to bear your memories of, and emotions associated with, similar past experiences, in an effort to cope with every particular situation. It also monitors your habitual behaviours and enables you to acquire new ones, should you so choose. As such, it has more survival value than instincts, which are the relatively inflexible, unconscious memories of the species rather than the conscious and subconscious memories of the individual. But in human beings, consciousness has the further value of permitting you to build images and models of the world which you can 'play with', and continuously compare with experience, and contemplate as approximate truths. But whatever you do, you should not confuse your Self with this temporary mental construct: your consciousness is merely a useful, but temporary manifestation of your true Self, which is the centre-of-gravity, so to speak, of your whole mental life - most of which is unconscious."

Me: "So you are saying that most people confuse their ego-consciousness with their Self?"

Mediator: "Yes, and it is the fear of losing this 'ego' that most often gives rise to a fear of death. But it has become quite obvious to most people by now that you will inevitable lose your consciousness when you die—which is why so many non-religious persons, and even some religious ones, have given up any kind of belief in a life after death. (You personally haven't lost consciousness here and now with Us, because you are not dead, and furthermore, you are privileged to have this very special experience to report back.)"

Me: "Very well then. Tell me more about this Self, which you say is my 'true Self' and distinct from my conscious ego."

Mediator: "Your consciousness is the mental aspect of just some of your brain functions. Your whole mind—most of which is unconscious—is the mental part of your total physicality."

Me: "You mean the rest of my brain and perhaps the rest of my body?"

Mediator: "O yes, that and much much more."

Me: "What 'more' is there?"

Mediator: "Have you forgotten already what we were saying about your extended self: those personally characteristic patterns in the ongoing present which you have constructed in the course of your life?"

Me: "Of course. Yes, I had forgotten them–too much to take on board and keep in mind. So you are saying that part of my unconsciousness is an unconscious mental aspect of this extended 'image' of my Self which I have impressed upon the world, and the people I've met?"

Mediator: "Yes, and will keep on extending throughout your life."

Me: "And when I die, that is all that will be left?"

Mediator: "Effectively of this life, yes."

Me: "That sounds a bit evasive: as though there is more."

Mediator: "Yes there is: We were hoping you might think it out for yourself."

Me: "I suppose we haven't considered what might be the part of my Self that corresponds to the part of your island model that lies permanently below sea-level. Is that it?"

Mediator: "Yes, indeed. This part of your unconscious has been called by one of your psychologists 'the collective unconscious': does that give you any clue?"

Me: "No, not really. Does it mean that I share it with others–my contemporaries for instance?"

Mediator: "Something like that. I wonder what you think will happen to your extended image in the world after you are dead."

Me: "I've no idea. I suppose it will slowly get mixed up with all the extended images of others and then slowly be diluted or fade away–not a very exciting prospect, but I cannot envisage anything else."

Mediator: "Well go away and think about it. Take a stroll in the garden and then sleep on it."

So I did as I was told.

Cycle Fourteen:

Re-engagement NOW

I lay awake for some time worrying about the thought of living on beyond my death in some unconscious state or other. I thought of my parents too, and others, and could make no sense of it, or see any better prospect. If, as *HeShT* insisted, this NOW was the only Reality there was for us, then there seemed nothing for it, but to just lie around waiting: if we are to survive after death at all.

"Right, you can stop pretending now. We can see that you are getting nowhere and only worrying yourself to death. Wake up and let's get started", said *HeShT*.

Me: "Believe me, I want nothing better."

Mediator: "You seem to have understood that when a person dies and their body is returned to the cycles of nature, all that remains of them is the pattern which they had impressed upon the Reality of the ongoing Present."

Me: "Yes, I have got that; though I cannot say that I'm entirely comfortable with it. But go on."

Mediator: "Thank you! Let me direct your thoughts to the deep unconsciousness which makes up the bulk, so to speak, of your mind. This is a body of dispositions which you did not acquire in your lifetime, but which can still influence your behaviour profoundly, all the same. Where do you think they come from?"

Me: "Perhaps they are the mental equivalent of my animal instincts–a memory encoded in my genes from my animal ancestry?"

Mediator: "Well done–but that applies only to a part of one's deep unconscious–the part that was modelled by the seabed in our picture of the archipelago of islands–what about the perpetually immersed slopes of the island itself?"

Me: "You mean that part of my personal unconsciousness, which came neither from my forgetting, nor my genes?"

Mediator: "Yes."

Me: "I cannot imagine. What else is there in my personal experience except my own life and my genetic inheritance?"

Mediator: "What about previous engagements with this life?"

Me: "You mean some kind of previous life?"

Mediator: "Well?"

Me: "O dear me no! That's for Far-Eastern religions and Californian cranks: all that living and reliving, reincarnation and stuff! I can't believe that. I don't want to believe that."

Mediator: "I can see you are prejudiced."

Me: "It's not prejudice–it's common knowledge."

Mediator: "Quite a good definition of prejudice, We would say."

Me: "O dear. I feel quite let down. Who was I last time? Napoleon or Marie Antoinette?"

Mediator: "Isn't it interesting, that when considering this idea, people always think they must have been somebody famous! The chances must surely be against it. It is for the same reason that you are taken in by lotteries. Anyway, We see we have some work to do convincing you of this truth. Part of your problem is the misapprehensions you have about the whole idea. These stem from the commonly held belief that you are your consciousness, which you have not yet disabused yourself of."

Me: "O well, go on: convince me."

Mediator: "Let Us try to outline the sequence of events that occur when creatures like you pass from one lifetime to another. Human beings have crossed the evolutionary threshold which gives them, in any particular life, some conscious freedom to respond positively or negatively to the the lures of Beauty, Truth and Goodness. By means of these responses you build up an unconscious, extended Self that is a sort of record of the kind of person you are. When you die, this 'record' is all that remains. The ordinary conscious ego, which you were 'lent' in this life, disappears together with the body which was its immediate material aspect. However, your deep, personal Self–the mental aspect of your extended material Self–remains. Now this is where you must try to forget your prejudices and take on something new. Part of this extended Self now becomes focussed again upon a new, potential human being–usually a developing foetus–so that a new life of conscious engagement with Reality begins, with the legacy of unconsciousness from previous lives. This new conscious ego does not, of course, usually remember past lives, which is just as well."

Me: "How does it become focussed, as you say, upon a new baby? Does it have any choice in the matter? Is there any rhyme or reason for the choice? Does it run in the family, for instance?"

Mediator: "These are questions to which full answers cannot be given to you: partly because you could not understand them, and partly because it would serve no useful purpose to know them. Suffice it for Us to say, that the time, place and potential person for your new engagement is governed by laws of nature which you have not yet discovered for yourselves."

Me: "Will we ever do so?"

Mediator: "Very probably, but that time is still some way off. A few of your great minds, reflecting upon this possibility, have recognised that there must be some meaningful relation between the kind of life you lead in one incarnation, and the situation in which you will find part of yourself in the next; though they have often thought that the relationship was a much tighter one than it is: generally a case of making the 'punishment fit the crime'. The Holy One is more merciful than to work in that rigid way. We will only tell you that the particular kind of body in which you will find yourself re-engaged, with its particular array of strengths and weaknesses, will itself usually be a part of your on-going extended physical Self."

Me: "I have just had a thought. If what you say is correct, both my parents could be alive again somewhere in the world–I may even have met them unknowingly! Surely you know this: if you do, please tell me."

Mediator: "No, that would not do at all. I can just see you rushing off and blurting it all out. That would get you, and the whole notion into disrepute. No it is better that you do not know that sort of thing; just as I would not reveal to you who you were previously–before you get around to asking. As far as you are concerned, your parents may or may not be re-engaged in the world at the present time. They will be, when it is appropriate, and, in any case, you will all meet again, eventually, in a manner which is quite beyond anything you can imagine now. But only when the time is right."

Me: "All this is so new an idea to me, that I don't know what sort of questions to ask. You appear to have put the most obvious ones out of bounds to me–those that relate to me personally. I must try to clear my mind and assemble my thoughts."

Mediator: "Perhaps a summary of where we have got to in your own words would be a useful way of going about that."

Me: "Very well. Putting it in personal terms. My present life, with my current self-consciousness, is a temporary form of engagement with Reality, bearing unconsciously the dispositions which I built up in previous lives. These are encoded in the patterns in the world which I previously constructed in those lives. So I am much 'bigger' than is apparent from my current identity. When I die, my present conscious personality will disappear, leaving this life's addition to the accumulated greater Self, as an unconscious aspect of all the ways in which Reality is different on account of all my engagements with it in past-presents. Then, according to some law of nature unknown to current science, part of this extended Self will be appropriately refocused upon a new biological life which will develop its own characteristic conscious personality. It will have all my unconscious previous Self as its mental hinterland. How is that?"

Mediator: "Yes, you have grasped the main points, and your summary should help you to know where to go next."

Me: "Perhaps, but just at this moment I feel very confused, and cannot for the life of me see the point of it all. But I'm beginning to realise that I have much more to learn than I had previously recognised. I shall try not to be so belligerently critical in future!"

Mediator: "O don't worry about that. We are used to it. In any case, such little emotional outbursts as you are capable of here, show that you are properly involved and are more likely to profit from the exercise."

Me: "Thank you. I feel a sleep cycle coming on."

Cycle Fifteen:

Realistic Eschatology

I awoke and declared, "I still don't think I much fancy the prospect of living in the world over and over again."

Mediator: "We are quick off the mark this time! Well in fact, you will have no choice in the matter, just as you didn't choose to happen in the first place–but you will thank Us in the long-run. So you don't relish being perpetually engaged in the task of co-creation?"

Me: "Well, putting it that way sounds a bit more interesting, but I still don't really like the sound of it."

Mediator: "What would you prefer?"

Me: "I suppose I never really thought about life after death. It was something I didn't want to face, or supposed one could not know anything about, for certain, anyway. I think I hoped, like many people, that if I behaved myself well enough, I might expect to get to heaven."

Mediator: "Oh, and what and where is that?"

Me: "You ask me?–I should have thought you would be telling me."

Mediator: "We want you to say what you think you mean by 'heaven.'"

Me: "You put me on the spot again. As I said, I had never thought very carefully about it. I suppose heaven is thought of as some sort of place, 'out of this world', where one can rest blissfully from the labours of life, and live in the presence of God. How is that?"

Mediator: "All right, let us examine that statement. Do you think it likely that this incredible universe (not to mention the other universes We told you of) is a sort of transitory antechamber to heaven: a mere training-ground for human beings, in preparation for a state of perpetual rest? Ultimately destined to be scrapped when humanity is finished? What a waste, apart from anything else."

Me: "You have a way of rubbishing my ideas by recontextualising them. Put that way, the idea of heaven sounds like an escapist's dream."

Mediator: "Sorry to seem so callous. Let me ask you further, why should you wish to 'live in the presence of God' as you put it? Why would that be so desirable, and in what do you suppose it would consist?"

Me: "O dear, once again you have unearthed one of my vague ideas. Isn't 'being with God' supposed to be the most desirable thing?"

Mediator: "Doing what?"

Me: "Just being, I suppose."

Mediator: "Really? Is that your view of a preferable post-mortem existence? Isn't 'just being' indistinguishable from 'not-being at all'?"

Me: "Well, worshipping then."

Mediator: "O come! Now you are just mouthing religious platitudes. How do you envisage 'worshipping'–endless hymn singing, or well-constructed prayers, or heaven forbid, playing harps?"

Me: "Now you are mocking me."

Mediator: "No, We are trying to shake you out of your religious rut."

Me: "All right, why don't you just tell me the answers and let me try to understand them?"

Mediator: "Very well. Perhaps you have suffered enough for the moment.

Let's open up some other considerations. Ever since you human beings crossed the evolutionary threshold that allowed you to develop so-called self-consciousness; to become aware of a personal responsibility for the future, and to begin to construct an elaborate, unconscious, extended Self in the material world of persons and things around you, we have watched you wrestling with the problem of death. You recognise that death seems to negate the promises which life offers. There is all this Beauty, Truth and Goodness, and the sense of personal achievement in being creative with it, and then along comes death and puts an end to it all, without any apparent compensations. Death seems, in fact, to be the ultimate evil, that crowns all the other evils which frustrate the higher things in your life generally, taking your loved ones away, and so on.

In response to all this, human beings have wrestled with the problem and have found (and been enabled to find) various images that help you to cope with an issue whose true solution is still well beyond your ability to comprehend. It is literally not possible to convey to you the exact Truth about your ultimate future in Reality; all that you can have are some suggestive images. Otherwise you have to proceed by faith. Call it 'faith in life' for the moment."

Me: "Well, why not just leave it at that. Why not just say that we should have faith that all will be well in the end? Something like: 'The God who made us first time round can make us again in whatever manner He wishes'."

Mediator: "Yes, there are robust persons for whom such an etiolated statement is sufficient. But most human beings have never been content with minimalist visions of this sort. Throughout your history, attempts have been made by philosophical and religious persons to fill out the vision of post-mortem existence as a way of giving some substance to their hopes. The best of them recognised the provisionality of all such visions, which are properly called 'myths'. But these have a very important place in human culture, leading to much artistic endeavour, for instance. Many of them are, in fact, approximations to the real truth, although none of them have, or could, tell the whole of it.

Me: "Oh I know some people who claim to know exactly what will happen to them and others after death."

Mediator: "O yes, so do we; they are to be found on many worlds. Such beings are really deeply anxious about their lives, and are grasping frantically for some absolute certainties in a matter where certainties are not available. Living before the uncertainty of life after death, is better than living with some supposed, but wrong, 'certainty' about it."

Me: "What about those persons today, who hope to use biological advances to live for ever?"

Mediator: "It is rather sad really. 'Living for ever' it could not be, as a moment's thought should show–not even your sun will do that! And while there is likely to be some success in prolonging the average human life by a few decades, or even centuries, just think about the increasing anxieties such long-lived persons will have. For instance, about the possibility of accidental loss of life, or death by some new disease! They would probably live lives that are increasingly obsessed with personal safety–that is if they are not bored out of their minds first, having exhausted their personal resources for creative living. Prolonging biological life in this way is irrelevant in the context of eternity, and it may also pose some very difficult practical and social problems for the societies which develop it."

Me: "Why did you say that living in the face of the uncertainty of life after death is better then living with some supposed certainty of it?"

Mediator: "Because the prospect of personal death, if faced and acknowledged, tends to focus the mind upon ultimate questions, discouraging you from dissipating your energies in the pursuit of hedonistic trivialities and mere distractions.

Let's get back to our survey of human attitudes to death. Most early human cultures regarded the world as 'only' a few thousand years in age (long in proportion to an individual's life, certainly) and to have been 'created' in a form very similar to the present, with human beings as part of it from early times. They also saw very little reason to believe that it could change much in the future. When they coupled this with their experiences of its manifest unsatisfactorinesses (despite the promises of beauty also found in it) they considered that any desirable, ultimate future world *would have to be a 'new' creation*–somehow quite different from, and unattached to this one. You know now, however, that the world is an evolving system, which has in it the potential for radical change, so that any 'new' creation must nowadays be envisaged by you as the result of the development and perfecting of this one, not a wholly new replacement. One can say that neither the knowledge of your ancients, nor their imaginations were up to the job of foreseeing a change to the current world of such a magnitude. It remains to be seen how long it will take your species to embrace this new vision: it has the knowledge–it just needs the will and the imagination: a great task for your artists of all kinds."

Me: "This will require a very radical modification of religious views, and religions are notoriously resistant to this sort of change."

Mediator: "True. However, they have done so from time to time. Take the Jewish-Christian religious adventure, for instance. Two hundred years before Jesus of Nazareth and the Emperor Augustus, an attempt was made by Hellenists to destroy Judaism. Now the Jews, up to this time, had refused to develop any clear picture of life after death–having no evidence one way or the other. But when they saw all their good men and women being cynically massacred on the sabbath, because they would not defend themselves on that day, they turned to the Persian religious insight of a post-mortem resurrection to life in this world, to express their belief that God would restore the righteous to life in this world at some future date. The Jews never developed this idea very fully, preferring wisely, to leave such speculative matters at the level of images.

Then several centuries later, when Christians, who had had direct experience of resurrection and who were wrestling with what they saw as the problem of what would have to happen to imperfect human souls after death, to make them fit 'to meet God', came up with the idea of *'purgatory'*–a place of correction and refining, where the soul would have to reside until <u>ready</u> to come safely into God's presence.

These are just two examples of human efforts to clarify what they believe *must be* some aspects of post-mortem existence. The images of 'heaven' and 'hell', as places to which souls may be sent as rewards or punishments for the kind of lives they have led, are other examples. These are notions which testify to the recognition of the seriousness of the consequences of what one does with one's life. Many more instances could be given. It is always important when one is considering traditional teachings on matters of this importance, to ask yourself–not what words did they use–but *what were they really trying to get at <u>in your terms</u>*, and to recognise that they were necessarily using the mythical method to express their insights in such matters. When you have done that, you may be able to come up with a contemporary expression of the same idea, modified by any new knowledge and philosophical dispositions which you now have. Your own task, when you return from your operation, will be to spark off thoughts of this kind in some of your contemporaries."

Me: "I look forward to that and to the new religious insights that will flow from it."

Mediator: "You don't really suppose that they will believe you, just like that, do you?

Me: "Oh I am beginning to think the case is persuasive enough."

Mediator: "Such naivety! Radically new ideas are rarely acceptable to the faithful. They may even be a source of danger to you personally. However, allow people to consider them a 'mere myth', so that they will get under their skin surreptitiously and be entertained lightly, while permitting the preservation of their precious intellectual or theological integrity."

Me: "I'll try to remember that. Thank you. Now it's time for me to sleep again."

Cycle Sixteen:

My Extended Self and Others

I opened my eyes and found myself already looking down at my body, stretched out on the operating table below, as if trying to 'earth' myself. I saw that the mask was off my face and the crew had lost the anxious looks in their eyes. However, it still did not seem that very much had happened since I last observed them.

Mediator: (reading my thoughts) "It hasn't, but I can tell you that the crisis is past, and you are on the mend. We still have plenty of our time here, though, and I suggest we begin. Would you care to try to summarise, and make sense of, how you now see your whole Self and the nature of your immediate future after death?"

Me: "Very well. My conscious self, centred on my ego, is a small, temporary mental aspect of my whole Self which is more extensive than either my consciousness or my body. My body is a quantum-bio-physical entity, the product of the exertions of millions of my biological ancestors (pre-human, as well as human), which has been 'lent' to me, so to speak, as a temporary means of engaging in the world-process NOW. It has a normal developmental pattern of birth, maturation and death. The mental aspect of it consists of a personal consciousness (when I'm awake and alert) and a personal unconsciousness, comprised of the residues of forgotten experiences, which none-the-less still influence how I behave: it is the basis of my acquired habits. How am I doing?"

Mediator: "So far so good–go on."

Me: "During the course of this life I have extended both my physical and mental Self in the form of the sum-total of ways in which the pattern of Reality in the present moment is characteristically different because of the ways in which I have acted wilfully in it. The physical aspect of this is all the artefacts and personal consequences which are now in the world because of me, and the mental aspect is the wave-component of these physical patterns. This 'projected' or 'extended Self' is what this life of mine could be judged upon. All right so far?"

Mediator: "Yes, very good. Now finish it off as best you can."

Me: "Well the projected Self, which I have constructed in this life, is a further extension of the Self which I have already made in previous engagements with Reality (incarnations), whose mental aspects make up my deep personal unconscious. (Are these what Jung called 'archetypes'?)"

Mediator: "Yes, partly. Go on,"

Me: "I suspect that there is an even deeper mental aspect of my Self which could be called 'the collective unconscious', but I don't know what to make of that."

Mediator: "What about your anticipated future after death?"

Me: "O yes, you asked about that too. Well, as far as I can see, the implications of all this are that when I die this death–that is this biological body ceases to function–I will survive in the dual aspect of the physical patterns in the present due to this and all my previous 'lives', and the attendant mental aspects, which, initially at least, will be unconscious. (Is this perhaps what Paul meant by the 'sleep of death'?)"

Mediator: "Yes, he had an inkling of this aspect of the way things are."

Me: "However, it appears that a part of this extended Self in the present, will eventually become (by some law of nature, as yet unknown to us) focused upon another biological 'engine' which will be strategically placed to continue some aspect of what I had achieved or mismanaged in my previous lives. This sounds a bit like the law of 'karma' in some Eastern Religions–is that true?"

Mediator: "Yes, it is what they were reaching towards. The truth is, however, that the relationship between what one does in one life, and the kind of environment in which one finds oneself in the next, is a much more subtle one than some of these religious systems, with their rigid notions of caste, and so on, have often envisaged."

Me: "Let's see, what more should I say? I can't think of anything else to add, except to ask some questions."

Mediator: "Go ahead."

Me: "At what sort of time intervals do these 'incarnations' occur? Does one keep to the same sex? Is there a perceptible advance in character between one life and the next–for instance is a famous person, even more famous in the next life? And what is the point of it all–where, if anywhere, is it all going?"

Mediator: "That should suffice for this session! The intervals between lives vary greatly. Sometimes the rebirth is immediate; sometimes it is only after many of your centuries have passed. You didn't ask where it occurs with respect to the last life. The answer to that is, usually quite close and in the same cultural environment, because that is where the most opportune continuities are most likely to be. However, it may be far off–even, in fact, (though so-far rarely) on other planets in your universe.

And no, you do not necessarily keep to the same sex; that depends entirely upon what your calling is in your new life. That is, what aspect of your Self and the Selves of others *you would be best placed to develop, mitigate or excise.*

Then you ask, 'If you are a prominent person in society in one life, will you be even more so in the next?' No not at all. 'Prominence in society' is a rough measure which *human beings* use to assess the significance of a person. You usually call it 'being remembered by history'. However, even apparently very obscure persons can make a hugely creative contribution to how things develop by acting properly at a critical moment. Such contributions, significant as they may be, could, none-the-less, go completely unnoticed by your recorded histories. To take one obvious instance, you may sometimes have wondered how many remarkable mothers or wives lie, unacknowledged, behind the lives of 'famous' men. Since, to date, your histories have tended to be written by men, this possibility has either not occurred to them, or they have ignored it. In fact, it is often true that the real moving force behind a significant event in human history has been a mother, or teacher or other unrecognised influence on a celebrated life. Similarly, highly significant lives from your perspective may not seem so important from Ours.

And another phenomenon you might like to consider in the light of your new knowledge is that of so-called 'genius' children, who seem to be born already old: their 'unconscious memories' are very influential in their current life. And yet another one is the apparent 'possession' of one person by the powerful extended self of another–even one who is deceased.

Finally, you ask 'What is the point of it all?' That is a good question, and we are working around to some kind of answer which will satisfy you, but we will have to leave that for the present. Suffice it to say that there are some good, in-principle, partial answers, even if you would not be able to understand the full ones. Let me leave you to ponder another observation. So far, you seem to have considered your Self as a rather <u>isolated</u> individual entity. What do you think to be the significance of the observation that you, including <u>your</u> 'extended Self', has been the *recipient of the actions of many <u>others</u>* - all those persons, known and unknown to you, down the ages, *who have influenced you*, in this and previous lives?"

Me: "My mind boggles at the notion. Goodness me, what am I to make of that. All those thousands, perhaps millions of Selves, somehow 'in me'! Help, the more I think of it the more amazing, and even alarming, I find it!"

Mediator: "Why alarming?"

Me: "It implies that I am responsible for their extended Selves as well as my own, and that how I respond to their 'influences' will be significant for their development also!"

Mediator: "You are beginning to catch on to this new perspective. Something more, in fact, for you to digest while 'asleep.'"

Me: "Help! Good night."

Cycle Seventeen:

Me in You and You in Me

I came around to hear a loud humming, like the sound of a great power house. I was apparently suspended above a huge grey cloud. Some parts of it were black and strangely menacing, while others seemed bright and promising. Away in the distance there was a slowly pulsating and beckoning light.

"Yes, just focus your mind on that light and you will approach it", said *HeShT,* speaking behind me.

Me: "What am I looking at? Is it the galaxy again?"

Mediator: "You will understand soon–just go in closer."

So I did as I had been directed, and urged my mind towards the pulsating light. It felt a bit like racking up the zoom on my microscope. As I neared the object it seemed oddly familiar, and then with a cry I recognised what I was looking at: it was me, or rather my body, lying in the operating theatre!

Me: "What on earth is going on? What is all this?"

Mediator: "Look around you."

I refocused on the vague, white, black and grey shapes around my body and saw many familiar objects and faces and was puzzled to see that they all had their eyes shut. Greatly confused I asked: "Please tell me what I'm seeing–it's giving me the creeps."

Mediator: "Draw back again and watch carefully."

So, I racked back my zoom, as it were, and felt as though I was backing through a host of well-known objects and persons. Eventually I found myself looking down again at the great grey cloud where I had started.

Me: "I still don't understand what all this is, or why you are showing it to me."

Mediator: "This is a representation of how We see you–rescaled to fit your imagination–it is your extended Self, NOW."

Me: "What! Is all that me? I don't understand."

Mediator: "You are being particularly slow this time. Do you not remember what we were saying, about you being really a psycho-physical entity dispersed in the form of all the ways in which Reality is characteristically different, on account of how you have acted in it in this and your many previous engagements?"

Me: "O yes, now it comes back to me. It doesn't look very pleasant, does it?"

Mediator: "It isn't–yet. But you do have some redeeming features: they are the lighter bits."

Me: "You mean that all that greyness is the average me. While the light-bits are where I have got it more-or-less right and the black bits (I can hardly look at them without horror) are the consequences of where I have gone wrong?"

Mediator: "That's correct. Let Us draw your attention to some features."

At this point a grey area began to pulsate slightly, and without being bidden I knew that I had to home in on it. As I drew close I recognised some sleeping students with whom I had spent a rather disappointing week-end. And I remembered feeling that I had let them down by not preparing well enough and of not being interested enough in their concerns–I hadn't even remembered all their names. I thought to myself, 'Yes, that's average me, all right.'

Mediator: "Good. Now let me show you some other features."

There then began an incredible tour in which I revisited many memories of decisions made: good, bad and indifferent. *HeShT* explained that when I died this sort of tour would be extensive, and would be part of the preparations for my being refocused appropriately on a new life. Little would be omitted, and it was bound to be very humbling. For now, I was privileged to have a quick look, avoiding the darkest features. I was allowed some brief glimpses of the current consequences of previous lives, but not long enough for me to be able to identify them clearly (not relevant now, I was told). I even saw an ancient Self flaking flint-stone weapons on an African shore. Then, just as I was getting fascinated, *HeShT* interrupted.

Mediator: "That is enough of satisfying your curiosity for now. We must get on. Look at this."

I found myself drawing back from the grey cloud which was my true Self, so that other areas which I had not visited continually came into view over the horizon, as it were. Then we stopped.

HeShT said, "Watch." Then I saw another cloud appear, seemingly at an angle to mine, but intersecting me at many points.

Mediator: "This is your mother."

Me: "Really! How astonishing!" I made to focus in on this new image, but HeShT intervened.

Mediator: "No, there will be time enough for that when the proper moment comes. That is not our purpose now. Just watch and consider."

Disappointed, I concurred, and observed as HeShT added many other intersecting Selves. I soon became aware of the fact that I was not an isolated entity, but rather an individual enmeshed in a network of dynamic Selves all interacting with each other. HeShT was saying each time: "Now here is your father... your sister... your friend John... your companion Anne... and here Beethoven... the Beatles... Plato... Kamau... A.N. Obody..." Very soon I cried out, "Enough, enough! I appreciate the point, and I can't absorb any more."

Mediator: "You have caught a glimpse of how We see things all the time. For We are present NOW to everyone, currently dead or alive, as We are to you, and We see you all whole, and in your relationships with each other. Can you begin to understand what are the implications of all this for your personal relationships?"

Me: "Very well, I'll try. If this is all true and all our personal interactions are enmeshed in the form of the Present moment, then it means that we are all continually working upon each other's extended Selves. How I react to someone's influence upon me has an effect upon the form of their Self. And when I influence someone else, that effect becomes part of my Self, and their reaction to my influence is then a modification of me. It therefore follows that we are all responsible for each other at a far more intimate level than I had ever realised. When I do something dreadful and hurt many others in consequence, I create a black-mark upon my Self; but those whom I hurt, by their own responses, can either deepen that blackness–also adding to their own black-spots as they do so (say by taking revenge), or they can, by loving and compassionate acts, mitigate the effects of my failures, and help us all on our way towards becoming something better."

Mediator: "Very good. You have begun to appreciate the wider implications of all this excellently. Now let me give you a few last views of this aspect of Reality. Let's draw back even further from this representation of your extended Self."

With that I found myself flying away, so to speak, and suddenly my Whole Self came into view. It was a mottled grey, rather fuzzy, vaguely humanoid form, with its eyes shut and a dim light in its head. *HeShT* said: "There you are–still taking shape, but with a long way to go–many more lifetimes should do it. Let me show you brief glimpses of other persons–one at a time–don't worry, I won't overwhelm you again!" I then saw passing before me, many forms, some more distinct than others, and some much whiter or less grey than me. I thought I recognised a few of them as they briefly appeared before me. They all had their eyes shut, which I took to mean that they were still largely unconscious and therefore like me, incomplete. Perhaps the light in their heads represented their current incarnation?

Mediator: "You have concluded rightly. Your joint destinies are to become, eventually, a blaze of light, and fully conscious of both your whole Selves and of each other. You will have a complete memory of all your previous engagements with Reality and know how, and by whom, they were corrected and integrated (just as We do). You can perhaps appreciate that that is a state of being which is beyond anything you can possibly comprehend or imagine at present. Now I think you deserve a rest. So let Me return you to 'Eden.'"

I found myself back in the marvellous garden which I had experienced earlier, only this time I was not alone. I have extreme difficulty in describing what followed. I had with me now a marvellous, multiple companion. *He/She* was sometimes alongside me sharing the same joy, and sometimes dispersed all over the garden, appreciating independently. My companions' faces were many too, and it gradually dawned upon me that I was being accompanied by a sort of composite of the better parts of all the good friends I had ever had, and all the spouses with whom I had ever shared a life, and I wept with joy and excitement. We moved among the marvels, sharing our wonder, sometimes separately, then at other times fused as one. All the while, the air was filled with a harmony of all the music and the scents I had ever known, and I realised that I was being given a brief glimpse of an aspect of how things might one day be for us all, and was filled with a sense of infinite gratitude and love and hope for this 'existence', or happening, in which we all find ourselves. I began to wonder where it came from.

In the end, utterly and pleasantly exhausted, we lay down on a bank and fell together into a deep sleep.

Cycle Eighteen:

Our Unimaginable Future-Presents

I opened my eyes to find *HeShT* before me as expected, and immediately asked, "Do you never sleep?" "No" *HeShT* replied, "We have no need of that, and in any case, I must always be present to share our Being with 'happeners' like you."

Me: "You have awakened in me a great curiosity about our future-presents. If you can't, or won't, tell me about mine in detail, perhaps you can give me some, in principle, descriptions about the human future in general?"

Mediator: "I like 'future-presents', which shows that you have started to work with the new view of time we taught you. You will continue to stumble over the idea for a while, because it is so contrary to the very structure of your language, which imposes an ancient way of thinking upon you.

You ask about what the present will be like for human beings 'in the future'? May I remind you that We are unable to give you any precise facts about this for at least three reasons: firstly, we do not actually know yet what human beings will choose to do–that is the nature of your freedom; secondly, We know possibilities for you, partly on the basis of what other higher beings have chosen, which it would be unwise to reveal to you, since you should forge them in the course of your own history; and thirdly, there are possibilities which you would not be able to understand were I to tell you of them. However, it is appropriate at this time, that I give you *some* notions to go away with."

Me: "It sounds as though I'm going to have to settle for less than I had hoped for."

Mediator: "It will still be more than you bargained for. Let's get on. Perhaps we should start with your summarising where you think we have got to."

Me: "I understand that the Universe and the human race, has many future presents ahead of it (billions of years of them in our terms). I understand that I, and all other persons, will continue to have a presence in it, in the form of a series of opportunities for mutually perfecting each other, which will continue as, mostly unconscious, aspects of the structure of the present. Each conscious personality will be a partial implementation of the Self, which has been situated by a special law of nature, so as to maximise the usefulness of that life. But I don't have any idea of the content of these future lives, or of what exactly is the point of it all."

Mediator: "You are coming on. However, we invite you to change the emphasis of what you have just said: you spoke of the developments in the future, as though they were for the sake of humanity only. Let me remind you that you are a part of Nature as a whole, and it is Nature who is advancing when you do. Also, were you to see them, you would probably not regard some of your descendents as human."

Me: "That sounds alarming. However, thank you for that correction. I'll try to remember it in future."

Mediator: "In this next millennium, We can predict for you, that you will begin the great adventure of moving off this planet into a Solar existence. Your understandings of biology, information technology, energy transformation, and many other things, will ensure that the details of living, both on this planet and off it, will continue to change radically. There will probably also be major changes in the ecology of your planet: some of it as a result of your own activities, but also others, perhaps even more significant, as a result of other natural processes. You have lived through many millennia of relative calm on your world which provided a window for the emergence of your civilisations. But there is no guarantee that it will always continue like that: there are powers in nature far beyond anything you can muster–at present anyway. It could be that you will need an ark in space to survive at all. But this is something which some of your thinkers are already aware of. You will be glad to know that you personally, but of course, not as Enni Boddy, will likely play a useful part in all this."

Me: "I would dearly love to know just what."

Mediator: "Yes, wouldn't you, but not even We can tell you exactly what. You ask about the distant future also. The 'in principle' answer here is that the distant future-present will be as different from the present-present, as the distant past-present is from it.

Let Me invite you to consider the life of a white cell in your blood and lymphatic system. Each cell is a little organism. It has a life-span and a job to do. It has a sort of home in your lymph glands from where it sallies forth to scavenge for dead and dying cells in your body. From time to time it may be enlisted to join in attacking an invading foreign organism, and could even lose its life in doing so. In other words this little cell has a life and purpose of its own, which it discharges competently. Although it has its own simple view of things, it has no notion either of you, or of its 'real' purpose in your life. It does not see itself as a functional part of a relatively gigantic living thing. From your perspective the white cell is a sort of primitive organism, and even looks very like one under the microscope. Similarly, from the perspective of the future form of humanity, you are a primitive organism, and you would have as much hope of understanding that state, as your white cell would have of understanding you."

Me: "Surely, the fact that I can understand that idea puts me in a different category from the white cell. Are you saying that there are things about the world and especially its future that not even our cleverest men or women could understand?"

Mediator: "Yes."

Me: "So bang-goes all those attempts to formulate the ultimate theory of everything and all that?"

Mediator: "Well, not entirely. They are very remarkable achievements of your species, and We are very impressed and gratified by them, but they are not anywhere as near the last word as some of your people would like to believe: Nature has many mind-blowing surprises up her sleeve for you yet!"

Me: "All right. So you have given me some sort of picture of a distant future-present, very different from the present one. You have assured me that we will all still be present and involved, even when it has changed out of all recognition. But you have not yet given me any sense of what it is all about: *What is Happening?*"

Mediator: "Yes, that is the question, and we are now perhaps just about ready to approach some sort of answer to it. You will remember earlier We asked you to try to say what 'perfection' meant?"

Me: "Yes, I remember, and you said it was a state beyond the comprehension of an imperfect being like me, but that the idea was a sort of direction of thought."

Mediator: "Good. And can you remember what feature of your experience we recognised to be the best pointer to perfection?"

Me: "Yes, Beauty."

Mediator: "Good. And what was the highest natural human response to beauty?"

Me: "Love."

Mediator: "Splendid. So we have a cluster of ideas: Perfection, Beauty and Love. I wonder if you would sleep on those and then come up with some idea of your own about the point of it all?"

Me: "I suppose, one could add Truth and Goodness also?"

Mediator: "Of course, but let's contemplate Beauty first."

And with that I drifted off to sleep.

Cycle Nineteen:

Yeshua

There appeared to be something different about *HeShT* when I next came to. Looking carefully I recognised why: amongst the array of many faces which appeared and disappeared all around me were some belonging to my own friends and spouses who had been with me in the garden a cycle or two back–only, their eyes were now closed. They had been there all the time. I had just not noticed.

Mediator: "Yes, what you see is the better parts of them which have already been partly taken over the threshold into the new level of psycho-physical reality."

Me: "You are going to have to explain all that."

Mediator: "You will remember the lighter parts of yourself in the vision I showed you? Well these represent those dispositions which you have acquired–by your efforts and those of others on your behalf–which are sufficiently compatible with the per-fectibility of Nature, to be already transformed, although still unconscious. What you are seeing here in some of Our many faces are those metamorphosed dispositions of persons whom you have known personally."

Me: "I think I've got the gist of that. Does this also mean that parts of me are here also?"

Mediator: "Well you are here are you not?"

Me: "Goodness, you are full of surprises."

Mediator: "You haven't seen anything yet!"

Me: "Good Lord!"

Mediator: "We wondered when you would get around to that."

Me: "O my goodness ... O How blind I've been... I almost daren't think of how disrespectfully I've behaved, I'm sorry, I'm sorry... There I go babbling again...! O dear, O dear, what do I have to do or say now?"

Mediator: "Never mind all that: it gets rather tiresome at times. Just keep on as you are, and think of Us as your constant companion, with whom you can argue and grumble as much as you wish. It's time We opened up another stage in your enlightenment. Have you any ideas, or shall We prompt you?"

Me: "Yes, I have one. Several times in our recent discussions I have found myself wondering about Jesus, the Jew from Nazareth. Where does he come in all this–if at all? Is he still being reincarnated down the centuries or what? Or is it all a myth anyway? Shouldn't we now be talking about religion?"

Mediator: "That rather depends upon what you mean by 'religion'. Religions are a system of humanly devised beliefs, commandments and rituals which have developed in response to a particularly vivid religious experience or set of experiences of its founder or founders. As such, all 'religions' are, to a degree, deeply flawed and incomplete institutions, which are always in need of correction and advancement. In a way, Jesus the Jew, can be seen as proclaiming the ultimate end of 'religion' in this sense, though he thought of himself primarily as a reformer of Judaism. In his historical life he had such a natural and spontaneous relationship with the Holy One, whom he called his 'Father', that he really had little need for all the trappings of human religion. However, he recognised also, that the human frame required props of various kinds, but envisaged them as being minimal: a few words said over grace at meals; the arrow prayer 'Father' at any moment, were sufficient. That has not prevented some of his followers from going over the top, and inventing an elaborate religion in his name. The real problems however, come when any such system proclaims itself as the one and only true way to relate to The Holy One."

Me: "Why do you keep speaking mysteriously of The Holy One?"

Mediator: "Let's leave that important matter aside for the moment, and concentrate upon Jesus– or Yeshua, as he was really called in Aramaic–his native language."

Me: "Very well. Where does Yeshua come into all this?"

Then, just for a moment, all the faces and stars that was *HeShT* seemed to collapse and coalesce into a single, androgynous figure with piercing, but kindly eyes, regarding me. But before I could even gasp, *HeShT* resumed the flickering, multifarious form that I had come to recognise and feel comfortable with. I knew I had been given some sort of answer to my last question, but did not dare pursue the matter immediately.

Mediator: "Very wise: Let's stick to 'history' for the moment shall we? You will know that Yeshua was an artisan from Galilee, in what might be called Northern Israel. He and his mother, brothers and sisters lived far from the historic centre of his faith in Jerusalem. They were a pious family, all well-versed in the prophetic traditions of Israel. You have some knowledge of the traditions about him so can you take the story on from there?"

Me: "I'll try. I recently read up on what some modern scholars had to say on the matter. When he was about thirty years of age he left his family business in the hands of his younger brothers and went to identify with a new prophetic religious movement started by a cousin of his called John the Baptizer. John had resurrected the ancient prophetic call to the Jewish people to repent and expect an imminent visitation from God. At the time, the territory of the Jews was a recent addition to the Roman Empire. They were a subject people and resented it. They also considered the occupation to be an insult to their God, and were constantly on the edge of rebellion and on the look-out for suitable leaders to free them from the Roman yoke.

Furthermore, the Roman tax-system meant that wealth tended to collect in the hands of a few. As a consequence, peasant farmers, whose families had owned a little plot for generations, found themselves having to sell their lands and eventually themselves and their families as slaves to greedy land-owners.

To make matters worse Judaism, under pressure from this terrible history, had gone into one of its legalistic phases, under the leadership of a well-meaning, but ultimately ambiguous, religious group called the Pharisees. They managed to produce such a sense of guilt in the population for failing to keep God's Laws, that there was an epidemic of psychosomatic disease. Poverty, illness, malnutrition and guilt, combined to produce large numbers of people who were crippled, blind, deaf and suffering from 'leprosy' and other debilitating conditions. In this situation John the Baptizer induced a tense atmosphere of expectation that God was about to intervene decisively on the side of Israel.

This did not come out of the blue, of course, since the insight that God played a part in the nation's history was an ancient one–at least as old as the Exodus from Egypt (more than a thousand years earlier)–not to mention the Exile to Babylon (six hundred years before). So it was with this teaching, especially its call to national repentance, that Yeshua identified himself, by going to be baptised by John in the river Jordan. He saw it as a call from God.

After his baptism, Yeshua immediately found himself precipitated into the front line, as it were, as God's chief executor. In the ancient Israelite religious vocabulary he knew himself to be, in effect, a special 'Son of God'. He soon took over leadership from John the Baptizer, who was promptly killed by King Herod Antipas as a dangerous agitator and critic. Yeshua seems to have recognised that he had little time in which to act. He appeared first in his home territory of Galilee, teaching that the Reign of God was at hand. His teaching was given much weight by the fact that wherever he went with it, the sick and the suffering were healed. Soon, of course, (our human nature being what it is) there were huge crowds pursuing him, wanting to be cured of their ills or to witness spectacular miracles. Others saw him as a possible military leader, whom they called the 'Messiah'. Only a small proportion of them were at all interested in his real teaching. However, he continued to heal all who came to him, out of compassion for them. He showed an incredible skill in teaching religious truth by simple story. He had little time for the legalistic hair-splitting of the Pharisaic type. His parables teased the mind of the hearer, so that those not ready for a particular truth would not see the point, while those who were, found themselves challenged to change their ways radically.

Mediator: "Good. What would you say was the core of his teaching?"

Me: "The sum total of his teachings and his activities in the short time which he had, before the authorities caught up with him, were 'That God is Love, and requires us to respond with love, and to love everybody else–including our enemies'. He seems to have left it vague, just how we should work out these two 'commands' in practice. Such a simple basic programme required no elaborate books, or confessions, so he didn't write any."

Mediator: "Yes, and much of subsequent Western history has been an attempt–only very partially successful–to implement them. It is early days still, however. Please go on."

Me: "Early days? O very well. The real test for Yeshua came, when he went up to Jerusalem, in effect to challenge directly the religious authorities to acknowledge that his teachings were from God. They would not do so however. Instead they connived with their Roman overlords to have him executed as a potentially dangerous, political agitator and blasphemer. Still he responded to all this hatred with love. So one Friday afternoon, in about what we call 30 CE, Yeshua of Nazareth was put to death by crucifixion, along with a couple of felons on a hill just outside the walls of Jerusalem.

Mediator: "So, that was that–failure?"

Me: "No. That should have been the end of the matter, as far as the authorities were concerned, but is was not. His followers, mostly Galilean fishermen and a few women, began a religious movement which soon spread into the Gentile world. One of their early converts was a fanatical Jewish Pharisee called Saul of Tarsus. Before the first century was out, these Jews, who believed in the One God, the Father Almighty, maker of heaven and earth, were soon producing a propaganda literature about Yeshua which, in effect, treated him as divine. This is a very remarkable phenomenon which our historians have found very difficult to account for, even when they have made serious attempts to do so."

Mediator: "Yes and the literature they produced is gathered into the collection called the New Testament, or New Covenant. It represents a first century attempt, written mainly by these Jews you speak of, to convey the belief that the historical Yeshua of Nazareth, who you have just described, and who was disgraced and executed by crucifixion, was, in fact, God's most beloved person while alive, and after his death, was elevated as God's right-hand man: a status he had had, in some sense, from the beginning of the creation! The question you have to ask therefore is–What sort of person must Yeshua have been to have given rise to this sort of incredible belief amongst Jews? Not a mere Israelite prophet surely? And what, in particular, could have convinced them of this high status before God? Furthermore, the movement which started in his name became, within only four hundred years, the official religion of the Roman Empire itself, and of its Emperor–a change of situation which was not without its problems either."

Me: "Well, this is all very interesting and most people who know this story can see that he was a very remarkable person. But all that was a long time ago and in a completely different culture. So many are wondering what possible relevance it could have for us now."

Mediator: "Why do you go to church?"

Me: "Out of habit, I suppose. Ours is a radical liberal congregation and most of my friends are there too."

Mediator: "Just as I knew already, but We wanted you to say it in your own hearing. You say that all this happened a long time ago, but remember what we said about 'All is always NOW', so this talk about 'then and now' is irrelevant. Also, there is one more significant event in the story of Yeshua which you have not mentioned in your outline, isn't there?"

Me: "I suppose you are referring to his so-called 'resurrection'?"

Mediator: "Why do you say 'so-called'?"

Me: "Well, nobody believes all that literally any more do they? I mean, people don't rise from the dead, leaving behind an empty tomb? 'Resurrection' is presumably a sort of metaphor for discovering a new motive for living after great disappointment."

Mediator: "I realise that that is what you have been telling yourself for some time. We have news for you, but that will have to wait until the next cycle, your eyes are getting heavy."

Then I was gone again.

Cycle Twenty:

Resurrection?

I awoke saying, "No I can't believe it: nobody rises from the dead; it is scientifically impossible."

Mediator: "So much the worse for your science. What makes you so certain that you know enough of the truth of how Reality works to dismiss the possibility out of hand?"

Me: "Well it feels impossible to me. If it is true, why don't we witness it happening all around us? What was so special about that man? In any case I cannot believe it with intellectual integrity."

Mediator: "We will grant you that last point. However, you are here to learn things which are beyond what your intellect yet knows."

Me: "Doesn't that violate your prime directive–not to tell us things we should discover for ourselves?"

Mediator: "No, because they won't believe you anyway."

Me: "Then I can't see the point of your telling me."

Mediator: "It will sow a small seed of doubt, which will eventually undermine certain pernicious certainties which get in the way of people's better recognition that ultimate truth is always mysterious."

Me: "You have an answer for everything. I'm sorry, I'm being petulant again. Where shall we start this time?"

Mediator: "We were reminding ourselves about the story of Yeshua of Nazareth. Paying special attention to the remarkable fact that so soon after his death by crucifixion, some of his Jewish followers were proclaiming him worshipful: they called him, not just 'Messiah' (Christ) but 'Lord'. There seem to have been two sorts of grounds for this remarkable belief—can you recollect them?"

Me: "Let me see… firstly, you were suggesting that he made a great personal impression on those who knew him; and secondly… I suppose you are referring to the resurrection, which I'm having such difficulty in accepting or understanding."

Mediator: "That's correct. The impression he made upon those who met him in the flesh was very decisive: very soon after any such meeting, a person found it difficult to be indifferent, and would either love him or hate him. In fact, a problem was to arise when his followers came to record his ministry, because his relations with individuals were so personal they could not be easily generalised. So they were reduced to trying to make images of what it felt like to meet him: these are the Gospels. The authorities, however, concluded that he was dangerous and should be put away. Would you like Us to remind you quickly of the final events of his life?"

Me: "Please do."

Mediator: "I will use your names for the days of the week to keep it simple. On the Thursday night of the last week of his life, Yeshua had his final, Passover-tide, secret meal, at which he presided, with a handful of his men and women followers in a hired room in Jerusalem. (That year the Jewish Passover Festival began on the Friday evening.) After the meal, Yeshua and his small band of followers went out of the city to the Mount of Olives to rest for the night with the thousands of other pilgrims. They had a patch in a private garden. All of a sudden, late into the night, a group of armed guards arrived determined to arrest Yeshua while everybody was asleep and off guard. They had been tipped off about Yeshua's whereabouts by one of the disciples who sought to force his hand. Yeshua was taken to the Jewish and Roman authorities, who were hastily convened to have him condemned, before his wider followers could get wind of what was happening, and possibly mount a protest. Early on the Friday morning, a rent-a-crowd was used to force the Roman governor to accede to the wish of the Jewish religious conservatives to have him executed. There were also a couple of other Jewish rebels of whom the Romans wanted to make an example, so Yeshua was included with them in a public crucifixion–as was the Roman custom. He was first flogged and mocked by soldiers, since a rumour had been spread that he considered himself 'the King of the Jews'. Then he was taken away to a small hill just outside the walls to be nailed through the wrists and feet onto a cross of wood, before being hoisted up for all to see, and left to die a slow, agonising death. While he was being impaled Yeshua gasped out, "Father, forgive them, for they don't know what they are doing." At the time that this was happening the Passover Lambs were being sacrificed in the Temple nearby. Then, after about three hours on the cross, he gave a great cry using words from a Jewish psalm of protest (but of ultimate faith): "My God, my God, why have you deserted me?" Shortly afterwards, he died.

Now Friday is also the eve of the Sabbath, which this year also happened to be the Passover, and ran from sunset on Friday until sunset on Saturday. During this period no work was to be done, no long journeys could be undertaken, and certainly no man could be left hanging on the gallows. So they sent soldiers in the late afternoon to break the men's legs, in order to effect a quicker death by asphyxiation. However, they found Yeshua to be already dead, and so didn't break his legs, but lanced him through his right side–just to make certain. Now one Pharisee, who was also a member of the Jewish Council, and a secret follower of Yeshua, used his rank to obtain permission from the Romans to take Yeshua' body and bury him in a private tomb nearby, rather than have him thrown into a shallow public grave–where the feral dogs would probably have found him, as they usually did."

Me: "I thought it had been shown that Yeshua had certainly suffered just this fate, along with the thousands of other crucified bodies which have never been found by archaeologists?"

Mediator: "Yes, and that shows the limitations of your 'scientific' historical procedures: they may be able to show what probably would have occurred, but without detailed evidence they cannot deal with exceptions. We can assure you, Yeshua was hastily laid out in a garden tomb near to the hill where he died, just before sunset and at the onset of the Sabbath. By this time most of his male followers had fled the city for fear of their lives, but were unable to travel very far because of Sabbath restrictions. They were a very bewildered bunch We can tell you. It seemed to them that everything they had hoped for from this man had failed to materialise, and they simply did not know what to do, except to sit out the Sabbath.

Meanwhile, his women followers, who according to custom had the task of performing the final funeral rites, had been allowed to carry out hastily the preliminary stages of burial. They did not wash his body since it was covered with his blood, which they believed he would need for his resurrection. (You will remember that many Jews at the time, believed in a general resurrection.) They simply packed a large quantity of aromatic herbs around him, and laid his body on a burial shroud which was then reflected back over his head and the bales of spices, down to his feet. They tied up his jaw and secured his wrists together in front of him. Reluctantly they then had the tomb sealed and left, intending to return as soon as practicable after the Sabbath (that is, early on the Sunday morning), in order to complete the funeral arrangements according to custom. The women, unlike the men, could count on not being obstructed in these normal duties or arrested by the authorities."

Me: "I imagine it must have been agonising for them: their beloved leader being taken so easily by the authorities and put to death in such a horrific and humiliating way. Presumably they must have had doubts about their previous high estimates of him."

Mediator: "Indeed they did. There was much agonising discussion that Saturday. All his followers were grateful to the Pharisee who had had Yeshua buried decently, and the women were confident that they would be permitted to complete the funeral arrangements. But the men, racked with fear and shame, were undecided as to whether they should dare to return to the city and risk arrest, or whether they should run off home, which for most meant distant Galilee."

Me: "This is the point where one would normally expect such a story to end. But it is here that the peculiar Christian difficulties arise. So I shall be particularly interested to hear how you continue."

Mediator: "As you say, there then followed the fateful events of the early Sunday morning. The women arrived at the tomb to find that the great stone by which it had been sealed had been rolled back. On entering they found that Yeshua's body had gone, though the grave cloths were still in position. There was a young man sitting on one side who said, "You are looking for Yeshua? He is not here. *Look where he lay.* He has been raised and has gone on to Galilee where he will meet you again. Go and tell his disciples." Needless to say, the women were absolutely terrified and confused, and at first said nothing to anyone. They simply fled from the tomb. One of them, however, called Mary of Magdala, soon decided to go and find two of the disciples who had had the courage to stay in hiding in the city. She told them of the empty tomb. These two came and saw it for themselves and confirmed that the body had gone. They also saw the grave-cloths spread out without a body in them, but they did not see the young man.

In the middle of all this, something happened that completely changed their lives and their estimate of the significance and importance of Yeshua. The accounts of it in the New Testament are full of religious imagery and are to some extent apparently garbled and contradictory (you will learn why later). They were granted what was, for them, irrefutable evidence that Yeshua was no longer dead *but was still alive in a new manner*, quite unlike the life he lived before his death. It was these experiences which included visions and auditions of a risen Yeshua, which changed bewildered and discouraged men and women into fearless witnesses to the *ultimate significance* of the man they had known as Yeshua from Nazareth."

Me: "Yes, but it is just the nature of that evidence which I have difficulty with–not to mention the problems I have with the notion itself. It seems to me scientifically impossible that any such thing could happen. I hear you when you say that this is something unique and beyond what my science knows, but I need a bit more information before I can take it seriously."

Mediator: "And, twenty first century sceptic, you shall have it. But first, let Us try to put into words which you can understand what actually happened to Yeshua and why. Be prepared for some surprises.

Up until his life as Yeshua of Nazareth, this individual had been re-engaged with the historical process leading up to it <u>in many life-times</u>. The details need not concern us here, but you get a clue in the event called 'the Transfiguration' in which Yeshua was witnessed by the select Three disciples (Peter, James and John) as being in <u>renewed</u> conversation with 'Moses' and 'Elijah'. To cut a long story short, Yeshua's re-engagements in various forms went right back to the very beginning of the creation of your Universe. Very slowly, under the guidance of *The Holy One,* the entity which was to become Yeshua of Nazareth, helped prepare the way for his appearance in history. The Hebrew Old Testament is a human testimony to the last stages of this preparatory evolutionary process. Of course, in the early engagements at the human level, the persons (men and women) who were to emerge eventually as Yeshua, did not have a clear idea of what they were up to: they had an unconscious extended Self just as you have. But by the time the re-engagement which you call 'Jesus Christ' happened, *he was fully conscious in his whole mental life*, and, moreover, *remembered his whole past history.* Of course, he was not able to share this knowledge with his disciples–whose own past engagements with reality-present he also knew–since this would be far beyond anything they could cope with. This personal knowledge was one of the things that gave Yeshua the air of being more than normally human. The transfiguration story is an attempt to capture an occasion when he tried to share as much of all this as he could with the inner core of three disciples. One of these (brother John) had a part in the writing of the Fourth Gospel in which the author writes "We beheld his glory, Glory as of the only Son of the Father". This Gospel, unlike the others, also gives some impression of the inner spiritual life of Yeshua. But not even this disciple and author really understood what was going on.

Me: "All this is mind-bogglingly new for me, and I suspect would be for everyone I know. But tell me more about the final nature of Yeshua?"

Mediator: "I assure you they will not believe you readily. Yeshua was his final re-engagement with Reality at the level at which you are still operating. He was fully human, but as one who had attained to a life of complete love, both of God and human beings–including his enemies–he was fully human in the way that none of you are. This is the reason why death could not hold him (any more that it will eventually be able to hold you– but you have a long way to go yet)."

Me: "But what happened to his body–that was just a bit of stuff–it couldn't just vanish could it?"

Mediator: "The matter which happened to make up the physical side of the pattern in the present which was Yeshua of Nazareth, shared also in his perfection, so that when his absolute love was finally proved by his willingness to die rather than compromise with evil, even this matter crossed a threshold into a new state still unknown to your science. It will be in this phase that all the 'living' matter in the universe which is compatible with the perfection which the Holy One purposes for Creation will emerge in the Present, to survive the eventual disappearance of the rest (as already predicted by your cosmologists). "

Me: "So we are talking about a great miracle?"

Mediator: "We do not like the word 'miracle' as used by you human beings. You employ it to imply some violation of nature. No, what happened–uniquely (so far)–in the death and subsequent resurrection of Yeshua, was simply the implementation of a new, emergent law of nature: namely, as the perfect evolves, it cannot be destroyed.

You should recognise that exactly what happened at the resurrection is quite beyond the reach of your current understanding and science. However, I can give you a notion to chew upon. You remember earlier, we were discussing the nature of your experience of Reality as a quantum simulation based upon immediately past events but anticipating the present? In other words, you are not able to experience just what is happening NOW, but only this simulation based upon what had more-or-less <u>recently happened?</u> Well, to help you to visualise how it is possible for Yeshua to be present now and everywhere, for all time and space, just think of his psycho-physical pattern of Reality as happening just 'ahead' *of what you are simulating,* in the Real, ongoing, NOW. Human souls who are very experienced in prayer and loving action can, in fact, have their consciousness raised to the point where they <u>are able</u> to experience something of this risen Christ in the Real Present, but this is far beyond your personal capacities and its elementary spiritual condition."

Me: "I feel utterly exhausted. You have given me so many impossible things to consider: ideas which are so strange and difficult to understand that I feel utterly bewildered, and even a bit angry, though I don't know exactly why."

Mediator: "It will pass. Your pride is piqued. Some of it you will grasp in time. The rest you will be able to report, more or less accurately, even though you are doubtful about it, or cannot make it out at all. You have more shocks ahead of you, so you would do well to rest now and let your poor brain digest what you have got!"

Me: "Oh, very well."

Cycle Twenty One:

The Appearances and The Key

I lay for some time, turning over in my mind what I could remember of the very varied, and often contradictory, accounts in the New Testament, of the so-called 'resurrection appearances' of Yeshua. Twentieth century scholars seemed mostly to have concluded that these could only be <u>legends</u> intended to convey the disciples' discovery of a sense of a kind of new-life when they lived and prayed to God <u>in Yeshua's name</u>.

<u>The earliest account of Yeshua's resurrection</u> appearances was written by Paul of Tarsus (about 25 years after the event and quoting an established tradition). He gave a list of names (including Peter and James) and groups (no women), including five hundred people at one time, *who claimed to have seen the risen Yeshua*, and 'were still alive' to be questioned. He also seems to have had a vivid experience of the risen Christ himself, when he was on the road from Jerusalem to Damascus, hunting down Christians. This experience famously resulted in his conversion from persecutor to missionary. In some of his letters he wrote explicitly, that unless one believed that Yeshua rose from the dead one could not be one of his followers and expect to be raised oneself. He envisioned a spiritual body'–whatever he meant by that.

Then there are <u>the Gospel accounts</u>, written between thirty and seventy years after the event, but based upon continuous oral traditions. The earliest written Gospel was that of <u>Mark</u>, who was possibly reporting the disciple Peter. He has the women (Mary Magdalene, Mary the mother of James and Salome) discover the empty tomb on the 'Sunday', and seeing a 'young man' inside who says that Yeshua is risen, and that they are to go and tell Peter and the other disciples to return to Galilee where he will meet them! But the women are too terrified to speak to anyone and the Gospel ends very abruptly <u>without any account of 'appearances'</u>.

The Gospels of Matthew and Luke, which generally follow Mark in their structure and substance, both differ radically from him, and each other, from this point on. A fact which cries out for an explanation, and is often taken to imply that <u>legend</u> has taken over.

<u>Matthew</u> has only 'Mary Magdalene and the other Mary' discover the empty tomb. There is an earthquake and a numinous angel appears and rolls back the stone which closed the tomb, terrifying both the women and the guards. The angel tells the women that Yeshua is risen, and invites them to come and see the place where he lay, and then commands them to go and tell the disciples to return to Galilee to meet Yeshua. On the way to the disciples, the women are encountered by Yeshua himself, who repeats the command. Meanwhile, the guards report what they have seen to the authorities, who tell them to say that the disciples came and stole the body in the night. Then the disciples go to Galilee as instructed, and there the risen Yeshua meets them and commands them to take the Good News to all the world. Some who saw him worshipped him, <u>while others doubted</u>–a curious statement!

<u>Luke</u> refers only to unnamed women, who go to the tomb, find it empty and are met by 'two men in dazzling apparel' who ask, 'Why do you look for the living among the dead?' and remind them of Yeshua's foretelling his death and resurrection. The women go immediately to tell the eleven disciples. He names them now as 'Mary Magdalene, Joanna, and Mary the mother of James, and other women'. In some ancient copies of this Gospel, Peter is said to have gone to the tomb at this point: to have stooped to look in, seen <u>only the linen cloths</u>, and then to have gone home wondering what to make of it all. Next, Luke has the

famous story of the appearance of Yeshua to two, uncertainly identified disciples, on the road west from Jerusalem to Emmaus. On the way, before they recognise him, he teaches them from the scriptures of how the Messiah <u>had</u> to suffer 'before entering his glory'. They press him to have supper with them and he presides at their meal. Then, as he breaks bread they recognise him and he vanishes! They hurry back to Jerusalem with their news to tell the eleven (who must have returned to Jerusalem), only to find them all full of the fact that Yeshua had 'appeared to Peter'. As they were talking, Yeshua himself comes into their presence and eats some boiled fish! He opens their minds to understand the scriptures, and instructs them to remain in Jerusalem until they receive the Holy Spirit. (This occurred forty days later at the feast of Pentecost.) Meanwhile (as told in Luke's second book–the Acts of the Apostles), Yeshua 'presents himself to them alive by many proofs' until he is taken up to heaven before their very eyes at the Ascension.

In the last of the official Gospels, that of <u>John</u>, written down perhaps seventy years after the event, Mary Magdalene is apparently the only woman to discover the empty tomb (although the presence of others is implied). She immediately runs to tell Simon Peter and the 'other disciple' saying 'they' have taken the Lord out of the tomb. The two disciples rush to the tomb, see <u>the empty linen cloths, including the napkin which had been on his head, rolled up by itself</u>. The 'other disciple' is said 'to have seen and believed' (I wonder what?). Then they return to their homes. Mary is left weeping in the vicinity. She is approached by Yeshua, whom she mistakes at first for the gardener–until he says her name. He tells her not to touch him but to go and tell the disciples that he is ascending to his Father. Then in the evening, Yeshua appears to nearly all the disciples, who are hiding indoors, and shows them his wounds and breathes on them the Holy Spirit. However Thomas, one of the disciples, was absent and when told all this he refused to believe the stories. So Yeshua appeared again a week later, and Thomas was overwhelmed saying, 'My Lord <u>and my God</u>'. The risen Yeshua is said to have done many signs in the presence of the disciples. Finally, in what looks like an appendix to the Gospel, he appears to some disciples while they are fishing, back in Galilee, by the Sea of Tiberias, and cooks some fish for them. It seems that they had returned to their previous occupations, and Yeshua came to commission them to be missionaries instead. Peter is told three times to 'Feed my Sheep'.

These accounts are obviously <u>very different from each other</u>, and can only be roughly reconciled by rather tortuous interleaving. Most Christians are probably unaware of the problem (as with the birth stories). Innumerable hymns and famous pictures have all conspired to give us a rather vague amalgam of all of them in our minds.

Apart from these sources, there are also fragments of other ancient 'gospels' which were rejected by the orthodox church, but which sometimes report interesting features; though they are usually derivative, and are quite obviously more legendary. I remember, for instance, the tradition that the Lord gave <u>the linen burial cloth</u> to 'the servant of the priest', before going on to appear to <u>James</u>, his brother.

Mediator (who had been reading my thoughts): "Well, well! For someone who is supposed not to know much about the Bible, that was very thorough. It is surprising what one can remember if one tries. However, it is understandable that it should leave you feeling very sceptical about the historicity of the events. As you will see, the earliest witnesses of the resurrection were in a great dilemma about how to convey their experiences in such a way that others would also recognise the risen Lord, *but without giving away the basic facts of the nature of their own experience.*"

Me: "That sounds very mysterious, what can you mean?"

Mediator: "They had a KEY: one of the best-kept secrets there have ever been, which a minority of your scholars have only recently begun to investigate seriously, which I will explain to you in a moment..."

Me: "Well, aren't you going to tell me? Why the hesitation?"

Mediator: "I'm anticipating your reaction, and giving you time to prepare."

Me: "OK, I'm ready for anything."

Mediator: "Even you seem to have picked up, in the thoughts you were just having about the Gospel accounts, the quite frequent references to the burial linen. Don't you find this slightly odd? They become more frequent in the later accounts."

Me: "Yes, there does seem a peculiar emphasis on it. But as you say, they are late, and presumably reflect a developing interest in details. … O for goodness sake, you are not going to talk about that Shroud are you?"

Mediator: "You've got it."

Me: "O no. But that has been shown to be a mediaeval fake!"

Mediator: "You should not use words like 'fake' about artefacts, unless you know for certain the motives of their creators. Even if the Shroud had been made artificially, there could have been perfectly proper liturgical motives for its production–whatever use may have been made of it subsequently by others. However, this interpretation does not arise, since the Shroud is authentic."

Me: "Then how do you account for the ^{14}Carbon dating to the fourteenth century CE, by sophisticated scientific methods?"

Mediator: "These were perfectly respectable on the basis of their own reasonable assumptions. But there are several systematic biases in the material of the Shroud which caused your dating techniques to be quite incorrect (As has also happened with other ancient, archaeologically interesting objects). We don't intend to spell these out for you; some of your researchers are investigating them already. Suffice it to say that a few are a matter of better techniques, which you can still apply, while others depend upon physics which you have not yet discovered."

Me: "So, you are saying that the famous Shroud is, after all, the linen cloth in which the body of Yeshua was wrapped, and that the full-length image of the front and rear of a crucified man is a miraculous representation of his appearance? How would one prove such a thing?"

Mediator: "There you go again with your 'miraculous' and your barely concealed incredulity. Yes the Shroud is authentic, and the image is that of the crucified Yeshua. As to 'proving' it: even when the dating is finally shown to be compatible with the possibility of it being authentic, this will not prove it. After all, it may have belonged to someone else–if you could account for the image. In this area you are not dealing with proof, but only reasonable, and question-raising possibilities."

Me: "Well it would certainly raise some questions for me, even if the dating was found to be compatible. Even so, I still don't see how a burial Shroud should make such a difference, either to me or to to the disciples."

Mediator: "For you it can indicate that something radical happened at the physical level in the resurrection of Yeshua, and why the accounts of it are so various. To appreciate what it meant for the disciples, you need to know something about Jewish religious beliefs and practices, as well as having a degree of empathy with those who discovered it. Let Me remind you that Jews abhorred images of any kind–it was forbidden by Law–and that grave cloths were ritually 'unclean', and had to be destroyed if discovered isolated from a body. Then, if you add to these features, the fact that the disciples, though they were utterly devastated by the unexpected execution of their leader, had nevertheless been partly prepared by him to expect some remarkable sequel to his 'suffering' in Jerusalem. They also had a general belief in the notion of a resurrection from the dead. Then ask yourself what could they possibly do when they found this astonishing image on his grave clothes, and he himself vanished? Once again, as in life, he had faced them with a religious dilemma. Here they were with highly suggestive, physical evidence to support their inclination to believe that he was still really alive in some new sense, but how could they ever let it be known exactly what the nature of the evidence was? If the religious authorities got wind of it, they would undoubtedly have confiscated and destroyed the Shroud. Both, because it was a grave cloth, with blood on it, and because it contravened the law against images. Even the male disciples were reluctant to touch something they had been conditioned to regard as ritually 'unclean'. (Later, the church was to have problems with Gentiles, since they tended to treat the object superstitiously.) When the disciples got used to it, the experience of seeing the image on the cloth (which was more distinct then than it is now), precipitated visualisations and auditions of the risen Yeshua in those who had known him personally. The sense of his real presence was overwhelming. However such experiences arc only self-authenticating to those who have them, while remaining dubious to others who merely hear about them. For some of his followers, at least, the image was seen as a 'miracle' from God, the like of which had never been reported before. It helped to authenticate Yeshua as God's chosen, and seemed to promise his return quite soon. Others, however, then as now, were doubtful, suspecting some natural, magical or demonic cause. We suggest that you go away and try to imagine yourself in the disciples' shoes, with what I have just told you in mind. And then in the next cycle I will outline for you what happened to the Shroud, from that fateful Sunday onwards."

Me: "It seems rather a little evidence on which to build a whole religion!"

Mediator: "Well We didn't build the religion on it did We? Only the first disciples–for the most part those who had known Yeshua personally–had their faith bolstered in this way. Once they had digested the fact and remembered what he had been like and had taught them, they appreciated its significance, but decided to keep its existence a secret. Now you go away and do as We have said."

I had to comply, and feeling very dubious, went away to sleep on it.

Cycle Twenty Two:

The Key

I awoke again.

Mediator: "Well, can you put yourself in the shoes of the followers of Yeshua, when they heard about his empty tomb, and then saw the KEY: his burial Shroud with his image on it?"

Me: "I'm beginning to. But I find it difficult to dismiss the feeling that Shroud mania is just another example of Roman Catholic preoccupation with supposed holy relics, which plagued the church in mediaeval times."

Mediator: "You are quite right to be cautious. But We can assure you that this really is the exception. The other, so-called 'relics' were a useful smoke-screen for Us at the time. So, have you been able to empathize with the disciples' dilemma–just supposing that it was true?"

Me: "Very well, I'll try. I can see that for them, his death in disgrace had raised the possibility that they had been mistaken about him all along: he could not have been a man from God after all. They asked themselves, 'Would not God have intervened on his behalf and stopped him being killed in that terrible way?' It was true, they also remembered, that he had warned them often that when the time came, and the hostile authorities caught up with him, he and they too probably, would suffer and possibly be killed–like some of the prophets before them. But they had been unable to accept this as likely: Yeshua seemed to them such a powerful man of God.

But now, with the empty tomb and this mysterious Shroud, with its 'illegal' representation of his battered body (which few, if any of the men had actually seen at its end, because they had fled when he was arrested), they felt, on the one hand, much shame that none of them had been prepared to die with him, and on the other, a sense of great excitement and relief, mixed with disbelief, that he may still be with them in some mysterious way. Perhaps he would return again soon 'in the flesh', so to speak; maybe even, to settle some scores?"

Mediator: "You have begun to feel something of what they went through. Remember that because of the ban on images, none of them would ever have seen a full-scale pictorial representation of a person before, so the Shroud image was deeply upsetting and provocative for them. Further, they had got so used to his presiding at their daily meals and reciting the conventional graces that the presence of the Shroud at meals would have made his personal presence very strongly felt. They also had, ringing in their ears the words he added to those graces during the last meal he had had with them: 'This bread–broken, and this wine–poured out, are my body and my blood: in future when you consume them, remember me.' You can perhaps appreciate that when they came to have their common meals again, and broke bread and poured wine, giving thanks to God, they sensed his continuing presence very strongly. So strongly, in fact, that some of them actually saw visions of him and heard him speak. These are natural responses, of course, of people in the distress of bereavement. But in this case they were quite right–he was still present with them, and always would be–and not just at their common meals. Though neither they, nor you, could understand fully the manner of his presence."

Me: "So what did they do then?"

Mediator: "They prayed, as they had never done before. What were they to do with the Shroud until their Lord returned? What should they tell people, including new converts? And what was God requiring them to do, now that Yeshua was dead, but apparently alive in a new way?

As to the last question: What did God want them to do? They soon found themselves impelled to go out and make known that the one whom the authorities had rejected, God had accepted by raising him from the dead, so that he must have been the long-expected Jewish Messiah after all. This was really too much for the Jewish authorities, with the result that many of the disciples were driven out of the Holy Land to go, first to the Jews of the dispersion, and eventually to sympathetic Gentiles. In this way We saw to it that the Good News of the nature of God, culminating in Yeshua, which had been revealed to the Jews so vividly in their history, would now become known to all the world. This is, as you know, now nearly complete on your planet, though with some very regrettable side-effects. It is, however, early days yet, and with vital lessons learned, the message has yet to begin its long voyage into the galaxy. Your species is the vanguard of this realisation, though it might not seem much like it at the moment."

Me: "What an awesome thought, but can we get back to what happened to the Shroud?"

Mediator: "Yes, We are prepared to give you an outline of what happened to it in the earliest days under Our watchful eyes. To start with, only the women felt confident to handle it–they were not subject to the legal taboos regarding defilement. Soon, however, Peter and the others began to touch it themselves. It was as though Yeshua was reinforcing the teaching he had given in life that petty religious regulations were to be transcended. As they did so (and this happened in the very early days, whilst they were still in hiding in Jerusalem) they began to think about the implications of what they had, and to plan how to convey those implications to others, but without actually giving away to them the literal truth of the Shroud. So the varied Gospel accounts of the appearances were slowly created.

They realised, both from this shocking relic, and their developing sense of Yeshua's continuing presence with them, that he was indeed still alive and active. His empty tomb meant that his actual body had somehow been taken up into an invisible, ever-present state. As Jews, some of them already had a belief in the general resurrection of the righteous dead at the end of history, when God was supposed to wind up his creation and reward those who had been his faithful followers with a new life on the renewed and perfected earth. Naturally they started expecting that their risen 'Lord', would return again <u>quite soon</u> as the first-born from the dead, to supervise the rising of all the human dead and to judge who should be rewarded with eternal life, and who punished for ever in hell. This was a quite common pattern of popular Jewish religiosity, and as such was a mixture of true insight and human error. They could not have appreciated either the limitless nature of God's love (which is incompatible with a perpetual hell) or God's 'patience' expressed in the cosmological time-span of the evolution of Creation.

Anyway, let's get back to the Shroud. You can perhaps see, that the resurrection narratives, so different from one another in the four Gospels were the product of imaginative attempts to convey the truths that Yeshua <u>was known with certainty</u> to be still alive–moreover in a form that was <u>still physical</u>, because his body had vanished leaving only an image of it. They attempted to convey this by saying that he could be seen, felt and could eat food, and had the capacity to be everywhere simultaneously. There was no agreed form to these stories, though they did mostly acknowledge the primary rôle of the women and the interpretive leadership of prominent men like Peter and James. In fact, in the first decades after the crucifixion, knowledge of the image was confined <u>only to very few</u> of his followers, and was not referred to directly in the written accounts. Later, it was mentioned only obliquely, evident only to those in the know, by short references to the grave-cloths. The Gnostic heretics also preserved the rumour of some 'secret teaching'.

There now began an extraordinary history during which We had a long, and at times, alarming, job of trying to keep the Shroud in existence until the significance of its true nature would be appreciated. The disciples soon realised that Jerusalem was a dangerous place for it, and a last showing was given to the Jerusalem followers–the basis of Brother Luke's account of the so-called 'Ascension'. Furthermore, some of the men of Yeshua' family, including James, had seen the Shroud and heard the stories of the empty tomb and, in consequence, became believers.

Anyway, the Shroud was bundled up and sent to Galilee for safety where, on one momentous occasion, it was shown to a select group of five hundred of his northern disciples. They were all sworn to secrecy before and after the showing. Some of them were persuaded by this evidence while others remained unconvinced. The sceptics sensed that this sort of evidence put the Yeshua they knew above and beyond even the rôle of Messiah. And since they had not been ready to give up every-thing to follow him, as he had bidden in life, they were reluctant to take this even larger step. So they died calling him Messiah only, not 'Lord'.

However, such a large public event could not escape the notice of the authorities entirely, and the Pharisee who had been put in charge of tracking down the leaders of the emerging new movement got wind of it. This was, of course, Saul of Tarsus, a Hellenistic (Diaspora) Jew, who had sat at the feet of the great Gamaliel, and was a fanatical opponent of this new messianic sect. He came up to Galilee but found nothing because it had been hurriedly dispatched to some converts in Damascus for safe keeping.

Saul set out in pursuit (as We knew he would, for we had long been preparing him for this). He caught up with the caravan, somewhere on the road near Damascus. He demanded a search, not having the least idea what he might find. 'Open that load', he demanded, pointing to an embroidered carpet-bag. The party members, who knew it contained the Shroud were aghast, and their faces gave them away. 'Come on, open it', Saul reiterated, convinced that he had found something of significance. When nobody moved he dragged it off the donkey which was bearing it himself, and tore it open. He found a white linen sheet and, not recognising what it was at first, dug into it looking for some hidden object. Then he saw the blood-stains and a moment later the image. He immediately recognised that it was a funeral Shroud which had once wrapped a crucified body and realised that, in consequence, he was ritually defiled (which, especially for a fastidious Pharisee, would entail a lot of ritual cleansing). Then a moment later he recognised <u>whose</u> Shroud it must have been, and why it was so significant.

He, like any good policeman, had 'done his homework' and he knew that the messianic sect believed that Yeshua had been raised to new life by God 'according to the scriptures', so We had primed him, so to speak, to be likely to recognise this undeniable evidence. When it happened, Saul was so overwhelmed that he was blinded and heard Our voice asking why he was persecuting Us. He was taken into Damascus by believers, a broken man. In time, after much turning over all he knew of his Jewish faith and the stories about Yeshua, he became a convert, changed his name to Paul, and eventually became the chief Jewish Apostle to the Gentiles in the Eastern Mediterranean."

Me: "That is quite an extraordinary tale–even convincing, coming from you. However, I still cannot see why there should be such a fuss about a piece of cloth, and how on earth did it survive until the twentieth century?"

Mediator: "The Holy One moves in mysterious and often unexpected ways. When HeShT became a human creature, it was as the apparently illegitimate child of a peasant woman from an obscure place in a troublesome backwater of a mighty Empire– not with great fanfares as, say, a long hoped for royal prince at the head of it. The use of a burial shroud to teach a fundamental lesson is of a piece with all that. The Christian religion is the most materialistic of all your religions–the chief source of your secularisms, in fact. The career of Yeshua of Nazareth is significant for the whole of your cosmic, physical reality, and this religion emphasises the immense importance of Reality as it is NOW, and how it is imperative for you to become engaged with it as it is, in order to share in its development towards loving perfection–however far off that may seem. The shroud is a symbol and reminder of all that, and an antidote to certain 'spiritualising' tendencies which take religion 'out of this world'.

You ask, how did it survive until today? That is a complicated story, involving many remarkable events, 'coincidences' and vicissitudes. It would serve no purpose, except to satisfy your curiosity, for Us to tell it to you. Moreover, it would spoil it for your historians and scientists who are working away to find out for themselves! However, you may try out on Us some of the things you may have heard."

Me: "Very well. I heard that it may have spent many centuries East of Turkey, folded and disguised as a cloth with a miraculous face upon it. Then the Muslims were persuaded to sell it to the Emperor at Constantinople, where it was re-discovered to be a 'folded-in-four' burial shroud bearing an image 'not made with hands' and for a time was used in religious processions. Then, during that infamous episode, the fourth crusade, it was stolen by Templars and taken to France. There it possibly became the Templars' Great Secret and may have given rise to the legend of the Holy Grail. Eventually it began to be exhibited in public to provide support for a small chapel in the South of France–just another relic, in an age used to the notion of relics, and so the Shroud entered history. How is that?"

Mediator: "Yes, very interesting. And is sufficiently like what happened to satisfy our requirements here. There were certainly many times when the Shroud was threatened with destruction and We had to employ all our powers of persuasion to ensure its survival until a time when its significance could be better appreciated. Does that satisfy you?"

Me: "You have told me a convincing story, though it has many gaps in it, and without some sort of special 'protection' of the kind you claim to have given it, it seems unlikely that it would have survived this long."

Mediator: "Yes, but there are still dangers associated with its interpretation. Beware of the 'believers': those credulous persons who almost worship the object and will accept anything reported about it, so long as it supports what they want to believe. Just as impossible to deal with are the determined 'unbelievers' who refuse to look dispassionately at the evidence. Of course, the Shroud, of itself, can 'prove' nothing. It can only support the faith of someone who trusts in the Holy One on other grounds. It will also serve to keep open the possibility of resurrection, in the minds of doubters in empirically-minded ages like yours."

Me: "Now I would like to hear, how this 'Physical Resurrection of Yeshua' fits into what you were telling me about the evolution of the Cosmos. And what relation, if any, Yeshua of Nazareth has with the divine Christ of Christian belief."

Mediator: "Very well, next time…"

Then darkness descended upon me again.

Cycle Twenty Three:

Evolving Christ

"Tell me about the 'Christ' in 'Jesus Christ.'" I said as I came around.

Mediator: "Gladly, please tell Us what comes to your mind when you hear the title."

Me: "'Jesus Christ' is the person whom Christians worship as God. He is said to be 'the Second Person of the Holy Trinity'–which puzzles many of us–and I've heard him described as a God-Man, which is equally enigmatic"

Mediator: "Why do you find it puzzling?"

Me: "Well, I just can't get my head around the idea that any being could be both human and divine at the same time, and what relevance this would have if it were the case. Also the teachings of two other great world religions, namely, Judaism and Islam, flatly deny the possibility. Even those Jews, who have lost their prejudices, to the extent that they can see that this man is the most influential Jew that ever lived, are not prepared to take on the notion that he is also God 'incarnate.'"

Mediator: "You have put an ancient dilemma in a nutshell: it was, to some extent, the product of the tension between the Semitic way of seeing things and the Greek one."

Me: "Explain, please."

Mediator: "For the Semite, reality was a sequence of events, rather than a collection of things. The attitude arose while living a semi-nomadic existence where possessions were few, and events were more significant than objects. Whence came also, their picture of God as one who directs history, and who calls himself 'I cause to happen, what happens.' In Semitic languages, the verb, or action word, is primary, with the words for things mostly derived from verbs. The verb 'to be' was not prominent, except in the sense of 'It happened' or 'It came to pass'. While for the Greek, on the other hand, reality is conceived of as a collection of beings to which, or to whom, things happen. Indeed the objects we can see and touch were often thought of as a poor representation of some ideal reality 'behind them' that just IS. Substantives, rather than actions are at the root of the Greek view of reality. For this reason the verb 'to be' is very prominent in all Indo-Aryan languages and philosophies. In fact one can say that the Greek intellectual dream was to discover what everything IS."

Me: "OK, but how does that relate to the question of 'Jesus Christ' the God-Man?"

Mediator: "Well, most of the expansion of early Christianity occurred in the countries which surrounded the Mediterranean Sea. At the time, this area was dominated by the Roman Empire which had espoused, as far as it could understand it, the Hellenistic world-view, derived from Greek philosophy, and disseminated by Alexander the Great and his successors. This meant that Christianity had to express itself for gentiles in the categories of Hellenistic thought. When a Jew asked the question: 'Who was Yeshua?' he or she, would expect an answer in terms of his function in the designs of God. For instance, that he was the long-expected Messiah, and so on. But when a gentile from the Hellenistic world asked this question (Who was Jesus?), he or she wanted to know what he WAS, in some ultimate, ontological sense."

Me: "Did they succeed?"

Mediator: "Not really, since it is not possible for you human beings to know such things. But they made a remarkable effort over about five or six centuries, and came up with some succinct statements of belief called 'Creeds' and 'Definitions'. These were both a good and a bad thing for the emerging religion. They were good, because without them it would not have

147

commended itself to the culture, and would probably therefore have disappeared altogether, and a bad thing, because these very human statements came to be regarded as God-given, unalterable statements of absolute truth, rather than a type of intellectual myth. It has taken many centuries for Christians to begin to have the courage to break with this view–in fact many versions of Christianity still haven't done so."

Me: "Can you say just how these efforts were inadequate?"

Mediator: "Yes. They were predicated on the belief that it was humanly possible to know what 'Jesus' WAS and what God WAS, and then equate them. As an attempt to do justice to WHO 'Jesus' was, this was a truly excellent insight, but the wisest thinkers always recognised that this kind of talk was only an attempt to express the ineffable. However, most of you are not capable of those sorts of subtleties, and a rather crude notion of the identity of God and Yeshua became the norm. (You are remembering that 'Jesus' is the Greek form of the Aramaic name 'Yeshua'?)"

Me: "Yes. But why can't we know what something or somebody IS?"

Mediator: "We thought about this a few cycles back, remember? You, as a Western European, still influenced via science by the Hellenistic world-view, tend to think of an entity as a bundle of 'properties'. You think that when you have listed these properties you know what that entity IS. But this is the wrong way to think of it. Such an approach may be a good one for practical purposes, since you are normally interested in what you can do with the thing in question, and its properties are therefore important in your terms. But, in fact, no entity is an isolated thing, with its own set of properties which define it completely. An individual entity, whether a thing or a person, is an abstraction from the whole of Reality. What it IS, is the sum total of ALL its relationships with ALL the other entities that make up the WHOLE of Reality. No human being can ever know all the relationships which any entity has with the whole: only the Holy One knows that. This applies to persons, as much as it does to things: you ARE the sum total of your relationships (conscious and unconscious) with other persons and things, living and dead."

Me: "Do you mean that the Universe is one thing and we are just parts of it, or something like that?"

Mediator: "Something like that. Remember that the Universe does not exist continuously in time, but re-happens moment by moment–as the Holy One sustains it. As to its oneness, you have a clue in some recent discoveries of your physicists. They have found that certain quantum entities, when they are separated in space experimentally (even by huge distances), still remain mysteriously united, so that if you do something to one of the entities, the other one responds instantaneously. If you now reflect on the fact that all the objects which make up your universe emerged twelve billion years ago from a single entity of immense energy, then you can see that the Universe is still, in some sense, one thing, despite its apparent size and diversity."

Me: "That is too big an idea for me to make sense of at the moment. I would like to get back to 'Jesus Christ' now, and see what all this has got to do with him."

Mediator: "Very well. There is just one other 'big idea' which needs to be added to your 'intellectual tool kit': namely, that the Universe of your reality is evolving. The idea of evolution originated among you as a technical theory about how the diversity of organisms arose on your planet. Some of you have recently extended the notion to the Universe as a whole, and even, very speculatively beyond that, to the relationships between Universes in the wider Cosmos. Evolution has had a bad press in some religious circles, because it is seen as a mechanism whereby nature is portrayed as creating itself, whereas these believers want to think of God as doing the creating. This is a typical either/or dichotomy that oversimplifies the issue: both are partially true. The Holy One gives the energy of happening to all beings, without which they would not happen at all:

149

and then invites them to respond by co-creating, within certain bounds. But we must return to these issues later. Now, let's now get back to 'Jesus Christ', as you have asked.

In Yeshua of Nazareth–creature and human being–the purposes of God for Creation *were realised for the first time in its evolution*. In the messiness of the everyday, in the still incomplete Creation, <u>a creature attained to an existence of perfectly loving response</u>, both to the requirements of the *Holy One*, and to those of all the people he met–including those hostile to him. Even when he was angry with them, and upbraided them for their blindness in not recognising that he was doing the work of God, it was still with the purest of motives of trying to get them to change their minds and hearts. He was prepared to maintain this attitude of loving concern, right to the end, even in the face of sustained, deliberate insult and the determination to have him killed horribly. In this, he and his heavenly Father–*the Holy One*–<u>were perfectly united</u>."

Me: "But doesn't this make him some sort of super-human? That is, someone who is capable of acts and behaviours far beyond what is possible to the rest of us. Perhaps we should rather think that it was just God acting through him?"

Mediator: "O no, you must never fall into that trap. Yeshua of Nazareth was a human being, and creature of this universe and you must never lose hold of that by importing a 'God-part', as it were. As to being 'super-human', this could be a way of putting it, provided you understood it to mean 'perfectly human'. Early theologians had an image of Yeshua as 'the second Adam'. According to Hebrew thought, the world had gone wrong because the first Adam and Eve (the representative human beings) had disobeyed God. In this myth, Yeshua achieved, in the messiness of a 'fallen' world, what the first Adam and Eve had failed to do. In other words, you (that is humanity, and Creation itself, with God's help) achieved perfection within the human frame in Yeshua of Nazareth, the truly representative human being and creature. He is therefore, the chief reason why you should be proud to be human beings, as well as ashamed of what you are revealed to be in comparison."

Me: "But doesn't this violate the theological notion that we human beings are incapable of good without God? If you say, Yeshua 'achieved' perfection, is that not something which we human beings are not supposed to be able to do; if so, how can he be human?"

Mediator: "What you must try to understand is that Yeshua of Nazareth, though perfectly human, was also the product of the age-long, focussed efforts of the Holy One to woo creation into perfection. The Old Testament which, you will remember, is a very human effort to record a people's historical encounter with God, shows you the Holy One continually at work in a particular people, educating them by prophet, king and priest (and even their enemies), to understand what was required of them in this life. Yeshua's arrival was just the end-stage in a divine effort, which began right at the start, and had been working towards the emergence of a perfectly loving creature from the beginning. We can say that Yeshua was 'in the mind of God' from the outset. Since there is a degree of freedom towards the future for all God's creatures, there was the possibility, approaching certainty that they would choose wrongly. For this reason the Holy One had to labour lovingly and persuasively right from the start, and Yeshua was the decisive product of that effort. For the first time in the long history of the evolution of creation, a Creature had responded freely to the most severe challenges of social and personal existence with Absolute Love. One can say that the purposes of God and creature came together and became One in him. That, in your terms, is what was being reached for in the ancient doctrine of the incarnation."

Me: "That sounds almost obvious when you put it that way. Although, of course there is still the question, why should anyone believe it? And why has it taken so long to get around to putting things in this way. What have our theologians been up to?"

Mediator: "Well it would take too much time for Us to take you through the whole story. Basically, your theologians have tended to overemphasise the insight that God was at work in Yeshua, to the detriment of his humanity and Creation's contribution in him. Today, there has been a tendency in the Western World, to react too far in the other direction, and reduce Yeshua to a sort of super-Jewish prophet and wise man. They have done this principally because they are unable to take a physical resurrection seriously, except as an image or metaphor, believing that science has excluded the possibility of its literal truth. We have seen that this is not so. It is important to recognise that the great work of Yeshua of Nazareth was an achievement of both God and God's Creation–not just God alone–and continues to be.

Can you see how this vision of Jesus Christ, as the culmination of the joint efforts of both God and creation, throws light upon the Gospel reports of his short ministry?"

Me: "Yes. It seems to me that we have allowed the success of our sophisticated scientific world-view to seduce us into thinking that we understand Reality better than we do. If Yeshua was the first example of what a human being (or any creature) should be like, then we cannot be certain of just what he was capable of achieving (and us likewise), since we don't have the data. I am thinking particularly about his 'miracles'. I suppose that the reports of some of them were just a sort of coded way of saying that he was divinely remarkable (turning water into wine, walking on water, feeding thousands on a few scraps, and perhaps even, raising the dead). But can we any longer be so certain what a truly good and loving human being, working in complete consonance with the purposes of God, would be capable of? Even, perhaps of things which seem impossible for us? In particular, I find myself much more ready to entertain the possibility that, as a perfect being, it was not possible for death to finish him off, or even send him into another round of finite, temporal engagement. After his death he crossed a new evolutionary threshold which made him real and present, everywhere and in every moment, in a new way; though I don't see how."

Mediator: "You are certainly beginning to understand what We have been telling you. This has been a rather sustained bit of thinking for you. Of course, being out of touch with your body, you are being even more than usually intellectual about it all. When you return you will find yourself capable of a much more rounded, emotional and active response to what you now know."

Me: "Thank you. I look forward to that, and of sharing these experiences with others."

Mediator: "That is what this is all about. Now rest."

Cycle Twenty Four:

Evolution's End

Me: "Goodness, I had almost forgotten my situation, and that I am supposed to be near death. What is happening down there?"

Mediator: "You may look, of you like, but be warned, you may be disappointed."

I directed my attention downwards as before, and the haze of light parted to show me, still lying there with my mouth open, and the surgical team just slightly differently arranged around me. *HeShT* said, "They are doing well enough."

Me: "Of course, I understand." And I looked away from the now very familiar and only slowly changing scene, and returned to my current situation and said, "Now I'm am anxious to learn more about the risen Christ and his relation to our present and future reality."

Mediator: "Say what you have in mind."

Me: "I understand that at his resurrection, he was translated into the immediate present in a new form. How did that relate to the image on the shroud? Why is it so significant?"

Mediator: "Very well, but you would have to know a lot more new physics to understand that properly. You can think of it as a sort of 'photograph' produced on the linen as the matter immediately associated with Yeshua at his death, was metamorphosed energetically and instantaneously into its new evolutionary form. This was not 'nuclear fission' of course, or your whole planet would have been obliterated! The effect of this novel, and up to now unique, physical process upon the atoms of the material, is one of the reasons why your dating techniques have got it wrong."

Me: "And this matter, where is it now?"

Mediator: "It would be perhaps more accurate to ask, 'When is it now?'!"

Me: "O very well, When is it now? though that seems an exceedingly odd sort of question."

Mediator: "You have lost touch, once again, with the understanding of Reality as always and only NOW. The Christ is present everywhere and with everyone, in this new embodied form: here and Now is the only where and when HeShT can be."

Me: "Why can't we see him then?"

Mediator: "Because you cannot yet consciously experience raw Reality here and now: though some of your mystics (in all your religions) have approached it. You will remember that I explained that entities like you, that is, beings at your stage of biological and spiritual evolution, experience reality second-hand, as it were, that is as represented by your real-time simulators. These operate as a slightly out-of-date, threefold impression of the present as past-present, present-present and future-present. Your consciousness is bound to this form of experience, and only higher consciousness can reach forward, so to speak, into the real present."

Me: "But what about drug-induced experiences of this so-called, 'higher consciousness'?"

Mediator: "These are generally illusions: a sort of physiological over-self-stimulation. It is possible to detach your simulator and let it float freely, which might give you either ecstatic or terrifying pseudo-experiences of Reality. In a few, individual cases, where the person has a properly developed spiritual maturity (and this requires much conscious application and disciplined effort over many lifetimes) the use of drugs may facilitate reaching higher consciousness, but more usually it is an illusion and a potentially dangerous distraction. It may also give you partial access to other people's minds and to distant events: this can be a seductive and spiritually disastrous power."

155

Me: "Very well, then what is the Christ doing in this advanced state of evolution?"

Mediator: "He is the growing point, or the leading-edge of evolution. He is supervising the gathering together into unity of all Selves as they become capable of true love! "

Me: "Please remind me what that is."

Mediator: "True love is an absolute concern for the well-being of the other, even if the only way of expressing it necessitates the loss of all that one values for oneself."

Me: "What happened at the crucifixion, in fact?"

Mediator: "Exactly; and before that, from time to time, right back to the foundation of the world."

Me: "I cannot see either myself, or anyone I know, attaining to that kind of love."

Mediator: "Some are nearer than you think–certainly nearer than you are. However, they tend to go unrecognised–not being highly regarded by human society as a whole, though they may be greatly valued by their friends. But, it is true; you all have a long way to go before you will be able to love perfectly, through and through, and so ready for full resurrection. The Christ is vastly far ahead of you in that respect, which is why he is 'in charge'."

Me: "Ah, now I begin to see the bigger picture, I think. May I try to put it into words?"

Mediator: "Go ahead."

Me: "We are all engaged in a process of trying to learn to live lives of love, over many lifetimes. At each attempt we are a different 'person' who is given the chance to concentrate upon improving some aspect of our extended Self, as well as contributing to the perfecting of other Selves: undoing past mistakes, building upon past achievements, and so on. As each of our extended Selves attain to some degree of true love, this aspect is incorporated into a higher form of existence towards which we are evolving, though, at first, our part is necessarily unconscious, because fragmented. This will go on until our whole Selves are integrated and perfected. How is that?"

Mediator: "All right, as far as it goes. But there is more, isn't there?"

Me: "Yes, it all sounds too much a matter of us pulling ourselves up by our own bootstraps, as it were. I don't feel that I, or anyone else, is capable of knowing the direction of, let alone working for, the kind of perfect state of which you speak."

Mediator: "Quite right, you are not. Neither would Yeshua of Nazareth have been, had he not 'stood on the shoulders' of many past heroes and heroines of the faith whose partial insights helped him along: including those of his mother and father. Furthermore, there were his efforts in his own previous lives. However, neither he nor his predecessors achieved all this alone: We were growing with them also, and mediated the Love of the Holy One."

Me: "I find that there are questions arising in me which I should like to ask about you HeShT, but which I'm not being encouraged to broach yet. Is that so?"

Mediator: "Yes, that is the case for the moment. We have quite a lot of work still to do before you will be ready for understanding Us in that way. Let's get back to the risen Christ. Are there any other traditional images which come to mind when you think about what we have been considering?"

Me: "Well yes, there is one which has been going through my head: it is the image presented first by Paul, I think, namely, that of the 'Body of Christ.'"

Mediator: "Good. Brother Paul suggested that you could think of your future forms, and indeed your present ones, as constituting a part of the risen Body of Christ, to the extent that you are faithful to him. This is exactly what we were examining a moment ago. All that you do in your lives, that is creatively

157

compatible with the ultimate purposes of the Holy One for Creation, is preserved as part of the form of the developing Body of Christ, which is a pattern of experienced happening in Reality in which your individuality will be preserved as a member in Christ's corporate individuality, but without violating your personal independence. Remember the image of the white cells in your biological body? You cannot picture this state of affairs in your present state of spiritual development, so there would be no point in Our trying to reveal it to you. In fact, it would probably not appeal to you at all. Remember when, as a seven-year-old, you realised with horror, that when grown up, you would not want to play with your toys anymore? But you can perhaps grasp the principles."

Me: "Yes, I think so.

Mediator: "Are there any other traditional images you can think of and which we can now reformulate?"

Me: "Yes. What about the ideas like the return (or 'second coming') of Christ at the Last Judgement, and the General Resurrection of everyone. These are traditional doctrines which don't seem to make much sense today."

Mediator: "Those are indeed big traditional images. We will have to take them one at a time. Let's leave the Last Judgement and the Second Coming for later cycles, and look now at the notion of a General Resurrection. That should not present too much of a problem for you to expound."

Me: "Yes, I suppose we have already covered it in a way. The basic idea of resurrection is that God, in his mercy, and out of Love for Creation, will eventually love everything into perfection so that we, as part of that process, can hope to be there to enjoy it. If this perfect state is identical with the Body of Christ, as a form of happening, beautiful beyond anything I can picture now, then that is what Christianity means by the expected General Resurrection at the end of time."

Mediator: "I'm glad you mentioned Beauty just then: it shows that you are still in touch with what We covered earlier, and will have to return to later. Yes, you have got the general idea, but don't forget that this will include other kinds of higher beings who are capable of love, from all parts of the Cosmos, some of whom have not yet heard the Good News, and won't do so until you take it to them."

Me: "There you go, blowing my mind again. That sort of thing is beyond me."

Mediator: "Just reminding you of the true context, and to stop you being 'a little earther', and a touch too self- and species-centred."

Me: "Time for sleep, I think."

Cycle Twenty Five:

Anne

"Hello Enni, Hello Enn!"

I woke up hearing a new, soft-spoken, and vaguely familiar voice. I looked and saw a fresh face in my garden. She had that same, rather somnambulant, look that my parents had worn.

I said, "Hello, who are you?"

"Don't you recognise me?" She replied, "I was *Anne*, your wife in a previous life. You were a man that time."

As she spoke, both her voice and her face became more familiar, and some dim memories began to stir. She continued,

"So you are Enni now, and a scientist with an unusual interest in religion, I understand."

Feeling very bewildered I replied,

"Yes, that is true *Anne*–did you say that was your name? And it's nice to meet you again–I think–but why are you here and how come you know all this?"

Anne: "You will have to ask the Companion that question."

Me: "Who? Oh, you mean HeShT?"

Anne: "*HeShT*? That's an odd name. I've not heard that one before."

Me: "He/She/It suggested it."

Anne: "O yes, I see."

Me: "Were you not with me a while back, with all the others?"

Anne: "Yes, but it's pleasant to be together again, just the two of us, is it not? I can still recognise you by your character, though you have developed a bit since we were one. You have had two lives since then, I'm told."

160

Me: "Have I? Perhaps you can tell me about them—and us, since I have no clear recollection of any of it, only a vague impression like a forgotten word permanently on the tip of the tongue."

Anne: "No, I cannot tell you: that is forbidden. The details of your other lives, as a woman and a man, are hidden from me anyway—as is your present body."

Me: "Then why is it that I cannot remember you as clearly as you, apparently, can me? And I really have no idea why we are meeting like this."

Anne: "The difference is, I am here awaiting my next life after my 'cleansing', while you are here only temporarily, after your accident, or whatever it was. You should take the opportunity to talk—you were never very good at it."

Me: "What do you mean by 'after my cleansing'?"

Anne: "After my last death—I outlived you by forty years—I was taken by the Companion (by *HeShT*) on a tour of my whole Self, black parts and grey parts and all. It was a long and painful experience. Stripped of all my self-deceptions, I saw how much of you had become part of me, and how much of us both had become parts of others, including our eight children. It was not always very flattering, I can tell you; though *HeShT* was very gentle with me. Apparently this is what happens every time, and is part of the preparation for making the next life an appropriate one."

Me: "You seem to have been waiting a long time for that?"

Anne: "O no. Time doesn't mean anything here. Most of your time I pass in 'sleep', and am oblivious to it all. Though I'm glad of opportunities like this to meet you again and see something of how you and I are developing."

Me: "You are still developing then?"

Anne: "Yes, though I can have little say in the matter. All the impressions I made on things and people, particularly people, are still active in the real present: some of them good and others bad. Some have increased the beauty of things while others have had to be undone by the good efforts of other souls, who are cleaning us up, so to speak."

Me: "'Souls', now there is a word I've not heard mentioned here."

Anne: "It means the same as Self–but not your ordinary, everyday self."

Me: "You mean not the 'ego'?"

Anne: "I don't know that word; it must be a new one since my time."

Me: "Well no, it is Latin, but I suppose we have given it a new slant. When do you expect to live again?"

Anne: "That I cannot know. In this state, we are exposed intermittently to who we really are and what others are making of us, knowing that, at the right time, we will be called to re-engage consciously as, a new 'person', with the world. We will be placed in a situation that will give us a chance to make some amends for past failings, whether passively, as a victim of the ills which we and others have committed, or actively, as someone placed to make a real, creative contribution to the way things are going. I also know that when that happens, I will forget all this, except deep down in my Soul–my real Self–which will still continue to influence, unconsciously, the kind of person I manifest temporarily."

We began to stroll around the garden, for all the world now like an old married couple. It was very strange for me, considering my commitments to my current life and family. I found myself imagining all the other, forgotten spouses and friends that I still 'contained' in myself. I began to understand why it was that *HeShT* said I could have no real conception of the future life, when we would all be conscious together, and yet not obliterated individually. I began to long to be getting back to my current mode of living, with the comfort of my present family, and its tiny, uncomplicated place in the vast scheme of things.

Then *Anne* said suddenly, "Right. I have to be going. The purpose of this meeting is now complete. I'm sure we will meet again in the not too distant future–I wonder what form that will take. I am more confident now that it will be good. We may even feel that we were 'made for each other!'"

The gentle, smiling face of Anne then rapidly shrank away and became reabsorbed into the multiple form of *HeShT*. I was disappointed, but had begun to get used to this sort of happening.

Me: "Thank you HeShT for that. I hope it has served some purpose. I certainly found it strangely pleasant, enlightening and a relief from all that hard thinking."

Mediator: "We are glad, and enjoyed your pleasure with you. However, we still have time in this cycle if you have any more questions you wish to ask."

Me: "Yes, it has just occurred to me. Why didn't Anne mention 'Jesus Christ'? As I vaguely remember, she was a devout Christian, and isn't this what we are concerned with at present?"

Mediator: "You should understand that We did not activate Anne completely for your meeting: she would have been too much for you. We thought it would be good for you just to meet her at a simple personal level and talk, as in the old days–that is part of the Christian life too, after all, is it not?"

Me: "Yes, of course. You remind me of my overactive intellect. Forever analysing, taking things apart and putting an intolerable strain upon others."

Mediator: "You will not remember this, but although Anne was a devout believer, you were certainly not. You were an 'Enlightenment man' and thought that religion was a thing of the past. When you died of the plague, everyone, except Anne, thought it was divine retribution. But her influence on you, her simple loving faith, is one of the reasons why you are now, at least a nominal Christian, with a small and wavering commitment to Us. You still bear a large part of her soul in you, and therefore have some responsibility for her too."

Me: "Now I begin to see why you arranged this meeting. You want to impress upon me that one does not live entirely for oneself. That everything one does is likely to carry a part of someone else's Self and to have an effect upon it. In that way we are all responsible for each other."

Mediator: "Correct. And, that the Christ, as the first creature to cross the new evolutionary threshold, now has the responsibility for supervising the gathering and maturation of the rest of Creation, as it follows him."

Me: "I'm not very comfortable with that talk of Jesus Christ being a 'creature.'"

Mediator: "That is because you have been brainwashed by Christian Orthodoxy which over-emphasised the divinity of Christ at the expense of his creature-hood; and this despite its lip-service to the doctrine that he was both divine and human. You will remember that Hellenistic thought was over-ambitious in its attempt to say exactly who Jesus Christ WAS, in ontological terms. It is better to understand that the will of God and the will of one of God's creatures became wholly aligned in Yeshua of Nazareth, as a consequence of the Holy One, and the creatures striving together from the very beginning. That same purpose of the Holy One, namely, to love Creation into returning Love freely (and becoming therefore wholly beautiful), is still operating; but now with the full co-operation of that one, truly great Creature and Person, together with all those who are aligned with him—whether they know it or not."

Me: "And when, after many lifetimes, the risen Christ has led us all into a state of perfection similar to his–that is, has incorporated us in himself–then we will all rise together in him, and enter the new state of Reality which he already inhabits?"

Mediator: "Something like that. Remember that saying of Origen, one of your early Christian thinkers: 'No-one will be saved until everyone is saved'. He got that right."

Me: "What about 'The Last Judgement?'"

Mediator: "That was an image which expressed the insight that everything you do is significant for the futures-present and that anything evil has consequences which have to be to be corrected, or converted into good. Nothing can escape having to be refined to some degree. Those who produced that image had no idea that Creation was a gigantic process, taking much time to complete, so they imagined a single climactic event-a great assize-when in fact it is a long, ongoing process, of the kind we have been talking about. Jesus Christ assesses every act as it is performed, and decides what We should try to do about it: Christ is the perpetual loving judge."

Me: "Now I think I can see what the image of 'the Second Coming' was all about: this evolutionary process, which proceeds under the loving guidance of the Holy One will come to a climax, when all that can be perfected, has been perfected in Christ, who will then appear, as it were, in full glory."

Mediator: "Something like that."

Me: "Why do you keep saying, 'Something like that'?"

Mediator: Well you don't suppose that you can get these things wholly right do you?"

Me: "I think I'm doing very well."

Mediator: "Do you really? We know that you are doing your best, and that is all that we could hope for. But clearly there are still some other things which you must get right before we ask you to go back."

Me: "With that warning, I think I had better retire."

Cycle Twenty Six:

The Human Future - Long Term

Me: "You have made me aware of the wider context in which my mysterious personal existence happens. You have taught me that I live a sequence of lives, during each of which an aspect of my wider Self becomes conscious in an evolving biological form. I have learned to appreciate that I am not an isolated individual but, in my extended Self (which is comprised of the sum total of the characteristic ways in which I have (over many lives) contributed to the shape of the ongoing present Reality), I am enmeshed with the extended Self of others: I am part of a wider whole, that is ultimately co-terminous with the Universe Itself. This entanglement means that we all have an inescapable and continuous responsibility for the development of one another's' Souls, until we are all perfected–an unimaginable future state of Individuality-in-Unity.

Now that you have shown me that I may live again in the coming millennia I confess to having a great curiosity about what sort of existence that will be. Can you give me <u>some</u> idea of that, *HeShT*?"

Mediator: "As We have already told you before, I cannot and should not give you any precise details. I can, however, give you some probable, in-principle possibilities which you may like to reflect upon."

Me: "Yes, I would like that."

Mediator: "Actually you may not like it at all. You should appreciate that your species has reached a particularly critical stage in its development. You now know enough about the habits of nature, as it moves from moment to moment, to be able to exploit these powers either for your own advancement or for your destruction. Since the great breakthrough, achieved by the Holy One and Yeshua of Nazareth, the ultimate success of your species and your multifarious descendents is assured. However, that will not prevent you from reverting to other 'Dark Ages' if you fail to be wise with the powers now in your hands: evolution is not a simple, linear process."

Me: "What sorts of powers in particular?"

Mediator: "The abilities to harness natural energies, to do with them what you wish; the powers to modify your biology and that of the entire biosphere; and the increasing ability to affect the brain, mind and human behaviour. Each of these has the potential, if misused, to put your civilisations back millennia or more in development."

Me: "What sort of things can we do to avoid such catastrophes?"

Mediator: "The possibility of acquiring the necessary wisdom does not seem on the cards. Your history shows that you are very slow to learn from it. Over and over again, cultures, religions, and powerful individuals, have fallen into the trap of self-centredness and self-indulgence, which are the essence of sin."

Me: "Ah, there is another word we have not heard in our conversations: 'sin.'"

Mediator: You will hear more about it, I assure you. But you ask, what can you do to possibly avert the likely disasters We outlined? Well, We have already encouraged the moving of your species off-planet. During the next two millennia, you will probably establish a large presence within this Solar System, but off the Earth. This will have a number of important consequences: it will relieve the pressures on the limited resources of your home planet; it will permit the continued growth of human populations without damaging the Earth's ecological systems; it will provide new, isolated environments in which scientific, sociological and political experiments can be undertaken without endangering the rest of you; it will provide an 'ark' should one of the major, natural disasters occur to the planet itself. These will happen if We have been unable to persuade huge numbers of lower entities to make the right choices within their limitations. They include: pandemics of new diseases, the possibility of meteorite or cometary collisions, exceptionally violent volcanic eruptions from within the earth, and hugely energetic astronomical phenomena in the vicinity. It would not do to continue to have all your eggs in one basket, if any of these were to occur."

Me: "Will I be involved in any of this–it sounds very challenging?"

Mediator: "I'm glad you find it so–not everybody would. As you already know, We cannot tell you that. You should appreciate that you will re-happen in a form that is appropriate for the good of the Whole, which is not necessarily at all what you might anticipate now. You could be simply one of the unadventurous, but essential, 'stay-at-homers', who remain to manage the old Earth: though somehow We don't expect so."

Me: "Will we get beyond the Solar System?"

Mediator: "That is anticipated eventually, though there is much to be done and learned by you before that can happen. There are 'laws of nature', as you call them, which you have not yet discovered which will change human capacities beyond all your recognition. Knowledge of these will contribute to your venturing far out into your galaxy, and eventually beyond. Sooner or later (and it could be sooner), you will encounter other higher entities. We have kept you apart until now since you would have been unable to cope with the experience. But you will meet eventually and share your knowledge and values. You also have to take with you the message of the empty tomb and the revelation of the ultimate power of Love–as the only way to attain to perfection. They, in their turn, will teach you things that you never thought of."

Me: "It all sounds rather rosy."

Mediator: "Believe me, it will not be. You can put all utopian dreams out of your mind. There will be great numbers of terrible disasters and much suffering in the course of all this development–just as there has been in the past. A knowledge of what is actually happening–so far as you can appreciate it–will mitigate the suffering to a degree, for here we are dealing with the only authentic instance of 'The End justifying the Means'. Every entity may know, within its limitations, that it has the power to contribute positively towards the ultimate End, but also that suffering is the inevitable concomitant of that process. Cutting teeth is always painful."

Me: "That all sounds rather callous."

Mediator: "It is a matter of perspective. Just as you, as a parent, have often suffered when denying your children something they really wanted, tearfully and desperately, because you knew that it was against their better interests for them to have it, so we suffer much with you, as we see you struggling to come to terms with what is often a terrible and frustrating existence and are tempted to take time off. Even your most intelligent, sophisticated and sensitive individuals can have no real idea of what is ultimately involved in all this, and why it has to happen in the way it does. The Cross of Christ might seem to be the ultimate, futile stupidity, though it was, on the contrary, the greatest triumph ever. That did not, however, remove the suffering."

Me: "Tell me more about the kind of form which we can expect to happen in, when engaged upon later stages of this momentous project."

Mediator: "You will remember from your study of biology, how evolution often proceeds by organisms of different kinds getting together and merging to form a new kind of life?"

Me: "Yes, it is called 'symbiosis'."

Mediator: "Many times in the course of the evolution of your ancestors, right back from the time when they were microscopic

169

organisms, there have been episodes when quite divergent creatures joined forces by symbiosis and formed new species with the combined virtues and capacities of both. Two areas of discovery which you have made recently (in addition to the ones just outlined) will make a considerable difference to your biological future. Firstly, you have begun to recognise that your biology is by no means perfect; that apart from the obvious genetic diseases, there are numerous ways in which your genetic constitution could be improved. Naturally there is a great deal of anxiety about the application of this knowledge, and this is one of the reasons why, for safety, some types of experimentation will only be permitted 'off-earth'.

Secondly, you have increased your powers of gathering, manipulating and calculating the consequences of information by the use of computers. You are well on the way towards providing an integrating nerve-net for your global society, which could make you all so interdependent as to be almost a super-organism: furthermore, the increasing miniaturisation of computational and storage devices, and their implementation in <u>organic</u> molecules, opens up the possibility of human/'computer' symbiosis. Much as the Cossack and his horse seemed almost to be one organism (so interdependent were they), so you will team up with information devices to become an even more advanced organism. These information devices will be incorporated into your protoplasm–even your genes, so they will be inheritable. That is, if you don't blow yourselves up first."

Me: "I must say I don't much like the sound of all that."

Mediator: "Well, I did warn you! No doubt your shrew-like ancestors would have found you pretty horrifying! Just imagine what even someone living as recently as the beginning of the nineteenth century would have thought of your world of the beginning of the twenty first, had they been given a vision of it. You can have little concept of what things will be like for you in a couple of millennia, let alone a few million years. You will find out however!"

Me: "Once again, you have given me much to think about, and if I don't like it, I suppose I have to accept that I asked for it."

Mediator: "Well, there you are. But don't worry–We will be with you all the way. That's enough for now; it's time for you to rest again."

Cycle Twenty Seven:

Evil, Chaos and Freedom

I lay for somctimc thinking about the immensities of Creation, the awesome beauty of it all, and the apparently very tiny place which we human beings have in it. Then I found myself wondering where <u>all the evil</u> came from. I did not know what was going on everywhere else in the Cosmos, but I felt suddenly overwhelmed by the sense of the futility of human endeavours. Not only did we seem so insignificant in the overall scheme of things—so recently on the scene and so small in proportion to the rest—but it also seemed that whenever we did achieve something good beautiful and true, it almost inevitably went wrong. Our creations pass away or are betrayed by our greed or envy or sheer bloody-mindedness.

Mediator: "We see you are ready to consider the question of Evil and Sin."

Me: "So it seems, though I am very reluctant to do so, since I was enjoying so much the visions of Reality you were sharing with me."

Mediator: "Alas, evil and sin are also part of Reality, and they have to be faced—including your own modest contributions—though they can wait for the moment!"

Me: "Thank goodness for that. Where do we begin?"

Mediator: "What do you suppose to be the root cause of evil?"

Me: "That's a difficult one to ask right at the start."

Mediator: "Have a go."

Me: "How about rebelliousness on the part of Creation?"

Mediator: "That is part of the answer certainly, but prior to that is Love itself."

Me: "What? Love! How can that be? Surely love is the answer to evil not its source?"

Mediator: "Our Love is the ultimate origin of your evil. We are responsible for the way things happen because we created you in the first place and for hoping, out of our Love for you, that you would respond with love in return. There is nothing We would not do, out of love, to receive you back to us in love. We work perpetually to this end. Moreover, it is love which prevents us from simply intervening and shoving you about."

Me: "But surely we have some portion of blame for how we behave?"

Mediator: "Mostly you do not know what you are doing, and yes, you are rebellious from time to time, but the bulk of the blame remains ours, and We accept that responsibility: which is the meaning of the crucifixion."

Me: "I am shocked and humbled; I had thought the responsibility was all ours."

Mediator: "Don't be too ambitious! Besides, you are not the only beings with a degree of freedom of will and therefore a capacity for going off the rails."

Me: "I think you had better begin at the beginning and lead me through this painful side of Reality."

Mediator: "Very well. As We have said, Evil is a consequence of Love. It is the purpose of the limitless Love of the Holy One that there should be another–The Beloved–who would respond to that Love with love. Love is the greatest power there is, and only Love can create love. But Love acts by persuasion not coercion. Love may sometimes circumscribe or hem in–set limits to the degree of freedom permitted, but it will never resort to overwhelming force. But when a beloved creature rebels and goes its own way–always therefore to its own detriment–Love is anguished and suffers pangs of remorse. So, We weep when, after all our efforts, the civilisation on a planet goes into self-destruct mode, and all that loving work comes to nothing."

Me: "I refuse to let you take the blame for our misdemeanours and failures to love in return."

Mediator: "That is very kind of you: You will be telling Us that you are proud of your sins next! No, the disparity between our power and yours is far too great for anything but a minuscule portion of blame to fall upon you. Not that it is therefore insignificant, for you are destined for perfection along with everything else and your failures hold up that process.

You should understand that since the World was made for reciprocal love, it had to have a degree of freedom of behaviour of its own: love can never be built-in, so to speak. So, given that Creation had a small degree of freedom, it was probable, to the point of inevitability, that it would sometimes use that freedom wrongly. Not that Creation lives in a perpetual state of having to choose between the right and the wrong action. No, many possible choices are neutral in this regard. Also, Creation has some space to be creative in its own right. The ultimate future-present of reality will have been a <u>co-creation</u>, as indeed is every present-present. We recognised this from the start and have been working perpetually to keep ahead, so to speak, with the way things are developing.

In your small-troop, primate past you learned both love and hate for your fellows - it was this that gave you survival value and caused you to be the most widespread primate on your planet. You have a basic instinct to love, care, and even sacrifice for your own family and troop, but, when threatened in any way, to hate, attack, or move on from any other human group that came your way. Civilization and religion have been trying to learn the tricks that extend your love for those who are different and diminish you instinctive suspicion and hatred of them. It is not exactly how We had preferred it to develop – but it was your choice."

Me: "I know from my own experience that we creatures have some freedom of choice about how we behave, and I can see that other, so-called 'higher', creatures could be the same. But are you saying that rocks and atoms also have freedom of will, so that natural disasters are also the result of evil-will and not just chance?"

Mediator: "You will have to listen especially carefully to my answer to that question; otherwise you will get it wrong. Yes, all actual entities, no matter at what level they happen, do have some degree of freedom about how they should behave. We woo them by lures which you cannot imagine, or have forgotten. However, many objects in your world are huge conglomerates of these free entities. So a mountain or a planet does not itself have any freedom of will, although the molecules and atoms which constitute it do–very little compared with you, of course. The 'behaviour', if we can so call it, of a mountain therefore, is not normally the product of any deliberate will, but rather the end-product of billions upon billions of minute wills acting independently, doing their own small thing. This emerges on your scale of living as 'chance'. We are saying that the 'behaviour' of a mountain, or other large collection of volitional entities, is not 'normally' the product of a deliberate will; that 'normally' is important, since the large-scale, activities of inorganic masses like mountains or cyclones often have minute initiating situations (perhaps even millions of years previously) when a free choice was critical for its future. This is the famous 'butter-fly' effect, modelled by your mathematics of Chaos. The sequence of present moments of reality is a dynamic affair, in which the habits of behaviour are often best described as unstable systems that grow from tiny beginnings. Even the slightest difference at the very beginning can make a very large difference to the way things develop in the end.

Think of the very simple example of trying to balance a pencil upon its point: this is a case of <u>static</u> inequilibrium. There is an almost infinite number of directions in which the pencil <u>could</u>

fall when released (as it inevitably would), and the direction 'chosen' would depend upon factors such as, the slightest initial deviation from the vertical, an imbalance in the bombardment on the side of the pencil by air molecules, tiny deviations in the shape of the pencil point and the surface on which it is standing, the gravity of a distant planet. If one were to try the balancing act many times, even in the most ideal circumstances, the pencil would probably fall in a different direction every time, *and you would not be able to predict what it would do*. All would depend upon minute differences in the initial conditions. (All this without considering tiny, unpredictable changes at the quantum level.) Now, suppose some absolutely momentous circumstance were to depend upon the direction in which that pencil fell, then that would give Us the opportunity to try to persuade the entities involved in those initial conditions (the molecules of the pencil or the surface or the air) to behave in such a way as to bring about that momentous circumstance. Do you understand all this?"

Me: "Yes, I think so. The world process generally waltzes along, moment by moment, in a regular fashion, with all us entities doing our thing according to acquired habits. But there occur moments when the future is very much in the balance. At such times you have an opportunity to use all your powers of loving persuasion to bring about the most desirable outcome, knowing that once it is launched the rest will follow inevitably."

Mediator: "Excellently put. But what do you suppose happens when Our powers of loving persuasion fail, when the entities refuse our suggestion and go off on their own course?"

Me: "Then an undesirable outcome is produced, an Evil one in fact, and you have to think all over again?"

Mediator: "Precisely, most of our 'time' is spent in this way. We are able to foresee much of the long-term developments from such critical presents, and have to plan to try to introduce corrections, if necessary, when they next arise. However, we cannot know exactly, how you creatures will actually respond when the time comes, with the result that we do not know exactly what will happen in future-presents. So what do you now think about the origin of evil?"

Me: "I can see that it arises when creatures, having some degree of freedom of will, choose to disregard your promptings at critical moments in the evolution of the present. Since you know what the consequences of all choices are likely to be, and also what would be the best choices to make, the failure to follow your promptings inevitably results in a bad outcome–an evil situation, in fact."

Mediator: "There, you have it. We love and love, and agonise over what you will choose, and suffer in consequence, and feel Ourselves responsible for it all, since you have very little understanding of the wider significance of what you are doing. Where you are culpable, is when you know from your traditions and your own small capacity to foresee the future, that what you are proposing to do will very likely cause others harm, you none-the-less choose to go ahead and do it. This is what is called 'Sin'. Such behaviour, as you have said, then causes Us to have to devise new stratagems to undo or make some sort of good use of the undesirable situation which has arisen in consequence of your wickedness."

Me: "And you do that for every person–everywhere in the Universe?"

Mediator: "Not only for every person, but for every free entity there is: every cell in your body; every molecule in every cell; every atom in every molecule; every proton in every atom…"

Me: "Stop, stop. I cannot imagine all that."

Mediator: "Don't worry. You just have to get on with your own thing. We are here for you completely, as we are for every other entity, in every moment of reality."

Me: "HeShT! HeShT! Who are you? I'm beginning to think that I have been taking you for granted and should have shown much more respect."

Mediator: "Don't worry about it. But give it some proper thought."

Me: "I will, I will."

And with that I lapsed into sleep again.

Cycle Twenty Eight:

Sacrifice

I found myself wondering about the notion of <u>sacrifice</u>, which seemed to be an aspect of most religions, especially ancient ones. Even in Christianity, there was the idea that 'Jesus Christ' was a sacrifice made by God for us. Was this a primitive hang-over, or was there something fundamental about the notion?

Mediator: "I see you have set the agenda for this cycle. Would you like to give Us some immediate associations which you have with the idea of sacrifice?"

Me: "It suggests to me giving up something in order to placate God or to persuade God to satisfy one's wishes. The item sacrificed has to have some value for the one sacrificing. It often, though not always, involves killing–even human sacrifice. In the Bible we have the story of Abraham being tested to see if he was willing to sacrifice his only and long-awaited son, Isaac, before being told to substitute a ram. And in Christianity, Christ is often described as a sacrifice for the sins of the whole world. Will that do to start us off?"

Mediator: "Yes. You are right to think that there is something fundamentally correct about the instinct to sacrifice in most religions. However, in its common, primitive form it was popularly thought of as a sort of bribe to the deity, usually to try to avert some disaster or other or to get the gods to do what you desire. (This was a carry over of the child's attempts to persuade reluctant parents.) As such it was founded on the misapprehension that God was manipulable by human beings. The same idea lay at the root of the orgiastic rites of the fertility religions: you wanted fertility for your crops, livestock or women, so you tried to 'turn on' the gods–very anthropomorphic!

So we can say that sacrifice, though necessary for religion, is not a matter of trying to influence God to do what one wants. Even Israelite religion, which had made considerable advances in the understanding of the *Holy One*, still continued the practice of substitutionary sacrifice of animals, long after it recognised that it was not a matter of bribing God. As you have remarked before, religions are very conservative institutions, and the practice of animal sacrifice was not given up easily, in fact, we had to engineer it. The sacrificial acts eventually functioned as a *symbol* of the true insight.

The Abraham story, however, shows the early recognition by Israelite religion that sacrificing one's first-born son in order to ensure that that would be more of them, was not a practice acceptable to Israel's God, though it was continued by some of Israel's kings long after this realisation. For Israel, the sacrificial system, which involved agricultural produce of all kinds–not just animals, was a system of *thanksgiving* to God for good harvests and abundant livestock, and a means of expiating *unwitting* sins (for which one could not therefore be contrite): a system given, they believed, by God Himself. In order to control these sacrifices, especially the beliefs which went along with them, they eventually concentrated the whole system in a single, central Temple in Jerusalem, under the eye of a priestly caste, where it functioned as a sort of sacred abattoir. This meant that most believers never got to see sacrifices except on pilgrimage. Eventually, after the Temple had been destroyed by the Romans, Jews and Christians learned that the whole business of animal sacrifice was not required by God at all."

Me: "But Christianity continued, and still does, to consider Yeshua's ghastly death a kind of sacrifice made by God on our behalf. What does that mean? It sounds terribly crude and callous."

Mediator: "Yes and some understandings of the notion have been both crude and callous: part of the answer to your question lies in your observation about the conservatism of religious language and practice. The earliest Jewish converts to the new

Messianic sect had grown up with a God-given system of animal sacrifices for coping with their sins, so they naturally sought another similar notion to continue the idea. This they found in the belief that Yeshua, as God's 'only Son', had been offered, once and for all by God, the Heavenly Father, as a sacrifice to ensure the forgiveness of the sins of the whole world. Attempts to 'explain' this idea in a more palatable form have been offered by your theologians down the centuries, but none has been universally accepted. Can you think of some possible ingredients for a contemporary one?"

Me: "O dear, here we go again. Er... God feels responsible for the world and allows his 'Son' to be immolated by it?"

Mediator: "Good, that image is a part of it. But what about the sacrifice made by Yeshua himself on behalf of Creation?"

Me: "I don't understand what you are getting at: in what way was Yeshua's terrible death a personal sacrifice? It looks more like others were sacrificing him."

Mediator: "Don't you see. Yeshua could have 'done anything with his life', as your common idiom has it. He had great charisma. He was skilled in teaching and healing. He had it in him to become a famous figure in history—even a Jewish Alexander perhaps, and so fulfil the popular expectation of a Messiah, who would galvanise the Semitic races against Rome and cast them out of God's own country. (Much as Brother Muhammad was to do for the Arabs, centuries later.) That surely is how the world normally expects great human beings to use their powers successfully. The tradition suggests that Yeshua was tempted to inaugurate such a programme himself, but he 'sacrificed' these potentials for the higher one of witnessing to God as Love, and paid the price by dying in obscurity and shame.

What do you think that tells us about the universal truth regarding the rôle of sacrifice in religion?"

Me: "Something to do with giving up what one wants in order to serve God?"

Mediator: "O dear me no, though that is another common mis-apprehension: think of something that one is good at and most wants to do or accomplish, and then 'sacrifice' it to God–what a terribly wrong idea. There is a germ of truth there, however, but it is hidden behind a gross and false view of the Holy One. Your skills and strengths are given in order to serve Reality, not to be thrown away. Of course, one can be mistaken about what one's primary strengths really are, only finding them when your secondary ones are given up. No, the true insight about the necessity for sacrifice is related to the notion of evolution."

Me: "Oh how is that?"

Mediator: "Well, think about it. Do you accept that you find yourself in an evolving Reality?"

Me: "Yes."

Mediator: "Would you say that it is likely to be right to work with the grain of this evolution?"

Me: "Ye-es, but I'm not quite sure what that means."

Mediator: "Well, is there not a danger that one would be tempted to use all one's powers and skills to set up a temporary 'comfort zone' of one's own, rather than run the risk of going with the flow?"

Me: "Ah yes, I begin to see the drift of what you are saying. To do the right thing, 'to go with the flow of evolution', as you say, might be a risky, and uncomfortable enterprise, involving great change and even loss. It would be much more tempting to set up a little world apart–to stop the flow and retire from the challenge. Yes, I see."

Mediator: "And do you see that to do this systematically all your life: always to use one's powers and skills, whatever they are, to advance the cause of what is right, even at the expense of one's own kudos, satisfaction and comfort, is what is meant by living sacrificially?"

Me: "Which is what Yeshua did?"

Mediator: "Exactly, and in a smaller way, many other good men and women (and other beings, high and low) down the ages–and not only Christians either. The instinct to sacrifice is the insight that since the world is still far from perfect; no-one has the right to use their talents or possessions to set up their own little utopia, in advance, so to speak. Not only is this futile, since 'you cannot take it with you', but also, in the scheme of things, any success in this direction is always at the expense of others: a life without sacrifice is always exploitative."

Me: "Then in what sense was Yeshua's sacrifice 'on behalf of human kind'?"

Mediator: "On behalf of the whole Creation, actually. Well, he demonstrated in real life that to live a life of absolute, self-sacrificing love, was possible for a creature, whatever the cost. As such he was at least an example, though one which passes judgement on the rest of you. But also, since it took him over the threshold of the next stage in creaturely evolution, it made him available to you at all times down the subsequent presents, as an understanding companion in your own, ever more creative attempts at sacrificial living."

Me: "What has happened to the idea that Yeshua' death was God's sacrifice of his own son?"

Mediator: "We will have to come back to that in a later cycle. We think it better for you to spend your time now contemplating the many ways in which you human beings avoid the sacrificial life: all the futile ambitions and life-styles and ways-of-being with which you fill your dreams and personal aspirations. They all come to dust, and lead to the suffering of others–both contemporaries and later generations."

Me: "I suppose a way of approaching that is to look at the obvious victims in our world today. I think of the poor and homeless in our society. Then there is the huge flow of refugees around the world. I think of political regimes in which a few powerful persons–usually men–have cornered the good things for themselves and their families, while their peoples do without and starve. Then there is the destruction of non-renewable resources for the sake of short-term financial gain. I am aware that, as a member of a very powerful and energetic society, I can inadvertently exploit members of much weaker and less energetic societies by requiring their work forces to produce things for me at much less than their true value–thus virtually enslaving them."

Mediator: "I wondered when you were going to recognise your own connivance in all this. It is so easy to analyse in an abstract way, as a means of not facing up to one's own faults. Good. Have We gone some way towards answering your question about the rôle of sacrifice in the religious view of life?"

Me: "Yes. I can see that while creation is still 'on its way', so to speak, it is wrong and futile to try to inaugurate one's own little 'heaven on earth'. Rather, one should devote what talents one has to the service of the Whole, even, if necessary, to the extent of depriving one's self of what most others would think as one's rights. We have other lives to lead, after all!"

Mediator: "That earns you a good rest."

Cycle Twenty Nine:

The Holy One

Me: "I think it is about time we considered another topic which we have been skirting around for some time: I want to talk to you about God, or what you seem to prefer to call 'The Holy One.'"

Mediator: "Certainly, you are ready for that now."

Me: "Well why do you speak of 'The Holy One', rather than God?"

Mediator: "The word 'God' is commonly used to point to the <u>idea</u> of divinity, while 'The Holy One' is the name one may use for the mysterious Ultimate who encounters you in your life. Most people, whether they say that they believe in God or not, think that they know what they mean by the word 'God', and happily engage in arguments about secondary problems, such as whether or not God 'exists' or how Jesus could be both 'God' and 'Man'. Which assumes that they understand what is meant by the big words in these extraordinary statements. For this reason it is often better to avoid the use of the word 'God', at least until all parties have defined to one anothers' satisfaction, just what they want to mean by it. So, do you want to talk about 'God'?"

Me: "Yes."

Mediator: "Very well, then what do you mean by the word?"

Me: "'God' is the word I use to describe the One who I believe created and sustains the whole of this Reality in which I find myself, and who is ultimately responsible for what happens, intending to bring it all to some consummation in the future."

Mediator: "Well that is certainly more sophisticated than some definitions We have heard. Many contemporary Western people still tend to think that God must be some sort of mighty Being away 'up there', far from this world, who might conceivably have designed and created the world in the beginning, but who now leaves it to run itself. The trouble with this picture, which was first put forward about three of your centuries ago, in response to the new scientific world-view, is that, in practice, it leads its believers into a style of living that ignores the god who apparently ignores them. You have picked up on the idea that God 'sustains' the world in being moment by moment. But why do you believe all this? What answer would you give to someone who challenged you?"

Me: "I was afraid you would ask me something like that, which is perhaps why I've been avoiding the topic until now. I suppose I have just taken the belief for granted, assuming that others have worked it all out. Aren't there things called 'The Proofs of the Existence of God', or something like that?"

Mediator: "There are, but they are not much use to unbelievers, and in fact, don't amount to proofs. But you are trying to avoid answering my question by putting one back to me What answer would you give to an inquirer? Think back to some of the things we have been saying during our time together here."

Me: "O dear, I had hoped to have got out of trying to answer that. I think I will want to get back to your statement that the 'proofs' don't work, but will try to answer your question meantime. I think I have come to understand that God is not another item, thing, or even person, to add to the other things we find in the world. I recognise that it is unlikely that I would be able to form any clear notion of God with my little, finite brain. God must be that, without whom, there would be nothing at all. Hasn't someone spoken of 'the ground of all being'? Though that sounds a bit impersonal. I suppose I have to say that my mysterious existence seems to make more sense if I think of it as having been called into being by a Someone or Something who has some good purpose for it. Otherwise, what is the point of it all? Why don't we just maximise our pleasures with all the energy and skill we can muster and leave it at that? That is the only alternative I can think of, and, although it has its attractions, it sounds pretty bleak to me in the long run."

Mediator: "Well that answer might impress some people I suppose, if the Holy One put you in the way of speaking to particular individuals in those terms, but there is a lot more to be said and clarified. The point you make about the sense of the mysteriousness of existence itself (or as We would prefer you to say, 'of re-happening itself'), is an important one. It is certainly easy for you beings to get so overwhelmed by the demands and distractions of everyday life that you lose sight of it.

Just think, you have no recollection of having asked to come into being; you just 'find yourself' here. You are also aware, in a way in which animals are not, that one day you will cease to happen in the world. That you will leave all your possessions and friends and lovers, and your precious body will rot, to be recycled by and for other living things. This you did not ask for either, and yet it is 'a fact of life'. The loss of those you love and care for, will be occasions which tend raise the ultimate questions for you, but most people try to put them out of mind as soon as possible.

Another kind of experience which may make you think about the meaning of 'existence' is that of suffering–one's own or others. Many have thought that the fact of suffering (and who doubts that there is much of it?) raises questions about either the almightiness or the goodness of God. 'How could a God who is both good and almighty permit the terrible things that go on in the world?' they ask. What would you say to that?"

Me: "One thing I have picked up from our conversations so far, is that God is so far 'above' us that we cannot expect fully to understand just what is going on. I recognise that if God creates by Love, and that love does not, in fact cannot, use force, then evils are bound to arise when we creatures go our own

187

way. An image has just occurred to me that of a parent, handing on a business to a maturing child. That child is certain to make mistakes, sometimes wilful ones, and then pay the price for so doing. But that is the only way in which the child will learn; the worst thing the retiring adult could do is to perpetually intervene when the going gets tough. I suspect that God's relationship to creation is a bit like that: a progressive handing over of responsibility for its own future, but with many mistakes being made on the way."

Mediator: "That is indeed quite a useful picture, but it runs up against the problem of justice. It would appear that much of the suffering in the world is 'innocent' suffering; that is people suffer unjustly for the wrongs of others, who may even appear to benefit from their misdeeds."

Me: "Yes, but haven't we gone some way towards answering that problem with the recognition that this life is not the only one we have, and that in future lives we will have to face, at least some of, the consequences of our current one?"

Mediator: "That is indeed so, and We are glad to see that you have now taken on that fact. But there is still more to the picture than some sort of one-for-one retribution. It remains true that many still suffer as a consequence of the wicked acts of others."

Me: "Nobody is wholly innocent."

Mediator: "True, and certain sufferings may indeed be the consequences of their own actions in this or previous lives, but that does not explain things completely: there is no cast-iron law of Karma."

Me: "Then I cannot see how justice can be met."

Mediator: "Would you say that the Creation deals justly with God?"

Me: "No. God treats Creation with unending Love, and Creation responds with rejection, incomprehension and even hatred."

Mediator: "So what does God do about it?"

Me: "God goes on loving; slowly wearing down the resistance, so to speak."

Mediator: "Does God complain about this 'injustice'?"

Me: "No. In fact, he seems, according to You, to accept full responsibility for what has gone wrong."

Mediator: "Well, what does that tell you about the proper human response?"

Me: "I suppose that we should also, out of love, show solidarity with those who suffer, and accept some responsibility for our own contribution to the ills of the world–even if they are not the immediate cause of the suffering in question; easier said than done."

Mediator: "Indeed. And how do you expect this to be received by those who feel this love of yours?"

Me: "They would probably crucify me… Goodness, what am I saying?"

Mediator: "Exactly. The fact is, the human view of love is often hopelessly sentimental. Love is a terrible and demanding power, and those who are offered it often reject it fiercely, since it challenges them to pass it on to others, including their 'enemies'. How does this answer my question about how you should answer those who challenge you with the question of the existence of God?"

Me: "There is no knock-down intellectual answer: all one can do is love them, and try to find the root cause of their questioning?"

Mediator: "There you are then."

Me: "All the same, can we get back to why you said that there are no valid 'proofs' for the existence of God?"

Mediator: "Well, what do you think would constitute a valid proof? What would you accept as such? And what difference would it make?"

Me: "There you go again: answering a question with another question."

Mediator: "It is surprising how many of you people think that difficult questions should have simple answers! In particular you fail to appreciate that all questions assume a certain valid range of answers. Problems arise when the answer lies outside that range. You seem to think that the human mind should be capable of providing a proof of the existence of God in the same way as it can prove that the sum of the angles of every plane triangle add up to 180 degrees. So I ask you what kind of demonstration would constitute 'proof' for you? Your question also assumes that you know what is meant by 'exist' and that that category is applicable to God."

Me: "O dear. Are you saying that God does not exist?"

Mediator: "Well, it all depends upon what you mean by 'exist'. In most peoples' minds, the word 'exists' refers to the being-present of the objects and persons around them. One could, in theory, add up the total of all the existents. If this is the meaning you have of 'exist', then God does not exist, since God is not an item in the world. One cannot point to God and say 'There God is'. There are many other usages of the word which we will not pursue here, you will have to go to your philosophers to explore them. One, however, is relevant: the word can mean that which is the perpetual source of all that happens–in which case God is the only One who does exist!– all the rest is derivative."

Me: "So what was wrong with the classical proofs?"

Mediator: "They virtually all assumed that God was one exist-ent among others, whose presence could be divined in some way. Or they glossed over the fact that the so-called evidence was ambiguous. Or they considered that existence was a 'property' of sorts which could be added to all the other properties which beings have. But entities are not sums of properties, but perpetual re-happenings in relationship. And being is not a property, only the source of all that happens. Furthermore, while creation is still incomplete, it can provide no unambiguous evidence of its origin."

Me: "Now you are beginning to lose me again."

Mediator: "Nevertheless we shall have to leave it at that. You will digest it in time."

With that challenge ringing in my ears, I fell into grateful sleep.

Cycle Thirty:

Aspects of Love

Me: "It seems that the Holy One can only be known as Love, rather than as the result of an intellectual enquiry. I think I want to consider further the mystery of Love."

Mediator: "Good. You have slept on it well. That is where we left off several cycles back, you may remember."

Me: "The word seems to have so very many meanings, is there something in common between them all?"

Mediator: "Yes, the meaning is on an evolutionary continuum from the most elementary forms to the most exalted. Many human languages have different words for the different forms, which perhaps helps to distinguish them, while obscuring their unity."

Me: "I had never thought of love as an evolving continuum!"

Mediator: "Yes, We have witnessed its evolution from the earliest moments of your universe. What you generally call 'love', in all the kinds you recognise, has evolved from the fundamental forces which attract and repel at the inorganic level."

Me: "Do you mean the electromagnetic and gravitational forces?"

Mediator: "And so on, yes. They are what bring and hold things together to form entities, while also ensuring that things remain distinct and capable of happening in new relationships: particles and waves again, matter and mind. These give rise to the emergence of new levels of organisation."

Me: "This is a long way from what I call 'love'."

Mediator: "Surely, but it is where it all began. Love is indeed 'What makes the worlds go round!' Would you like to try to say what you associate with the notion of love?"

Me: "Oh, attraction and the promise of ecstasy; frustration and agony."

Mediator: "Very good. And might one also add: jealousy?"

Me: "In my experience yes, certainly."

Mediator: "Human love covers a whole spectrum, from the animal level of sexual attraction to that of the most sophisticated, self-sacrificing desire to give all for the sake of the beloved. The Greeks had several words for these different kinds and aspects of love, and the first Greek-speaking Christians chose the, hitherto little-used, Greek word 'agape' to express that exalted love which Yeshua had shown and provoked in them–a level of love that still remains largely beyond the reach of most of you, except in odd, inspired moments."

Me: "But I wouldn't say that Christianity has exactly celebrated love. Rather it seems to have been very wary of it."

Mediator: "Yes, there is a curious dichotomy here. On the one hand, Christians have proclaimed that 'God is Love', and have repeated Yeshua's summary of the Law as 'Love God and your Neighbour as yourself'. But on the other hand, they have frequently attempted to repress ordinary human love, even regarding it as evil, and certainly not worthy of true believers."

Me: "Why is that?"

Mediator: "It is because biological love is so powerful, especially in some individuals, where it can virtually take over the personality and cause you to act in ways which you would otherwise disapprove of. This hurts human pride. It has been especially urgent for those who think that God is best served by being celibate. In the Christian religion there has been a strong tradition from very early times, stemming partly from the example of Yeshua of Nazareth, that really serious believers must be unmarried. Even today, some of your denominations insist upon it for their ordained clergy."

Me: "Are you saying this is wrong?"

Mediator: "We are saying that it is seriously muddled. It is true, and this was the case with Yeshua, that some individuals may be called to serve the Holy One in a way which would be hampered by close personal relationships–especially family life. But when you remember that any individual life is only one of a series, in which different demands may be made of you each time, then it is not too difficult to appreciate that The Holy One may properly ask you to be celibate in some of them. It is quite wrong for a Church to make it into a general test of sincerity and devotion: in fact it is dangerous and cruel."

Me: "Do you mean that only those with a weak sex-drive should attempt the celibate life?"

Mediator: "No, but it would certainly be easier for them. It is possible for anyone to sublimate their sexuality, or any other biological appetite, if they go about it in the right way."

Me: "Oh, and what is that?"

Mediator: "Well, you need to be strongly motivated, with a clear and coherent idea of why you want to behave in this biologically 'unnatural' way. It is important to recognise that sexuality is part of one's inherited biology and, as such, is a wonderful and beautiful thing. Long ago, in the evolution of life on your planet, We persuaded 'nature' to use sexual attraction as a sure-fire way to express the instinct for survival in creatures that were too simple to be able to understand death and therefore the need to produce offspring for evolution to proceed. This and other instinctive behaviours which you have inherited from your animal past are still part of the way you find yourself to be, and, properly expressed, they can be the source of much pleasure and satisfaction. But you human beings are no longer just simple animals: you have crossed an evolutionary threshold which permits you to over-ride the immediate expression of instinctive drives for the sake of higher ways of living."

Me: "So it is better always to over-ride one's instincts, for the sake of higher things?"

Mediator: "There you go again with your tendency to oversimplify and express things in either-or terms. No, your biological drives are a proper aspect of your current humanity and they have a perfectly proper place in it. In fact they should be enjoyed and celebrated as part of the Holy One's good world. However, you have also to manage them lovingly. They need to be tamed with gentleness–think of the way in which domestic animals can be persuaded to happily suppress their drives in order to please their owners–this you need to learn to do for yourself. In fact, one of the functions of consciousness is to permit you to develop new habitual behaviours to run alongside or replace old ones: think of how you learned to express yourself in another language or managed to give up smoking."

Me: "Yes, I've heard it said that human beings were the first domesticated animals–we domesticated ourselves!"

Mediator: "Actually, you first learned how to control yourselves by discovering how to control the wild dogs who attached themselves to your camps."

Me: "How fascinating! You are full of surprises as usual. Now, can we get back to my 'over-simplification' of thinking one should suppress one's instincts."

Mediator: "Yes, isn't it remarkable that when considering the place of sexual-love in human life people have often felt the need to go to one of two extremes: either to say that everything important is sexual at base, or to say that sex is evil and must be eliminated completely from one's life. So, there have been those who sought to show that every human drive, even the most exalted, can be 'reduced' to sex. Or, by that law which states that every extreme spills over into its opposite, others have attempted to show that this very basic feature of human experience needs to be eliminated in order to live a proper life. No, it is very important for the health, both of individuals and human society that you learn to celebrate love at the sexual level in its proper place, neither exalting it to the 'be-all and end-all' of life, nor trying to repress it altogether."

Me: "We seem to have spent a lot of time on sex."

Mediator: "Because it is a preoccupation of your current society. You are going through an experimental period–largely precipitated by the development of more-or-less reliable methods of contraception–in which you are seeking out the boundaries of proper behaviour with regard to this most elementary and powerful of drives."

Me: "We have run into some problems have we not?"

Mediator: "To what are you referring?"

Me: "To the breakdown of family life and the rise of new diseases like AIDS."

Mediator: "Yes, a mere reversion to an animal-like expression of sexuality will not do. You are a long-lived species whose young take a long-time to develop and whose adult maturation is itself a life-long process. Promiscuous sexual behaviour is essentially animal behaviour, and while you may find it to be entertaining for a short time, is inimical to personal growth, since this is usually best achieved in your present state of development in the rough and tumble of an intimate, shared and committed life with one other person. It is also a poor background for the upbringing of children who need an environment of stable adult relationships. Finally, as your societies have rediscovered many times, promiscuity provides an optimal environment for the evolution of venereal diseases."

Me: "What about single-parent and single-sex families, while we are on this sort of subject?"

Mediator: "We observe that both these forms of family-life can work, especially as they tend to be highly motivated to succeed.

Some of them even, are more successful as environments for the bringing-up of children than the average mixed-sex family. However, as a general rule, the best family environments for the maturation of both children and parents, are ones in which the parents are of opposite sexes and where there are also lots of contacts with a variety of other families, including relatives.

You speak as if, having got onto this matter, we have got off the subject of love: surely we have not. The family is the arena of love for most people, most of the time. It is here that you have the greatest chance of learning the meaning of the word, especially in its higher forms. Sexuality will, if it is managed properly, act as a continuing encouragement to the parents to develop mutually, throughout life, in the face of inevitable problems. But other interpersonal relationships in the family, that don't have a sexual basis, will challenge the development of the higher realms of love."

Me: "Yes I did think we were getting off the subject. What about homosexuality? Is this a legitimate form of love? You don't seem to be excluding it as a possible pattern of parenting."

Mediator: "Human beings, as you have already pointed out; have been 'domesticated' for a long time. That is to say, you have been so successful biologically, that you have set yourselves some distance from the severest honing of natural selection. One of the consequences of this has been 'genetic drift' or the accumulation in your genome of biologically valueless genes which would not have survived 'in the wild', so to speak. The sexual orientation of a person is the result of a subtle interaction between their inherited genetic disposition, the hormonal environment of their mother's womb, their sexual encounters at puberty and their fantasy life. Biologically, of course, homosexuality is valueless, except perhaps as a natural contraceptive! (Like the swarming phase of locusts, which is a kind of mass suicide to ensure the survival of a few grasshoppers!) But there are also other good reasons why human beings should value homosexuals, since they bring a fresh perspective to the rich mix of human creative endeavour."

Me: "That puts the matter in an entirely different light for me. Thank you. Can you say something about the vexed issue of the differences between men and women?"

Mediator: "This relates to the question of love, because it is part of what men and women find to be both fascinating and repelling about one another. It is important to distinguish between masculine and feminine ways of relating to life, on the one hand, and male and female sexuality on the other: they are not the same. All men and women, whatever their sexual orientation, have some capacity for both masculine and feminine ways of behaving. It is true that hormonal influences upon the way their brains develop can bias them, so that most men tend towards the masculine mode, and most women towards the feminine mode. These two styles of approaching reality, reflect the attraction-repulsion features of the forces of nature, including love. The masculine approach to things seeks to take control by analysing, taking apart, and then perhaps re-assembling in a manner best suited to one's perceived needs: while the feminine mode is to take control by harmonising, and relating the individual to the wider Whole–especially personal wholes. The one is analytic and the other synthetic. Since each of these have their rôle in a full life, but tend to act in opposite directions, they are a source of both the fascination and the frustration which characterises the relationship between your sexes. A fully-rounded individual can use either mode appropriately. One can see this very clearly in Yeshua of Nazareth who employed each of them seamlessly as the occasion demanded. Eventually, these polarities will be superseded–but don't concern yourself with that here and now."

Me: "Once again you have given me much to think about. Now I'm tired again."

Cycle Thirty One:

Origins of Love and Beauty

Me: "There must be a lot more to say about love: we have tended to get stuck at the sexual level."

Mediator: "Certainly, there is. And we are 'stuck', as you say, because your society is. All of you long for and need love, but you are confused about what it is and where to find it."

Me: "There is just one thing in this area, left over from our last cycle, about which I would like to hear what you have to say, since it has caused much trouble in some religious circles."

Mediator: "You refer to contraception."

Me: "Yes, there are those who consider it tantamount to murder, or at least to frustrating the will of God."

Mediator: "Yes. We remember the first time one of you brought fire into a cave in order to keep it warm. There were those present who shook their heads and said that it was completely 'unnatural', and that no good would come of it. They often went on to declare that fire was such dangerous stuff that many would die because of it, and so on. And, of course, they were correct–many millions of you have subsequently died or been terribly injured by fire–but who would seriously suggest that you would have been better off never to have learned to use it? The fact is, that it is 'natural' for you human beings to be 'unnatural' in this way.

Since the time when human biological success enabled you to live for many fertile decades, your women have had to bear the burden of having many children. It is no exaggeration to say, in fact, that, with the exception of certain biologically well-endowed individuals, you have been killing your women by multiple childbirths. It has also deprived human societies of feminine styles of leadership in public life. Torn between the powerful urges of sex, maternal instinct, the longing for life-long companionship, and the desire for spiritual love, you have tortured yourselves over this matter almost more than any other. Prostitution, secular and sacred, has been one very widespread and unsatisfactory 'solution' to your dilemma. The only, sure-fire, ancient contraceptive was extreme asceticism—living far from temptations, and on an exceedingly sparse diet, so that the biological urges were suppressed. When attempts were made to mitigate these extremes, in monasteries with more humane regimes, for instance, frustration, neuroses and sometimes outright hypocrisy were often the result.

Of course, as with the example of fire, all powerful, new technologies carry dangers with them, and this is true of contraception too. In particular, it can tempt people to reduce sex to mere entertainment. When this happens, personal relationships become quickly exhausted and you get a 'quick-change society' in which everyone is moving on to live with another, temporary partner or partners. This deprives adults, and any children who may be caught up in these transitory arrangements, of the kind of secure and challenging environment which maximises their chances of maturing properly. Your press is full of stories of rich, promiscuous play-boys and -girls, who in this respect, are simply big adolescents looking for the next playmate, and are deeply unhappy and unfulfilled in consequence. And those who cannot afford this life-style, dream about it. Contraception is potentially one of the great transformers of human society. It has already gone a long way towards liberating women from the chains of their biology. But you are going to have to work out for yourselves the details of the best way in which to use it, and how its dangers can be avoided."

Me: "You are not going to tell me from what age they should be used and all that?"

Mediator: "No, that is not your personal concern any more."

Me: "Thank you for spending so much time on the subject all the same. Can we now pass on to other aspects of love? Granted that love has its origins in biological urges, or even earlier in the physical forces of nature, what are we to say are the characteristics of the higher forms of love that have evolved from them in our species?"

Mediator: "Love is the ultimately proper response to beauty, both, when it is immediate and obvious, and when it is so obscured by ugliness or indifference that it scarcely more than a mere potential. Animal responses to beauty (and you still have these too) are purely instinctive. You human beings, however, are being led by visions of beauty, far beyond the biological level. And, insofar as you perceive these levels, you will feel the corresponding emotions of love."

Me: "Why do you say we are being 'led' by visions of beauty, and that love is the proper response to it?"

Mediator: "What do you suppose to be the origins of the lure of beauty or the agonising sense of its absence?"

Me: "I don't know: it is just something that I find I have, along with my humanity generally."

Mediator: "You appear to have forgotten what we were saying about the origins of beauty, truth and goodness earlier."

Me: "Oh, of course. Beauty is one member of the great, given triad of values by which we are challenged in every moment of our life. Ah, it is coming back to me now. Beauty is a glimpse of the way things ought to be–the direction in which perfection is to be found."

Mediator: "And what does that tell you about the current state of your species?"

Me: "That it is imperfect and incomplete?"

Mediator: "Exactly. In each of the lives you will lead in the present epoch, you will find yourself sensitive to some particular aspect of the beautiful (you can scarcely hope to perceive them all) and you will be aware of a certain range of things that are wrong, and of matters of which you are still woefully ignorant. These constitute your own particular challenge for that life, and their pattern arises partly from the way in which you lived your previous one. But you still haven't identified the ultimate origin of the lure of beauty."

Me: "It must be the Holy One, I suppose."

Mediator: "Why so tentative?"

Me: "I don't really know. Perhaps it is because I am so aware of the power of the beautiful to lead me astray that I'm loathe to attribute it to God."

Mediator: "That is hardly beauty's fault, is it?"

Me: "No, I suppose not. But much of our religious history has been governed by a negative attitude to beauty–especially personal beauty, so I imagine I'm reflecting all that."

Mediator: "Quite so. We have already seen how that could have come about–particularly for those who make celibacy their ambition. But it is also certainly true that beauty has given rise to a great deal of envy, acquisitiveness, greed, covetousness, and jealousy, so that it is hardly surprising that people have been afraid of it. But all of this was the result of wrong responses to beauty, whether one's own or another's–not the fault of the beautiful itself. An enormous amount of damage has been done to human society by those religious leaders who adopt a very negative and defensive attitude to lovely things, and people. This was one of the major causes of the historical back-lash against religion in your Western societies, and the seeking of refuge in hedonism. Wrongly directed, love can perhaps be best described as 'lust' or 'acquisitiveness'; can you try to distinguish this from higher love?"

Me: "I suppose 'lust' is love at the natural, animal level, whose energy we need to learn to re-direct. Higher love is concerned to enable things and people to be more as they should be."

Mediator: "How do you see this working in the normal response of men and women to physical beauty?"

Me: "One should try to look 'through', as it were, the beauty of the attractive person, and ask oneself just what you are being

202

invited to encourage. This may of course, lead to a close personal relationship, but it should not dissipate itself in a shallow episode."

Mediator: "Very well. You have just used the expression 'look through'–so can I ask again, to what do you suppose you are 'looking through to' when confronted by something or someone beautiful?"

Me: "I suspect, once again, you want me to say 'God' or 'the Holy One.'"

Mediator: "Indeed. And when you understand that you will have arrived at a very foundational matter. Beauty is one of the voices of God: one of the ways in which the Holy One addresses you, and invites you to co-create in the development of Reality. You may not always recognise this, in which case one can say that the revelation is 'veiled'. However, it is possible to experience beauty as the voice of God: especially easily perhaps in moments of ecstasy, for instance. Such occasions can help you to begin to recognise God behind all the other, less dramatic encounters, in everyday life."

Me: "Oh dear, I have hardly ever recognised God 'behind' the beautiful. However, I now realise that there have been peak experiences in my life, whose significance I did not appreciate at the time. Perhaps, when I get back, I shall be more alert to them."

Mediator: "We are sure you will. By the way, you still have time for a few more sessions with Us, before we have to decide whether or not to let you return. The medical team have you stabilised."

Me: "Oh, good. I feel that there is still a lot I want to know before entering the fray again."

Mediator: "You need to spend more time thinking about the deeper meanings of the lures of beauty, truth and goodness."

Me: "I'll do that. Good night!"

Cycle Thirty Two:

Love, Beauty and 'God the Son'

I woke up feeling heavy again. *HeShT* said, "You have slept through many cycles due to a pulse of anaesthetic."

Me: "Can I see how they are getting on?"

Mediator: "Of course."

I looked down through the window in the field of light. There I was, still lying on my back on the operating table with my eyes shut and tubes coming out of my mouth. Things hadn't changed much otherwise. The staff had moved a little further off and some had their eyes fixed on a digital readout–I presumed a cardiac monitor. Satisfied, I returned to *HeShT*.

Me: "Thank you."

Mediator: "We must begin by considering further the significance of beauty and love, now that you have had time to think about them. Would you please try to summarise where we have got to?"

Me: "The experience of Beauty in the ongoing present moment is a disguised encounter with the Holy One. It is the means by which love is invoked, and is a glimpse of the direction in which perfection lies. It is never perfect itself and may, in fact, be hidden under layers of ugliness, necessitating loving insight to perceive it at all. Beauty is never perfect because 'creation' is still under construction, as it were. Contrariwise, ugliness is the product of ill-will on the part of some entity or entities (high or low) in creation, who by commission or omission have failed to respond positively to the invitation of the Holy One, the Creator. How is that?"

Mediator: "Yes, that is fine. Now we must extend your understanding a bit more.

You will remember from your intermittent life in the church, that the Christian religion sees God as *Triune*: a Trinity of three 'Persons' in One God?"

Me: "Yes Father, Son and Holy Spirit: an extremely opaque idea."

Mediator: "Well, with which of the three Persons, as you understand them, would you especially associate the value of Beauty and the virtue of Love?"

Me: "At first sight, I suppose, all three, for 'God is Love': though I don't normally associate Beauty with God–only with nature."

Mediator: "Think of 'Glory.'"

Me: "Ah yes, of course: Glory could be the word for the absolute Beauty of God."

Mediator: "But accepting that Beauty and Love are associated in your mind with God, with which of the three Persons are they especially connected?"

Me: "Let's see. O dear, this is difficult. As I think of each in turn, they seem to fit equally well with all."

Mediator: "Even God 'the Holy Spirit'?"

Me: "Well no, I suppose not. The Holy Spirit has always seemed a bit vague in my mind."

Mediator: "We shall see why later. But go on."

Me: "That leaves us with God the Father and God the Son."

Mediator: "Yes, so ask yourself, with which of them do I feel, not think, Beauty and Love to be most strongly associated?"

Me: "Ah well, now it is clearly God the Son, meaning Christ. Because, although my image of God the Father is one of magnificence and rather austere love, Yeshua I can picture as one of us, and I suppose have felt something of his love from time to time. I have not often thought of him as beautiful though."

Mediator: "You should: he was a beautiful person who loved everyone, even his enemies, and taught beautiful truths by beautiful stories and sayings, and who died a truly glorious death."

Me: "I can't think of Yeshua's death as glorious–sordid rather, and ghastly. After all, he had been tried by the highest authorities in the land–including the religious authorities, and had been found guilty of treason and blasphemy. Then they had him executed in the most painful, humiliating and public manner in order to deter any others who might be thinking along the same lines. When I think of the cries, the agony, the sweat, the blood, the urine, faeces and flies in the hot sun, and the crowds mocking–I do not think of glory but rather of horror, failure and disgrace."

Mediator: "Truly the foolishness of the Holy One is wiser than the wisdom of men. Don't you see, it was not Yeshua who was on trial, but rather the authorities themselves? The test was: Would they, or would they not, see the Beauty of God in this beautiful Person who, even when challenged with the prospect of his own horrible death, still did not waver from the course of Love? Also, if you can learn to see beauty in this event, you will be able to see it anywhere."

Me: "I had not thought of it in that way before. Yes, I see now."

Mediator: "And it is still the case. Beauty and Love are not always obvious or ecstatic, but are found also in the sordid and secret byways of the everyday: wherever sacrificial love stands alongside in solidarity with the despised and rejected, wounded and suffering."

Me: "And that is how one finds beauty in the most unpromising places?"

Mediator: "Yes."

Me: "I would have liked to have met Yeshua of Nazareth."

Mediator: "You did, and you cried 'Crucify'!"

Me: "No I didn't! Surely I didn't! Oh please tell me that I was not one of those!"

Mediator: "Sorry, but that is the truth–however unpalatable you find it. You can take some comfort, though, from the fact that you have moved on a bit spiritually since then."

Me: "Oh dear. Oh dear. I feel ashamed. I had hoped that I would have been one of those who was always on God's side. I have always pictured myself thus in our Holy Week celebrations."

Mediator: "Really now! None of the disciples were–not even Peter, remember? You all deny Christ or desert him when it comes to the point. Or to put it in our terms here: you betray Beauty and Love with your feeble self-centeredness and petty hatreds."

Me: "I have much to learn, have I not?"

Mediator: "Yes indeed, and in the mercy of the Holy One you will have many lifetimes in which to do it. You characteristically make the mistake of supposing that because you can think clever thoughts about your beliefs, that these are substitutes for living them out in Reality. We are concerned to make you aware of this."

Me: "Yes, I'm truly sorry. I will get it right in future."

Mediator: "No you will not! Not right away anyway; though you will probably try harder."

Me: "Ouch … you appear now to be taking some delight in hurting and humiliating me. You can have no idea what it is like to be a frail human being."

Mediator: "We take no such delight, and you should stop taking refuge in self-pity. You cannot earn your way into heaven, or pull yourself up into perfection by your own bootstraps. But you can learn to live more lovingly, and allow yourself to be gently led up by it, in the knowledge that even your faults will be put to good use–remember what was done for you at Calvary. As for not knowing what it is like to be human: I remember very well."

Me: "You?!!"

But before I could take in fully what *HeShT* had just said, I collapsed in great alarm into profound unconsciousness.

Cycle Thirty Three:

Hope, Goodness and the Holy Spirit

I came around remembering that something surprising had occurred at the end of the last cycle, but I could not recall what.

Mediator: "You will when you are ready."

Me: "How frustrating. I don't think I am going to be able to get it out of my mind: it is there all the time niggling away."

Mediator: "You will soon put it aside when we get going.

Recall that we were thinking about the experience of <u>Beauty</u> (or its absence) in every present moment, its potential for invoking love and its association with the Christ, the second Person of the Holy Trinity. We must now consider the experience of the lure of the value of <u>Goodness,</u> and its associations."

Me: "Very well."

Mediator: "Can you recollect some of the ideas we discovered earlier when considering the matter?"

Me: "Let me see: the lure of Goodness comes to us through the futures-present face of NOW and needs the virtue of Hope in order to be responded to correctly."

Mediator: "That's right. But why is hope necessary?"

Me: "Because we can never know with absolute certainty what is the right thing to do in any circumstance, but have to use our imperfect moral senses, guided by traditions and reason. Without hope we would not embark upon morally difficult choices at all, nor would we persist with the course of action chosen when it runs into difficulties."

Mediator: "Does this mean that you do not expect guidance of any sort–other than traditions–when making difficult moral choices. After all, where did the traditions come from in the first place?"

Me: "Many would answer 'from God', but we have already seen that it cannot be a simple as that. Not only can there be quite contradictory claims regarding divine inspiration, but novel situations are always arising which have no precedent and are therefore without guidance from 'divine' traditions."

Mediator: "What about those persons who claim to have direct instructions from God on moral issues?"

Me: "How is one to know that they are genuine–assuming that they could be in the first place? One kind of clue, certainly, is the sort of life such claimants lead. If this is considered to be loving and exemplary, then we may be disposed to believe them. But so often such persons seem to be just subtle manipulators of desperate people: seeking the power over others which they have not been able to obtain in more legitimate spheres."

Mediator: "So what is the answer to the question, where does guidance come from?"

Me: "I seem to remember that we concluded that moral decisions needed to be corporate decisions. That is to say proposed moral courses of action needed to be considered publicly before they could claim to be the right ones. Complete consensus, of course, is often hard to come by, and compromise or confrontations are likely outcomes of any such activities."

Mediator: "Would you expect radically new proposals for moral behaviour to come from committees?"

Me: "No, perhaps not."

Mediator: "Then where would they come from?"

Me: "I suppose they are bound to occur first to an individual who is deeply engaged with the issue under consideration."

Mediator: "And where do you suppose that she or he gets the idea?"

Me: "I suspect that you are trying to coax me into answering 'God', but I find myself resisting that answer–it can't be that simple."

Mediator: "Good. And you are quite right. A clue is found in the observation you just made, that such moral innovations are likely to be suggested by committed individuals, within a living community that is wrestling with the problematic matter in hand. Only such persons will have explored the issues widely and become sufficiently deeply and existentially engaged. Those who do this (and it does not usually happen to people who live only isolated or superficial lives) will often have the surprising experience of suddenly recognising an entirely new course of action which had not occurred to anyone previously. Where do you think such innovative ideas could come from?"

Me: "I suppose from the person's own inner creativity–or from 'God', whatever that means?"

Mediator: "Exactly, it is generally impossible for you know whether such new insights are of your own creation, or whether they have been put into your mind by God. The Holy One is the perfect lover and teacher: never imposing solutions to your problems, but ever at hand to make tiny suggestions and leaving you to make of them what you will. Your own creative ideas, if they are compatible with the whole project for creation are also acceptable contributions and will be incorporated appropriately."

Me: "I'm very glad to hear that. I expect that my problem in this matter is yet another example of our human tendency to reduce things to a simple either/or. Moral solutions, we feel, must either come from human insight or from God, instead of recognising the possibility of a complex interaction between contributions that are not easily distinguished and attributed."

Mediator: "That is right. Now, can We go on to ask you again, With which of the Persons of the Holy Trinity of the Holy One would you most closely associate the lure of Goodness and the virtue of Hope?"

Me: "Once again, all of them, but I suppose most especially God 'the Holy Spirit'."

Mediator: "And why is that?"

Me: "Because God the Holy Spirit is the God of Surprises, the One who is always leading us into all things new, who may be seen as the One to offer aid in making novel moral decisions."

Mediator: "Very good. Very good. God 'the Holy Spirit' is indeed the Personal aspect of the Holy One who leads you wayward followers into their future–and not only the 'believers in Christ', but all moral beings, everywhere.

Now would you try to summarise what you have learned about the nature of your experience of Reality NOW, emphasising the place of the Holy Spirit in it."

Me: "Reality NOW is experienced by me as an on-going, three-faced Present Moment, of which one of the faces is the futures-Present present, offering us a range of options for the next Present Moment.

- We all have some sense of freedom and responsibility with regard to the choices on offer in every moment, recognising that sometimes such choices are very determinative of the future. This situation of finding ourselves to be moral beings is a great mystery and is simply given to us with our existence and it cannot be avoided.
- It is possible to make some sense of this situation, however, if we see ourselves as part of a great, divine enterprise, in which we are invited to share.
- We will be given repeated opportunities in new lives to re-engage in this process until it is completed, and can have some satisfaction in the realisation that our contribution,

minuscule as it is bound to be, may find its place in the final consummation.

- Returning to the futures-Present in every present: it is in this aspect of our encounter with the mystery of Reality that we are met by 'God the Holy Spirit', who points us the way forward and invites us to co-create the future."

Mediator: "Excellent. Now can you see why your image of God the Holy Spirit, is so vague?"

Me: "Yes, because it is in some respects God the Unknown. The God who opens our eyes to see aspects of Reality of which we had hitherto been ignorant, and which we may not welcome when they are revealed to us. Of 'God the Father' I can form a clearish image, since He is the God of the Holy Scriptures and the 'Father' of Jesus Christ. While Jesus Christ, 'the Son of God', and the second Person of the Holy Trinity, I can picture since we have the accounts of his ministry in the Gospels and the efforts of thousands of theologians and mystics to make him comprehensible. But 'God the Holy Spirit' is an aspect of the Holy One who is always ahead of us, leading us into often completely unknown futures. That is why my image of this Person is vague. Oh and by-the-way. Why do you talk of our actions having to be 'compatible' with the purposes of God rather than in 'obedience' to them, which is the more traditional word?"

Mediator: "The word 'obedience' came out of the hierarchical image of the relationship between God and creature which was only a half-truth: 'compatibility' is better–it recognises your co-creative activity.

Now, would you say it is especially easy to be encountered by the Holy Spirit and <u>not</u> recognise it?"

Me: "I suppose so. We tend to think that our good ideas and insights come entirely from ourselves and hope to get some recognition of the fact from our peers. We are also likely to blind ourselves to futures which will require us to change too much. Then there is the tradition in literary circles of the mysterious 'muse' who supervises one's creativity–I suppose that could be the Holy Spirit?"

Mediator: "And of course, not confined to Christians or even religious persons in general?"

Me: "No, I expect not. There is just one other problem I have with 'God the Holy Spirit'."

Mediator: "Yes We know–say it."

Me: "Isn't our experience of It/Him/Her, suppose to be ecstatic–a Pentecostal experience?"

Mediator: "Certainly it can be. But it doesn't have to be. When people who have been without any hope at all for their future, suddenly find one, they are bound to be ecstatic–don't you think?"

Me: "Yes, of course. Perhaps I will be more ready to recognise the Holy Spirit of the Holy One in future."

Mediator: "Well, We hope you have found your time with Us to be enlightening?"

Me: "Yes, very. Oh, you are not saying my time here is up are you?"

Mediator: "No, we still have a few more matters to explore before you are returned to full Reality. Go away now and contemplate 'God the Holy Spirit' and be ready for whatever HeShT throws at you."

Once again I drifted off, and despite the warning, did not appreciate the significance of *HeShT's* last remark, and in consequence was completely unprepared for what happened next.

Cycle Thirty Four:

I face the reality of my Self

"Hey you Enn, or whatever you call yourself, wake up! Come on, Wake up!"

Startled to hear a harsh, new voice, I came around abruptly. I was surrounded, as usual, by *HeShT*'s familiar sea of faces, but amongst them, and lovingly supported, was one that was shouting at me angrily. It was a black face, with prominent eyes and lips contorted with passion.

"Yes, you" he continued when he saw me become aware, "I thought it was you, and now that you are awake, I know it is."

Completely puzzled, I looked to *HeShT* for an explanation.

HeShT said simply, "Listen to him."

Black Man: "We have met before, man, and I wish I had hands to get at you."

Me: "For goodness sake why?"

Black Man: "You don't remember? How very convenient! Once, when my mother, my brothers and I were busy collecting roots and berries near our village in Africa, your slavers suddenly appeared and dragged us off. We were put in irons, taken down river by small boat and packed into your ship to cross the Great Sea. There were about a hundred of us in a very cramped space below deck. We were terrified and had hardly any food or water. We cried and cried and wondered what was going to happen to us. After a week or two in these terrible conditions, some of us got sick, my mother amongst them. Then you, Captain Whatever-your-bloody-name was, had those afflicted thrown overboard, saying they were worthless and if kept could pass on their fever! That was the last I ever saw of my mother."

He went on with his terrible story for a while until I cried out,

215

"I don't know what you are talking about. I have never been to sea and I would never do anything like that. *HeShT* tell him I wouldn't, please, please."

At this the Negro's face began to fade and merge into the others, protesting all the while. When he had eventually mingled with the rest, and his voice had faded away, I was left with *HeShT* regarding me gravely and rather more sternly than usual.

Mediator: "He remains very bitter, though he was a good man in his village and in the new world to which you transported him."

Me: "I am completely puzzled. I have no recollection of anything like this, and I'm sure that I wouldn't behave like that anyway."

Mediator: "No, not quite as bad as that now, but that is what you did then."

Me: "Oh I see, we are talking about one of my previous lives?"

Mediator: "Yes, slow coach."

Me: "When I appear to have been the Captain of a slave ship between Africa and America."

Mediator: "Yes."

Me: "And a pretty awful one at that."

Mediator: "Yes, though you were nice enough to your family, whom you loved dearly, and for whose benefit you did it all. You were eventually to retire and settle very comfortably in Jamaica, pacifying your conscience by saying 'They were only wogs, and didn't suffer the way we do'. You must have been deaf."

Me: "I cannot remember any of this and I'm having difficulty in owning it as something for which I am responsible."

Mediator: "Yes, it is a merciful feature of your type of being, that each instance of a conscious life forgets the previous ones. Not that you do so completely, since the bulk of you, so to speak, is your unconscious dispersed Self (remember?) which continues to influence how you behave."

Me: "I don't recognise any of this as being me at all, and I don't believe that my unconscious Self is influencing me like that either. Oh dear, I find all this all very distressing."

Mediator: "It is necessary for your self-knowledge, and to shake you out of your overly-intellectual approach to what you are learning with Us here."

Me: "Well, I'm certainly shaken and rather apprehensive of what you are going to reveal to me next."

Mediator: "We feel for you, believe Us. However, you should remember that in every moment, I take billions of beings like you through an even more searching examination of their souls after death, so We are well-acquainted with injured pride."

Me: "Oh, it is not a question of injured pride in my case: I just don't recognise myself at all. It is not as though you had brought to my attention some dreadful deed of my youth which I had conveniently forgotten, is it?"

Mediator: "No we spared you that–this time. You don't recognise yourself, because you don't know yourself well enough. It is true that you have made some advances spiritually in your several lives since the one briefly revealed to you just now, but don't deceive yourself into thinking that you have put all that behind you completely."

Me: "Oh but I have, surely. You will know of how well I behaved towards that African person who came to work for us in our laboratory some years ago. In fact, it was I who insisted that we should employ him, when the boss wanted to take on a less well qualified white–just because he was white."

Mediator: "Yes, and very pleased you were with yourself weren't you? There had been some flagrant examples of racism on the news and you were very glad to have the opportunity to distance yourself from such things–which was an advance, of sorts."

Me: "Yes, I was very proud of that action, and it surely shows that I have put all that previous-life stuff behind me."

Mediator: "Can you remember the man's name?"

Me: "Yes of course, it was…? Oh come on, it is on the tip of my tongue … Oh dear, I can't remember … it will doubtless come back to me in a moment."

Mediator: "You can't remember his name because you were never really interested in him. It was Kamau. He belonged to the Kikuyu tribe, from Kenya. Although he did indeed get the job, and worked well in your laboratory for a number of years, he was never made particularly welcome by any of you, and his discoveries were only acknowledged grudgingly. In the end he had to go to America to get proper recognition."

Me: "Yes well, he was an awkward character, and it cannot be said that he went out of his way to be likeable."

Mediator: "If you treat someone badly they tend to react badly, and so a vicious circle is set up and everyone thinks that they are the victim. Kamau came to your country, already smarting from the treatment he had had at the hands of previous white employers, so he was in no position to be magnanimous and understanding in the face of your deficiencies."

Me: "But I have just explained–I responded properly."

Mediator: "Yes, but that was less to do with him than it was with your own self-image. And once the incident was over, you joined with your colleagues, women and men, in virtually ignoring him. He was an awkward character, yes, and took umbrage very easily, but that is no excuse for your behaviour."

Me: "Oh very well. But I don't think that that was justification for subjecting me to the way I was woken up this cycle."

Mediator: "So you really think that you have put all that behind you, and that there is no relic in your prejudices?"

Me: "Yes, I do."

Mediator: "Then how do you account for what happened next?"

Me: "What are you talking about?"

Mediator: "The development with your daughter?"

Me: "Oh that–what about it?"

Mediator: "You are still refusing to face the truth aren't you?"

Me: "In what way?"

Mediator: "Let Us spell it out for you, since We all witnessed it, and you have clearly repressed all memory of it. Everything was going along smoothly, so far as you were concerned, though not particularly for Kamau, who felt lonely and isolated, when you daughter Jane came to work for you temporarily in her Summer holidays, and fell in love with him."

Me: "Oh no, he fell in love with her, as well he might, for she was a very attractive girl."

Mediator: "No, you have to face it: she fell in love with him and he with her. Also, he was a very attractive man."

Me: "Oh dear, I don't like any of this, please stop. I think it is time for me to sleep again."

Mediator: "No, it is not quite time yet. Let me remind you. When you two learnt of the affair, and of their plans to leave together for America, you put your foot down and threatened to have nothing more to do with Jane if she went ahead. There were some weeks of intense agony and mutual recrimination. Eventually Kamau gave in his notice and left alone. Fortunately for you, the relationship had not developed to the point where she would have preferred him to you. In the end she went on to marry somebody who suited you better. So you see, you have conveniently forgotten those developments. Do you really think that these racial prejudices have been completely expurgated deep down?"

Me: "Well no, I suppose not… No, no–on second thoughts, I'm not going to accept responsibility for these actions you have just reminded me of. They were the result of my background, social conditioning, and the way I was brought up, the attitudes of all my contemporaries, and so on. I am very angry that you should be trying to make me feel guilty for having attitudes that were perfectly normal and widely held at the time. No, you are not going to be able to get away with that–I won't let you, I won't, I won't. I want to go back now, I've had enough. Send me back!"

Mediator: "Tut, tut. That was some outburst. We wonder why there was so much emotion in it. Could it be that you have a conscience after all and that your pride has been hurt? Of course your behaviour is largely the product of the influence of others, and most of you have your values shaped most of the time by the society and times you live in, and you are no exception: this is the residual truth in your 'Doctrine of Original Sin'. Furthermore, the values you espouse in one life live on to influence you in the next. However, from time to time you are given the chance to break with such established behaviour patterns. Usually at the beginning of a slippery, downward slope you will find yourself wondering if you should stop and redirect your energies while you can. That is the moment when, by applying moral effort and imagining other ethically better ways of proceeding, you are given a chance to make a significant difference to the future. If you miss that opportunity it becomes progressively harder to break the common mould, and you laps back into just running with the crowd."

Me: "I'm sorry, I'm sorry. I have to accept that you are bound to know me far better than I can ever know myself. I feel thoroughly humiliated. Now I come to think about it, I am very surprised at my reaction to you just now–it was as though I was looking down into a dark and bottomless pit."

Mediator: "That was a glimpse of the ancient Enemy. The One with whom we all have to strive continually, helping beings, high and low like you, to resist It.

It is nearly time for you to sleep again. You can take some comfort in the fact that as a result of your wrong actions Jane learned a thing or two about forgiveness when she forgave you both. Also that the slave-trade incident with which we began was one of the things, which, when it became widely reported, was influential in bringing the whole sorry practice of the British slave-trade to an end. But, remember, that this good outcome was what We and others were able, in time, to make out of you and your actions, and not what you achieved for yourself, so you can take no credit for it.

Now you should go away and think about the *true* meaning of the notion 'that every moment of your experience of Reality has a future face in which you are invited by the *Holy Spirit* to pursue the Good with the virtue of Hope in the knowledge that you are privileged to co-create the future of Creation'!"

Me: "Now you are laughing at me."

Mediator: "Not at all. You will get over it. We know you well enough to be confident that, when you have had time to appreciate what has happened to you in this cycle, you will profit from it."

Then I almost scrambled into sleep.

Cycle Thirty Five:

Faith, Truth and 'God the Father'

I came around very reluctantly to this cycle.

Me: "I'm still smarting from last time. You certainly took me down a peg or two."

Mediator: "It was necessary, as you will eventually come to recognise, though We regret that you found it so unpleasant. You should find this cycle much more to you liking, for it is along your usual tack."

Me: "What is that then?"

Mediator: "Can't you guess?"

Me: "I can't imagine."

Mediator: "Oh come on, stop sulking and try. Think of the last few cycles–what have we been considering?"

Me: "Let me see. Oh yes, we were going over the business of the three faces of Reality NOW. We had looked at the experience of the Beautiful in every present-face of the Present, which ideally invokes in us the virtue of Love. Then we looked at the experience of the lure of the Good in the future-present-face of every Present, which requires the virtue of Hope. And then you chose to rub my nose in my shortcomings."

Mediator: "Just put all that behind you for now, and go on: all this should be old-hat to you. What important new insight were we covering in this matter of what you are really encountering in every present moment?"

Me: "Oh of course. The experience of the Beautiful is a veiled encounter with 'God the Son', and that of the lure of the Good a meeting with the alarming 'God the Holy Spirit'–the one, I note, who is often called 'the Comforter!' Some comforter!"

Mediator: "You really must leave off this self-pity. Can you remember how much cutting your teeth hurt? Would you rather you hadn't grown teeth? Now, can't you guess where we go next?"

Me: "Obviously it is something to do with the experience of the lure of Truth in every past-present-face of the Present which requires the virtue of Faith as its response… Oh now I see, this is a veiled encounter with 'God the Father'!"

Mediator: "Well done, that's better, you have completed the insight for yourself. Now let us examine more closely the three virtues which are associated with the triune structure of NOW, its three values, and three 'Persons' of God. What are the three great virtues again?"

Me: "Faith, Hope and Love."

Mediator: "What do they have in common?"

Me: "These are the three 'theological' virtues, identified by Paul in his letters to the young churches, as the prime gifts of God. Understood in their broadest meanings, they cover all that is best and highest in human endeavour. They are closely related, but not reducible to each other. They are constituents of every creative effort."

Mediator: "Why is human creativity necessary?"

Me: "I suppose because these three virtues are responses to the three values of Truth, Goodness and Beauty, which are all imperfectly manifested in life as we know it now–certainly our perception of them is. This requires much creative effort on our part. These efforts are our human contribution towards the maturation of Creation as a whole. I can vividly remember how difficult it was for us to arrive at the truth of the biological problems which I encountered in my professional life. It was amazing how different the truth seemed to equally committed researchers who came at the same problem from different angles. It often turned out that we were all partially right, of course. You have taught me to see that those advances in knowledge were increases of creation's own understanding of itself."

Mediator: "Excellent. So would you say that, in practice, what is considered true or beautiful or right is entirely a <u>human</u> construction in response to the challenges of life?"

Me: "Well not entirely–that is what humanists think. I see now that some guidance is available from the Holy One in our searching and wrestling. However, it may be impossible to know for certain whether any particular insight is solely our own or is a hint from the Holy One."

Mediator: "Very good. Would you please run through the three virtues again and say how they relate to your responses to Reality NOW."

Me: "Well, firstly, *Faith* <u>is the virtue</u> invoked by our realisation that the Truth is there, but our understanding of it is always only partial and improvable.

- Truth is what once happened in the present to make the present-present what it is, and this includes general truths as well as forensic truths.
- The universal human experience of the lure of the Truth is an encounter with the *Holy One:* God ('the Father')– whether recognised as such or not.

Secondly, *Hope* <u>is the virtue</u> required to face the fact that we can never know with absolute certainty what choices we should make from amongst the options offered to us in the potential future-presents we experience in every NOW.

- Having considered all precedents, and the likely outcomes of the various choices before us (the truth), we just have to launch out in the faith that our vision of the Truth is reliable and in the <u>hope</u> that we have made the best choice possible towards the Good.

- The universal experience of the challenge of what is right is also an encounter with the *Holy One:* God ('the Holy Spirit')–whether recognised as such or not.

Finally, *Love is the virtue* by means of which we discern the pale lineations of ultimate perfection of which we can have glimpses in every present moment.

- What we choose to love is also a creative act, since we can radically reverse our judgements with the development of deeper sensibilities. Anyone who has learned to appreciate a form of art which they previously could make nothing of, knows that love can grow and mature if one makes the necessary effort. It is also possible to learn to see something as merely sensational or even ugly which once one considered beautiful.
- The universal experience of the beautiful at the heart of every present moment is also an encounter with the *Holy One;* God('the Son')-whether appreciated as such or not."

Mediator: "Good. You have grasped that well. What would you say to somebody who complained that it was all rather abstract and impersonal?"

Me: "Just that it is an attempt to generalise human experience maximally, and that every individual person needs to learn to deal with their own individual encounter with Reality NOW. They need to be creative with their own virtues of faith, hope and love towards their own visions of Truth, Goodness and Beauty, and in this way put some flesh on the bare bones of this sort of exposition."

Mediator: "Very well, so long as you realise that many persons require much more help to get from these sorts of abstractions to their own reality–they need stories, drama, myths and other fictions."

Me: "Certainly–and the construction of those kinds of works of art are the creative products of those whose calling it is to make them."

Mediator: "You have understood that the experience of the lures of the three Values are veiled meetings with the triune Holy One, invoking the responses of the three Virtues on the part of human persons. Do you think the Virtues have any place in the Holy One's response to Creation?"

Me: "Let me think… Religions usually say something to the effect that God is Hopeful, Faithful and Loving, so I suppose that this can be worked into our typology somewhere."

Mediator: "Good, but let us leave the detailed working out of that idea for another cycle. It is enough for now to observe that the human responses of faithfulness, hopefulness and love are themselves *reactions to the corresponding virtues in God,* and that this is the way in which the Holy One woos the Creation forwards on its way its consummation.

Finally, can you think of any single idea which unites *the three virtues* we have been considering–in the same way as the three Persons of God are united in One God?"

Me: "No, I don't think I can. Haven't philosophers been trying to do this for ages?"

Mediator: "The unifying idea is Holiness."

Me: "Well, well. And what is the unifying value then?"

Mediator: "Perfection."

Me: "So, we have One God in three Persons;

> One aspiration to Holiness in three virtues;
> One vision of Perfection in three values, and
> One Present Moment of Reality encountered
> in the three aspects of NOW."

Mediator: "You and your systems! Very good. Can you begin to see also, that this is what was meant by the ancient insight that human beings *'were made in the Image of God'?* Now you can rest again, feeling you have achieved your sort of thing."

Cycle Thirty Six:

Glory, Holiness and the Unity of God

I woke up wanting to learn more about the *Holy One by* whom we are met in a veiled way in every present moment, in the form of the 'lures' of the values of Truth, Beauty and Goodness.

Mediator: "As I expected. We should begin by considering the notions of God's Glory and Holiness."

Me: "Oh, I expected you to give me some images which I could take away and contemplate."

Mediator: "No, images are for you to find for yourselves. While you are here with Us, and considering the sort of person you are, we will start with ideas derived from your experience.

Let's begin with <u>Glory</u>. What comes to mind when you think of it?"

Me: "Hadn't we already said that Glory was the Beauty of God?"

Mediator: "Yes, but we must examine the idea further. So far we have associated Beauty especially with the Person of the Son experienced by you in the pure Present. But, as you rightly remarked when I asked you, Beauty is associated with all three Persons not just the Son. So what do you suppose is meant by Glory?"

Me: "I suppose it is the Beauty of God as One."

Mediator: "Right. Glory is the Absolute Beauty of God as One. God is where the values of Truth, Beauty and Goodness converge to become the one great Value of Perfect Glory. God, in God's Self is Glorious. To you-wards God is veiled Truth, Beauty and Goodness. Can you think of an image for Glory?"

Me: "Yes, blinding light, like the sun. Light so powerful that it is hurtful to look at."

Mediator: "That is good. Certainly you could not look at the unveiled Glory of the Holy One and live. But you have wept at the sound of great music, or great and good deeds, and on encountering beautiful people. In these awful and ecstatic experiences of beauty you have also caught a glimpse of the glorious face of God. Another word for Glory, but more abstract and therefore less capable of being imagined, is 'Perfection', but we will return to that later.

Now let's turn to *Holiness*. If Glory (or Perfection) is the uniting divine <u>value</u>, what is Holiness?"

Me: "Once again, I think we have already seen that Holiness is the unity of perfect virtues. In God who is One, Faith, Love and Hope are also one, and that oneness is Holiness. How's that?"

Mediator: "Very good. God, in God's Self with respect to Creation, shows the virtue of Holiness, which you, one-dimensional-temporal beings experience as God's loving and hopeful faithfulness. What image comes to mind when you think of holiness?"

Me: "Activity towards me so pure that it becomes a terrifying, absolute demand that I become holy also."

Mediator: "Yeshua said, 'You must be perfect, as your heavenly Father is perfect'. And your response was to kill him, demonstrating how far you still have to go.

Holiness, therefore, is Glory in action towards Creation. Only a few persons, with strong spiritual constitutions, acquired by many lives of faithful living, have anything like a direct experience of the <u>singleness</u> of the Holiness of God in God's Glory. These are the founders and reformers of the great religions. For the rest of you, the encounter with God comes through the less overwhelming, <u>three-fold</u> experience of the faithfulness, the loving-kindness and the hopefulness of God in your everyday lives. Furthermore, because of your limitations, the experience of only one of these tends to be prominent in any particular phase of you life.

We must consider these three characteristics of the *Holy One* in more detail, so that you will recognise them better for what they are in future.

First then, let's think about what is meant by the *Faithfulness of the Holy One*. With which of the 'Persons' is this most closely associated?"

Me: "God the Father."

Mediator: "What therefore could be meant by your experience of it? Remember all the things we have been considering about the nature of Reality."

Me: "Reality is a re-happening, moment by moment, of an enormous Creation, of which we are only a tiny part.

-This Reality is evolving in a step-wise manner, each ultimate moment being a temporary, imperfect, pattern of entities that are invited to choose (under guidance) what pattern (closer to perfection) to adopt next.

-God *faithfully* sustains this process, giving energy of being to the entities, *faithfully* accepting their choices–good or bad–and perpetually adjusting *HeShT's* persuasions to correct for errors."

Mediator: "Good. And how do you personally experience this divine faithfulness?"

Me: "Oh, in the beautiful regularities of nature: the way in which day follows night and things generally happen in a predictable, 'lawful' manner. Also in the way in which our religious insights grow continually as the ages pass: the way in which the promises of God, as mediated by prophets and others are kept and even surpassed. I think especially in the biblical story of the promises made by God to Moses and the Israelites which were fulfilled, I believe, in the person of Yeshua of Nazareth."

Mediator: "And what does contemplating the faithfulness of God do for you?"

Me: "It fills me with thankfulness and a sense of the worth-whileness of life. It also encourages my faith in turn. I have to proceed most of the time with a very inadequate grasp of the truth and that requires faith."

Mediator: "Good. Now let's turn to the *Hopefulness of God* as another aspect of the Holy One's Holiness. What do you make of that?"

Me: "Considering the mess that much of creation is in, and how long it seems to be taking to evolve, God the Holy Spirit must posses almost limitless Hope that it will eventually be perfected. To continue faithfully renewing its being moment by moment, when we would have been inclined to scrap the whole thing long ago, shows a degree of Hope that is beyond belief. I suppose I experience this aspect of the Holy One in the encouragement which I obtain to continue with my own little projects in the face of disillusion, disappointment and even uncomprehending opposition."

Mediator: "Which leaves us with the last virtue: that of Love. What can you now say about the *Love of the Holy One* and your experience of it?"

Me: "Ultimately the Faithfulness and Hopefulness of the Holy One towards the Creation can only come from an almost unbelievable Love for it.

- Love is the capacity to be there, hopefully and faithfully, for the beloved, through all the vicissitudes of re-happening.
- I know this personally because, despite all my repeated failures to live up to even my own ideals, my sense of the presence of the *Holy One* has never deserted me, although it has sometimes grown dim.

- I suppose I must, through the many life-times you say I have had, have developed some capacity to recognise the loving presence of my Creator and Saviour, who continues to permit me to re-happen and offers guidance when needed.
- This kind of absolute and unconditional Love *enables my feeble capacity to love*, towards both God and God's creation–especially other people. All right, all right–some of them anyway."

Mediator: "Well corrected: We wouldn't want you to get away with failing to recognise the gap between aspiration and performance!

So you have shown some grasp of the idea that <u>Holiness</u> is the unity of the three-fold <u>virtues</u> of the *Holy One* towards Creation. The aim of this activity is to lead Creation towards a holy response: a process which is far from complete. You and your society's creative efforts of trying to lead a life of faith, love and hope, in response to the *Holy One's* Faith, Love and Hope, is your contribution–however small–towards this aim. The *Holy and Glorious One* will continue to be along side you until you join with all the others in Ultimate Perfection."

Me: "I feel that my previous ideas and images of God have been just too small and 'domesticated' to cope with the nature of Reality as I now understand it. You have helped me to expand my ideas and visions. Can we begin to tidy these up a bit. I want to see how they connect with traditionally expressed views, such as the Doctrine of the Trinity and so on?"

Mediator: "Certainly we can. So, until the next time, take a break."

Cycle Thirty Seven:

Creator, Redeemer and Sanctifier

I opened my eyes and launched straight away into: "We were going to be talking about 'God the Holy Trinity.'"

Mediator: "Gladly. You could begin by considering the common characterization of the Holy One as Creator, Redeemer and Sanctifier; what do you make of those three?"

Me: "Let me see–I once had to make an academic study of all this, but have forgotten most of it."

Mediator: "Try to think of it in the terms we have been formulating."

Me: "God the Creator is God, who faithfully renews Reality in every moment by giving over the energy that permits the evolution of every Present moment out of the previous one, and by respecting any choices that were made then: the God of all our 'pasts-present'.

God *the Redeemer* is God, who is *lovingly* involved with Reality in every present moment, ready to share our suffering in it, if that is what is required, who demonstrated this supremely and crucially, in the career of Yeshua: the God of all our 'presents'.

(I seem to remember that 'Redemption' is an ancient image drawn from the slave market. Redeeming a slave meant paying the price that bought their freedom. It was a useful religious image referring to the experience of being freed from the slavery of bondage to the *status quo,* and liberation to the new life of living freely under love.)

God *the Sanctifier* is God, who *hopefully* works continuously to support the evolution of Creation into a state of perfect Communion, by offering new choices for the next moment and any help necessary to make the best decision; the God of all our 'future-presents'.

(To sanctify means to make holy.)

All this is why we pray 'in the Name' of God, the Father, Son and Holy Spirit: the One who was, and is, and is to come. Amen.'"

Mediator: "You have learned well, and have grasped the gist of the way of seeing things which we have been showing you. Now will you dig out something from your memory of what you were once taught about God the Holy Trinity?"

Me: "God, who meets us in worship and the everyday, is not to be thought of as utterly singular, but rather as being a sort of community of inter-acting 'Persons', God the Father, God the Son, and God the Holy Spirit."

Mediator: "Would you say that this was an entirely satisfactory way of seeing the Holy One, even given that much more could be said along these lines?"

Me: "No, certainly not. Not only has it been the source of much puzzlement, but also it has given rise to a good deal of unlovely, contentious arguments about the best way to describe the relationships between the so-called 'persons' while preserving the notion of the unity of God. Even allowing for changes in the meanings of words, and the difficulties of translation from the ancient languages in which these ideas were formulated, I cannot help feeling that that whole approach is more of a hindrance to our understanding rather than a help."

Mediator: "The credal and doctrinal statements to which you refer were the product of several centuries of heated, creative debate by mostly Greek minds, who were trying to come to terms with what they recognised to be the enormous achievement and significance of Yeshua of Nazareth who was crucified and raised from the dead. They formulated their understanding of this in the categories of the philosophies of their own time–which are not yours of today. There has been a tendency to regard their remarkable formulations as divinely sanctioned, instead of seeing them as magnificent, though flawed examples, which should serve to encourage people in other ages to do something similarly appropriate for their own time."

Me: "Wasn't part of the problem to do with the language of scripture? They had to take account of the actual words and expressions which were already considered to be divinely inspired in the Gospels and the letters of Paul and others?"

Mediator: "Go on."

Me: "Well, on the one hand they had to take account of the ancient insight, attributed particularly to Moses, that God was One (and this in the teeth of the common religiosity of the time, which still recognised many gods–and goddesses); and on the other, the historical facts of the career of Yeshua, who they believed to be worshipful (and therefore divine), who had referred to the God of his people as 'Father' in the most intimate way, and who also promised to send them the Holy Spirit of God to guide them into all things new. So they were landed, so to speak, with God 'the Father' and the divine Son, and the Spirit of God, and the problem of how to continue to relate to these, while still thinking of, speaking of, and addressing God as One."

Mediator: "Exactly. We must pursue later the question of the nature of religious Truth, and the inadequacies of human language and thought for coping with it. But for the moment: you once were also required to make a collection of Gospel passages to illustrate the dilemma you referred to above. Perhaps you can recollect some of these now?"

Me: "I'll try. I had to assemble passages of a Trinitarian nature from the teachings and the prayers attributed by St. John to Yeshua on the last night of his life, after he had eaten his last meal with his disciples and before his arrest in the dead of night. Let's see if I can recall them.

Mediator: "You may be surprised how easy this will be for you here and now with Us."

So I continued:

"Yeshua said to his disciples: 'Set your troubled hearts at rest. Trust in God always; trust also in me. There are many dwelling-places in my Father's house; if it were not so I should have told you; for I am going to prepare a place for you. And if I go and prepare a place for you, I shall come again and take you to myself, so that where I am you may be also.

Anyone who has seen me has seen the Father. Do you not believe that I am in the Father, and the Father in me? I am not myself the source of the words I speak to you; it is the Father who dwells in me, doing his own work. In very truth I tell you, whoever has faith in me will do what I am doing; indeed they will do greater things still, because I am going to the Father.

If you love me you will obey my commands; and I will ask the Father, and he will give you Another to be your advocate, who will be with you for ever–the Spirit of truth. I will not leave you bereft; I am coming back to you. When that day comes, you will know that I am in my Father, and you in me and I in you. Anyone who loves me will heed what I say; then my Father will love them and We will come to them and make Our dwelling with them.

I have told you these things while I am with you; but the Advocate, the Holy Spirit whom the Father will send in my name, will teach you everything and remind you of all I have told you.

I have spoken thus to you, so that my joy may be in you, and your joy complete. This is my commandment: love one another, as I have loved you. There is no greater love than this that some-one should lay down his life for his friends.

When the Advocate has come, whom I shall send you from the Father–the Spirit of truth that issues from the Father–he will bear witness to me. And you also are my witnesses. I assure you that it is in your interest that I am leaving you; if I do not go, the Advocate will not come, whereas if I go, I will send Him to you. When He comes He will prove the world wrong.

There is much more that I could say to you, but the burden would be too great for you now. However, when the Spirit of truth comes, He will guide you into all the truth, for He will not speak on his own authority, but will speak only what He hears; and He will make known to you what is to come. He will take what is mine and make it known to you. All that the Father has is mine. I came from the Father and have come into the world; and now I am leaving the world again and going to the Father.

Then Yeshua looked up to heaven and prayed:

'Father, the hour has come. Glorify your Son, so that the Son may glorify you. For you have made Him sovereign over all mankind, to give eternal life to all whom you have given Him. I have glorified you on earth by finishing the work which you gave me to do; and now, Father, glorify me in your own presence with the glory which I had with you before the world began.

'I have made your name known to all those whom you gave me out of the world. They were yours and you gave them to me. Now they know with certainty that I came from you.

'I pray for them. I am no longer in the world; they are still in the world. Holy Father, protect them by the power of your Name, that they may be one, just as we are One. It is not for these alone that I pray, but for those also who through their words put their faith in me. May they all be one; as you, Father, are in me, and I in you, so also may they be in Us, that the world may believe.'

———————

I may have remembered some things wrongly, but I think that is substantially correct. It was wrestling to try to make unified sense of passages like that, that the early church fathers formulated doctrines of the triune God."

Mediator: "You have remembered well what was recorded by Brother John, and have identified the problem of language with which the early church fathers had to cope. (Isn't it remarkable also, how much you can remember when not distracted by the consciousness of your body and its everyday affairs?) You should also notice that you are now able to interpret these passages in a new way.

It is part of the wisdom of the scriptural method of conveying spiritual truth that any passage is susceptible to a variety of interpretations–whatever was the exact meaning originally. These verses attributed to Yeshua by John, are an expression of the understanding of the significance of Yeshua about seventy years after his death and resurrection, by some Hellenistic Jewish congregations in Asia Minor. You can now understand them in your own way–provided that you divest yourself of the mind-set that stems from the Hellenistic world-view of the following centuries.

There remain some philosophical problems regarding the truth about the image of the Triune God which we will have to look at another time."

Me: "Thank you. That was a useful session for me. I feel another wave of sleep coming on."

Mediator: "You did all the work this time! Sleep well."

Cycle Thirty Eight:

The Image of God

Me: "HeShT, I still cannot form a clear concept of God, the Holy Trinity."

Mediator: "After all we have said, do you really expect to be able to do that?"

Me: "Well, perhaps I want to form a clear concept about not being able to form a clear concept of God!"

Mediator: "Oh we are lively 'today'! Perhaps you had better try to summarise briefly the triune nature of your experience of Reality as we have been unpacking it so far, and then we can take it from there."

Me: "Right, here goes:

Reality, as experienced by my consciousness is an approximate simulation of the ongoing present moment, which has a threefold structure comprised of this present, its given past and its future potentials;

- each of these is valued as more-or-less beautiful, true and good respectively,
- which may invoke in me the responses of love, faith and hope;
- and these can be recognised as the veiled allurements of God: Son, Father and Holy Spirit,
- who is Loving, Faithful and Hopeful towards me and the whole of this astonishing creation of which I'm an almost infinitesimal part."

Mediator: "Why did you order that as 'Son, Father and Holy Spirit', rather than 'Father, Son and Holy Spirit' as is usually done?"

Me: "I suppose because I have to start from where my religious experience starts–with the loving beauty of Jesus Christ 'the

Son of God'. For me, any 'picture' of God has to begin with the example of that life and how it illumines mine, and only after that go on to Why and How anything is happening at all (God the Father), and What will possibly happen and Where it is all heading (God the Holy Spirit)."

Mediator: "It seems to Us that you have answered your own initial question."

Me: "Perhaps, but it is the stimulation of your company that enables me."

Mediator: "Thank you, We are happy with that. You are moving towards the recognition of the important distinction between knowing God in the sense of knowing <u>personally</u>, and 'knowing' in the sense of knowing <u>about</u> God."

Me: "I suppose I was asking for some information about God when I said that I could not form any clear concept of God."

Mediator: "But knowledge about God is not available to you, nor could your mind contain it."

Me: "But what about what we were saying about God being the Creator, Redeemer and Sanctifier, and so on? Isn't that knowledge about God?"

Mediator: "Not really. All you can have knowledge 'of' is what other persons (human beings in your case) have said speculatively and analogically about their own personal encounters with the Holy One. All that theology and religious language is a gigantic metaphor, which says, given that we have had this heightened experience of Reality, it is as if there is a Personal Being behind it all who is like this. You can have knowledge of your own and other people's reported experiences, but you cannot have knowledge about God.

Just think for a moment, so far as you can see, God is the One who intimately (faithfully, lovingly and hopefully) upholds the re-happening of <u>all beings</u> (from quark to quasar) in this, and in the near-infinity of other Universes, and leads them in a manner analogous to the way in which you know yourself to be led moment by moment, towards an end that is beyond your comprehension. How could you, a mere, higher primate on a tiny planet, hope to be able to have any real knowledge <u>about</u> such a God? All <u>your</u> so-called 'knowledge of God' is a matter of more-or-less true <u>speculation</u> derived from accounts of the religious experiences of more spiritually developed persons."

Me: "Oh, I see. The only important religious knowledge is personal knowledge of God."

Mediator: "Yes, and moreover, it is not knowledge that you can acquire by trying. You have forgotten that although you set out with some curiosity to find out what all this God-talk was about, in the end you knew yourself to have been found and addressed, since the actual experience was different from anything you had expected. The world went on in much the same way as it always did, but you saw it differently. This is not something you can explain to others—they have to make the transition themselves, when they are invited. The most you can do is enable them to recognise the call of God when they hear it."

Me: "And how do I do that?"

Mediator: "By inviting them to consider a deeper meaning to their own experiences of beauty, truth and goodness and the corresponding urgings to love, faith and hope in the particularities of their lives."

Me: "I remember a personal experience which may provide an analogy for the transition from a secular to a religious view of life."

Mediator: "We know what you mean, but go on, say it."

Me: "I once constructed a television set from component parts. After many months of effort I finally got it all assembled and was ready to switch on. Nothing happened, of course, and it was several more weeks before I managed to get the sound only of several stations. Then came the first day when I saw some rather flickery, black-and-white pictures: but there was no colour. Eventually, late one night, after several hours of frustrating fiddling with tuning coils, the black-and-white picture I was watching developed rather unstable colour. Several more days passed before I could get a good colour picture on demand. Since then, that hesitant transition from a black-and-white image of a TV picture to a coloured one has represented for me an analogy for my wanderings to and fro between an irreligious view of life and a religious one. So it seems to me that trying to describe the religious view of life to someone who hasn't experienced it, is rather like trying to describe colour to a colour-blind person–it can't really be done."

Mediator: "We like that. Much of Our 'time' and effort is spent trying to persuade souls like yours to make that transition. You are often very resistant to making the change, because of course, growth is often painful and may require giving up old patterns of life and relationships with friends for the sake of new ones, the long-term consequences of which you cannot as yet appreciate."

Me: "That reminds me again of my recognition, at the age of seven, that when I grew up I would no longer want to play with my toys. I could not imagine such a state, but I could see that grown ups did not do so–except when playing with me."

Mediator: "Yes and their playing with you helped your transition to grown-up play. There is a lesson in there about religious instruction."

Me: "I'll try to remember it."

Mediator: "It is important for you to understand that many people who are looking for religion want to begin from the apparently assured understandings of their own cultural history. They find it very hard to take on completely new ways of seeing things. They want to know exactly what to believe and how to behave, and are often attracted firstly to anyone who offers them the necessary assurance. It is important to begin where they are, and it would be cruel to try to plunge them straight into the sort of approach we have adopted here (not that this is particularly advanced, you should understand, so don't get above yourself!). All the same, perhaps you should try to summarise where we have got to in our understanding of the nature of the Holy One in relation to you and Creation."

Me: "I'll try. The Holy One is the triune mystery who lovingly sustains and addresses Creation moment by moment, in a three-fold, personal movement in which the loving experience of a still-unperfected beauty, and a faith that what has been achieved by love so far, gives hope that a Perfectly Beautiful Relationship will be attained by love in the End. Knowing that we are thus loved, means that we are enabled to love in turn: this is what is meant by *'being made in the Threefold image of God'*. How is that?"

Mediator: "Bravo. But do you think that you live up to it?"

Me: "Goodness me no! But I realise that though I fail to do so again and again and again, I am forgiven again and again and again, facilitates my trying in my turn to forgive again and again and again!"

Mediator: "It seems to Us that you have reached a new level of understanding which will take you some time to comprehend fully and put into practice. The thought forms and vocabulary, and what they mean about how you should behave towards one another will not come easily. By now you should realise that behind and beyond your image of God as Holy Trinity is the Holy One: the <u>God-Head</u>, who is beyond all images and comprehensions, but knowable in the depths of your soul."

Me: "Yes I understand, but I would value an examination of the status of the received traditions of scripture and doctrine, and how we should apply them. And further, how one should attempt to appropriate new insights, such as the ones I have learnt here, which may not be apparent in either scripture or tradition–including those of other religions."

Mediator: "You are obviously approaching the threshold of normal consciousness again. But we have time for a couple more cycles. Take a rest now."

So I went out yet again.

Cycle Thirty Nine:

Language, Scriptures, Traditions & the Nature of God

Me: "You have made me well aware of the fact that religious knowledge is a matter of actual personal experience and not just knowledge of facts, but I would still like to know the truth status of scripture and traditions, since these are considered by many to be determinative–in fact, some would stop at scripture."

Mediator: "Very well, let us consider them. Scriptures are the classical, core-writings produced by your higher religions. They are usually thought to have been written under divine guidance by the founder, or founders and their immediate followers, although it is often difficult for you to discover exactly who wrote what, and there may have been a long period of editing and rearranging before a final form emerged. There is also a strong tendency in time, to regard scriptures as having been virtually written by God, and therefore to be infallible guides to absolute truths about the deity (or the Absolute etc.) and how one is supposed to behave towards him (usually) and one another. What are the problems about all this?"

Me: "Well, apart from the widespread, time-conditioned, and inappropriate attribution of maleness to the Holy One, clearly, there are many different religions, each with their own scriptures and, on the surface at least, teaching different 'absolute truths' about God and human morals. How is one to judge which, if any, is the 'right one'. To absolutize one's own cultural tradition is a common intellectual cop-out. Further, many scriptures are written in what are now dead languages, or dead versions of modern languages, so that the usual problems of translating from one tongue to another are amplified. The cultural differences existing between the time when they were written and the present time are often very great so that there may be considerable differences of opinion amongst competent scholars as to just what they meant (or could mean now). In practice, different groups or denominations within any particular religion, adopt an interpretative schema of their own, having also their own 'correct' translation, and then tend to claim absolute authority for it. This becomes increasingly suspect in the modern world: how is one to adjudicate between the various contenders? Today we can only see scriptures as the productions of an interaction between the human and the divine–with a heavy load of the human in them."

Mediator: "You have outlined well the commonly felt difficulties with the claims that a body of literature is Holy Scripture. But, in so far as any particular religion has nurtured successfully the spiritual life of millions of people, you must surely allow that their scriptures are likely to be 'true' in some sense. Could you try to work out how that could be?"

Me: "If one is prepared to allow that a particular religion has been spiritually successful, then indeed, there must be some truth at its core, and its scriptures would be expected to witness to that truth. I suppose, that I would want to insist that scriptures are a creative human record of the religious experience of the earliest practitioners of the religion–including the founder, of course–and that they are likely to be composed of some truly fundamental insights embedded, as it were, in a more or less extensive body of very human, and often incorrect–and certainly time-conditioned–religious prejudices.

Mediator: "How do you expect that to go down with your more conservative brothers and sisters?"

Me: "O, not at all well. Most of them regard the bottom line as 'Scripture says…': all the rest, however, logical or persuasive, is just a liberal accommodation to secularism. How could one answer that charge?"

Mediator: "You have already drawn attention to the basic difficulty of how would one justify the claim that one's own Scriptures are the one-and-only true ones. But beyond that, it is rare for those who claim that their Scriptures are the literal words of God and therefore infallible or inerrant, actually to believe everything that is written in them. If they only studied the history of their faith they would see that their religious fathers often felt that they had to change their minds about what they should and should not believe: few to day, for instance, would believe that slaves should just accept their lot, or that all diseases were either punishments from God or the activities of malevolent demons. It is very difficult for some persons to give up the idea that their ancient scriptures contain clear statements of all that is necessary to believe about God and God's requirements: it is such an easy over-simplification of what is actually the case."

Me: "And what is that?"

Mediator: "Classical Scriptures, which were written at an unselfconscious time before the notion of a Holy Scripture was conceived, certainly contain the core-revelation that characterises that particular approach to the Ultimate Holy Mystery, but it cannot contain everything. Human language, subtle as it is, simply cannot do that: God and God's hopes for creation cannot be enshrined in any book. In the distant future we will be asking of you behaviours - appropriate to the time and circumstances - which you just could not begin to envisage now: one might just as well ask a cat to act ecologically."

Me: "So, it becomes essential, for modern practitioners–indeed for all followers in the future–to attempt to separate out the central insights from the temporary, cultural expression of them. (I note in passing, that Jesus of Nazareth did not write any scripture, which is presumably significant.)"

Mediator: "Indeed I didn't. Can you say more about the common notion that everything that is essential for the religion is contained in its classical Scriptures?"

Me: "I suppose this may be true in a general sense – Hello, what was that you just said?– Oh, very well, I'll go on… it may be true in a general sense, though it is surely essential to try to discover what this is, and then express it in contemporary terms. But has one to exclude the possibility that radically new insights into God may emerge in time? There would be problems of authenticating them, of course, but is the possibility excluded?"

Mediator: "How could they be, considering the need, continually to come to terms with other religions as they emerge, with different insights–unless one discounts the truth claims of other religions altogether?"

Me: "The belief that one's own religion is the only true one, and even that one's own version of it is the only authentic expression of it, begins to look like mere tribalism in the modern world. We should expect to be challenged by God to expand our understanding though the insights of other religions as they arise: so much for absolute and sufficient Holy Scriptures.

All the same I would value some guidance about how to relate to other religions. Historically we haven't been very good at it."

Mediator: "No, indeed you have not. But an in-depth knowledge of other religions is not something with which you should concern yourself personally–not in this life anyway. What We and they have been up to down the ages is far too much for you to assimilate. For you it is enough that you witness lovingly, faithfully and hopefully to the partial vision of Us that you have been given and have tried to articulate; leave the rest to us. As the millennia pass all your religions will learn to accommodate themselves to one-another's insights–it cannot be accomplished in centuries, let alone single lifetimes! What you must always beware of is the descent into hatred when faced with incomprehensible differences. Resort to violence and hatred is never justified in the name of, and for the sake of any religion."

Me: "It seems to me that most religions have the utmost difficulty in adapting themselves to new knowledge of any kind, let alone the insights of other religions."

Mediator: "Yes, it may seem so, but most of them have been doing so–if rather slowly and reluctantly throughout history. Would you really expect not to learn anything new about the Holy One's requirements as the centuries, the millennia and billennia pass? To do so, is to act like a know-all twenty year old, who thinks he or she has arrived because they have espoused the latest, fashionable ideology. It is worth noting that scriptures were mostly written at times when human society was lived very much more at the communal level than it is in many of your societies today. This means they are deposits of well-tried and tested human wisdom. However, even they cannot give guidance about new possibilities, such as artificial contraception, or the legitimacy of using weapons of mass-destruction, or whether it is proper for you to move off your planet and into space.

Now what about <u>traditions</u>? Most religions have, in addition to a body of scripture, a more-or-less extensive set of traditions. These may be commentaries upon the scripture or a set of doctrinal, liturgical and ethical developments of it."

Me: "I suppose that many of the same objections to absolutising scripture apply also to canonising traditions. Traditions in religions represent developments in, as it were, the second, third and other early, subsequent generations. Being generally not too far from the cultural milieu of the original revelation they represent the additions and expansions of insightful individuals with essentially the same outlook. Traditions may claim to include additional revelations, or they may aspire only to clarify, or re-express the original. Whatever their form, there is always a tendency to come to regard them as definitive, so that even if scripture is not itself considered complete, the early tradition is thought to have completed it. Many Christians, for instance, consider the Creeds to have done this for the Bible."

Mediator: "Why do you think that there is this tendency to canonise early traditions?"

Me: "I expect that it is an extension of the respect felt for the scripture and the belief that being near the fire, so to speak, their creators were well qualified to round off the revelation. Also there is the practical fact, that eventually there is often such a large body of traditional literature to be assimilated, that it could take more than an individual's life-time to master it fully. So it may seem arrogant for any single person to claim to be able to add to or correct it. But what are we to make of the claim to Divine Revelation anyway?"

Mediator: "Certainly, a proper humility is sometimes at work in the conservative mind, but it is more often intellectual laziness, or a lack of imagination and an unwillingness to take risks for the sake of helping those who simply cannot transport themselves back into an extinct world-view. Divine Revelation is always the result of our encouragement to people to do their creative best in the circumstances in which they currently find themselves. Such 'revelations' are never complete or absolute. Let Me illustrate by inviting you to try to stretch your mind around a new view of how you should think of God nowadays–a view which requires the new understanding of time and Reality which we have been considering."

Me: "Very well, I'll have a go."

Mediator: "The Greek mind, which first formulated Christian doctrines and creeds outside Palestine, had, as one of its fundamental ambitions, the aim of knowing what everything WAS - including, if possible God, as we have seen: 'Jesus was God incarnate' etc. Now it is possible to unpack statements like that in order to arrive a what they were really trying to get at - but at the level of its literal meaning such a statement is over-ambitious. Since none of you human beings know what either Jesus Christ or God IS, it is not intellectually legitimate to claim their ontological identity. What WAS being claimed–and that was large enough–was that in the career of Jesus of Nazareth, the purposes of God and those of God's Creation came together perfectly, so that the project of the re-divinisation of Creation crossed a critical threshold and was now successfully underway. The justification for this interpretation, was its congruence with the previous revelations regarding God's purposes for Creation (as revealed in Scriptures), and God's subsequent actions in history forwarding that end."

Me: "You mean that Creation was being taken up into God?"

Mediator: "Yes and no. Creation is really always a part of the Reality of the Holy One which has been 'set aside', as it were, intending it to become independently perfect under the influence of Love. But this is an infinite process since perfection is limitless. The Greek image of God was of an absolute, unchanging, Perfection, and this clashed with the Biblical view (which it regarded as primitive and anthropomorphic). Christianity has had to wrestle with this tension between Jerusalem and Athens throughout its history. But Perfection is endless and must therefore include Perfecting: a Perfection which is still perfecting, is greater than a perfection that has arrived at some so-called 'perfection'. This is rather like the recognition, that the idea of infinity includes the notion of an infinity of infinities: perfection, like infinity, is endless. That aspect of the Holy One which is endlessly perfecting, is what you call 'Creation'. Creation will approach Perfection asymptotically, that is endlessly more closely, and you all will always have a part to play in it, eventually, in time-dimensions beyond those you currently experience. In this huge enterprise you will join together with other life-forms, of which you now have no knowledge whatever, but with which We have dealings in every moment of Reality. Creation is, on account of its going its own way, a bleeding wound in the side of God. Jesus Christ is the point of healing of that wound: where Creation is being progressively taken up again into the Holy One."

Me: "I see what you mean by stretching my mind. Does this mean that the perfecting of Creation will never be attained?"

Mediator: "Perfection will be *in the process of* reciprocal Love which will become endlessly more perfect–not in some mere state, but dynamically. A good analogy for you is a so-called 'perfect' performance of a piece of music, such as one of our Mozart's wonderful Symphonies. 'On paper' this seems perfect, to even the greatest human musical minds, but all actual performances leave something to be desired. An individual orchestra and conductor can get better and better at performing it, but they are unlikely ever to be entirely satisfied. There would, in any case, also be an infinite number of different kinds of 'perfect' performances. That is what is envisioned for the consummation of the Holy One's Creation. It will also be so absorbing that time will appear to cease!"

Me: "Thank you for that analogy, it is very helpful to me. But why is it that Biblical religion seems to want to put an absolute distinction between Creator and Creation, if you are now saying the Creation is part of God?"

Mediator: "Well, there was such a strong tendency in ancient historical times to identify God with some object in the world (for instance the heavenly bodies) that it was necessary to say a very firm 'No!' to that tendency. But the Christian insight that Christ pre-existed in God shows that ultimately Creator and Creature are the same. This also makes it easier to understand the notion of incarnation–it is the first major step in a restoration of what is ultimately the case anyway. Incidentally, We are glad to see that you have broken out of your obsession with trinities! You must be coming round.

Me: "Oops–was it that bad? I think I shall have to retire to consider that carefully! Let me rest again now, and when we resume I want to learn about prayer."

Cycle Forty:

Prayer and The Mediator Revealed

Me: "From what you have been saying about personal experience being central to real religion, I suppose *prayer* must be important, but I have always found it very difficult to do and have never been certain that I was getting it right."

Mediator: "All religions practise it."

Me: "Quite, and extremely elegant and even beautiful some of their prayers and forms of worship are–I cannot hope to compete with that."

Mediator: "But there is no competition. It doesn't seem to Us that you are at a loss for words."

Me: "Yes, but what we have been doing here is just chatting about my various concerns, and very enlightening it has been, though extremely alarming at times."

Mediator: "So?"

Me: "You don't mean to tell me that I have been praying!?"

Mediator: "Think about it. I remember vividly the disciples asking the same question. 'Teach us to pray, Lord' they said, and We recall the astonishment on their faces at Our answer: 'When you pray, say "ABBA"'. There followed a stunned silence. Then they blurted out things like, 'Is that all! Surely not', and, 'But we cannot address our Heavenly Father with such an intimate word: it's what we use for our dads, uncles and revered teachers!' and so on. They, like so many of you, seem to think that only long, carefully composed and formal prayers will do the job, forgetting that We know far more than you do about what is going on, and what all your needs are, and are continuously at work addressing them.

However, as I also found out, while the spirit may sometimes be willing, human flesh is very weak indeed, so that you certainly need more than just an 'Arrow prayer' like 'Abba'. In fact, you have to take time to turn matters over in your mind, to wrestle with temptations, and to check that what you are proposing to do is in line with what you understand to be our heavenly Father's will, and not just an expression of your own."

Me: "But I can't go around muttering 'Abba' all the time; people will think me daft."

Mediator: "They will think that anyway, believe me, when they get wind of all this. No, you are quite right. The word (which is Aramaic) was the natural one for Yeshua to have used, since He had a particularly intimate relationship with his heavenly Father, as he was fortunate to have had with his earthly father also. This is not always the case with people, and 'Father' may not be the best word for them. (Yeshua could just as easily have used the word 'Imma' (mother)–had his culture permitted it.) The point We are making lies not so much with the actual word, as with the proper intimacy and brevity of prayer. Your life, as We have been emphasising, consists of a sequence of moments of joy, horror and decision (small and great), and it is at such moments that you will especially need to be able to make immediate contact with Us. At such times, all that is required is one pulse of thought–clothe it in whatever word you like–or no word at all. The irreligious life, on the other hand (and you now about that too), is one which never makes the pulse at all; it fails to recognise the 'vertical' dimension of Reality which intersects the 'horizontal' at every moment."

Me: "But there doesn't seem much content in the one 'pulse' or word 'Father'"

Mediator: "As in human life, where there is an intimate relationship, one word or gesture is all you need. However, We recognised this with the disciples, and so We gave them a slight expansion of the word Abba, which you know as 'The Lord's Prayer'. This was a sort of minimal explication of the idea, just to help its proper use."

Me: "I have read reams and reams on the Lord's Prayer, to no avail. Most Christians have, I suppose, learnt it off by heart and we can trot it out from time to time. But I feel it is a bit of a cop-out to regard it as one's main prayer–it's too easy."

Mediator: "Indeed, We have noticed. This is because the point has been missed. All those words you speak about, together with all the words that so often pass for prayer, and are so intimidating to would-be prayers, are in fact detracting from the point. True prayer is a personal impulse at a crucial moment, not a long speech, or worse still a lecture to Us. Though, as We found out, the human frame and brain is such that you need much conscious practice to acquire the right attitudes, in order to pray in this immediate way and to cultivate your intimacy with the Holy One. So there is a place also for periods of prayer in which you practice using classically prepared examples, or take your time to chew-over matters, and run your concerns for yourself and others before the Holy One. You need also to meet and share with other believers, to celebrate acts of public worship, and share in the symbols of communion, which can be anything from the most formal, magnificent, 'operatic' performances, to the clappily or quietly informal. And these can, of course, be a glorious anticipation of the Consummation of Creation. But none of that should detract from the fact that you should endeavour to make your normal, everyday prayer, a string of momentary communications of your Soul with Us, uttered in the rough and tumble of life. In fact, all that formal and public prayer is simply the proper background for your private communion with Us. It is rather like the difference between a big party and a family meal."

Me: "Tell me more about the expansion of Abba, which you say the Lord's Prayer is."

Mediator: "Recite it for me."

Me: "Now you put me on the spot again - I hope I haven't forgotten it!"

Our **Father** (Abba), in heaven:
Hallowed be your Name
Your Kingdom come
Your will be done on earth as in heaven.

Give us today our daily bread.

Forgive us our sins
- as we forgive those who sin against us.

Do not bring us to the time of trial
But deliver us from evil.

Mediator: "That's a correct modern English version. Notice that it begins by emphasising, that the point of prayer is to try to align what you are currently proposing to do with the purposes of the Holy One. It is necessary to remind people that prayer is not about trying to get what they want out of God, but rather of endeavouring to discern what God wants of them. Hence 'Your kingdom come–your will be done'. Only then does one ask for 'daily bread': that is, the wherewithal to live, and perform what God wants. There follows the remembrance that you have often been here before, and failed to do the right thing then. So you ask for forgiveness (and, as a token of your sincerity, and recognition of your own vulnerability, you undertake to forgive others any wrongs they have done to you–very difficult). Finally, there is a plea not to be 'tested' too far, and to be protected against evil. All these movements are contained in the one word 'Abba', and should likewise be in your own 'arrow prayers' of the moment."

Me: "What of the comment that I have sometimes heard, that the Lord's Prayer is not Trinitarian, and therefore cannot be THE model prayer for Christians?"

Mediator: "Of course it is not Trinitarian - I was not a Christian, and it took Our followers another four centuries to hammer out that sort of language. But the triune structure is there if you look. It begins with an inclination to 'God the Father' and asks that you will be given the power to re-happen appropriately(bread);

it continues with a petition to 'God the Son' to be forgiven for failing both his and your humanity; and it closes with a request to 'God the Holy Spirit' to be with you as you launch out into the unknown and possibly alarming future. We gave the disciples this expansion of the single word, and are pleased that they were not tempted to extend it much further. (They only added a 'doxology' for liturgical purposes.) Just compare what Brother Luke recorded of the occasion with that remembered by Brother Matthew, and you will see what I mean. Despite this, however, the extreme brevity of the original has often been lost sight of. Huge volumes have been written on the prayer with the result that sometimes people have become intimidated by the whole idea of praying. They also failed to notice its Triune structure, which We have just outlined."

Me: "Thank you for explaining all that. Now it occurs to me to ask– What about all the other religions: what truth value do they have?"

Mediator: "We think that you have quite enough to cope with for now–leave all that for your future engagements!"

Me: "But I want to know if they are better than my religion, or more advanced even."

Mediator: "Oh many will think that they must be the best because they are the latest, or the even the oldest, and as millions of years pass and your species spreads through the cosmos and advances into forms which you could not even begin to imagine, it will eventually dawn upon people that Our Ways are fathomless, and that your religious insights are never complete."

Me: "How do I cope with unbelievers?"

Mediator: "First try to understand them–they often have good reasons for not believing, and then just love them to bits."

Me: "Shouldn't I try to convince them of the error of their ways?"

Mediator: "We doubt that you are clever enough to do that: No, loving will do the trick."

Me: "Oh dear, I'm not very good at that."

Mediator: "That is true, but you can learn to do better.

Now it is time. Up let us go: you may want to give thanks and praise and glory to the *One* who makes all this happen for ever and ever."

Me: "I get the feeling that I'm missing something very obvious and important here but cannot get a clear focus on just what it is. I believe that in my befuddled state I have not taken in fully your significance HeShT, or properly appreciated what you have done for me in these many cycles. All the same, I want to thank you–whoever you are."

Mediator: "We are pleased for you. Your time with Us here is nearly finished. I have opened up your 'past' and shown you much of the truth about how you have got to this Present; I have been alongside you in this experience (including your agonies), while you expanded your understanding and vision of *'What is Happening'*. Now We commission you again to go back into your future. Go and write what you have learnt here–however imperfectly you have appreciated it–and share it with others so that they might benefit from it too. As We have been here and Now for you, let *us* be here and Now for others. Remember, We will be with you always."

Me: "Yes but who <u>are</u> you *HeShT*?"

Then, as if in answer, there emerged from the host of faces that was *HeShT*, a small dark Lady in blue. *HeShT* said, "Meet our Mother: without her enabling, steadfast Love, none of us would have been here and NOW like this–Does that answer your Question?" The lady then extended a graceful hand in my direction and I fell down in terror crying out. "O Lord, but why me? I can't write: Anybody could do better than me."

Mediator: "We know that, and they will. But if We had to wait until all of you were perfect We would have no helpers at all, would We? No, I'm happy to go with you–warts and all. Your deficiencies will encourage others. Have no fear: Before Adam was, I am. We are the Origin and Leading Edge of Creation, travelling before, with and in front of all you beloved 'Happeners' for ever and ever."

Then I heard again the harmonious roar of the Great Music, and everything began to surge around me. *HeShT* seemed to explode at an enormous speed in all directions. All the myriads upon myriads of faces contracted to become smaller and smaller until they composed the elements of a single, huge and shining Universal Body. I recognised too the Song of the Worlds which I had heard again and again, between previous lives, and felt moved to join in with a few notes of my own – croaks they were. Everyone seemed so fulfilled and joyous that I was elevated and terrified at the same time. Then I felt small and ashamed, but greatly privileged to have shared their company for a while. "Do not be alarmed", said *HeShT*, "We have protected you against recognising Us, since that would have been too much for you, and would have reduced you to horrified silence. Now that you know Us better, you should feel free to call on Me at anytime."

It was then that I saw that amongst the myriads of rejoicing faces were the founders of all the great religions and philosophies; and, just for a moment I caught a glimpse of the forms of strange beings from other worlds, other galaxies, and other universes of this incredible Cosmos!! I cried out in astonished excitement and abasement,

"*HeShT, HeShT, Yeshua, ABBA, my Lord and my God*! I'm sorry, I'm sorry, I'm so unworthy, I want to know more, much more–please don't abandon me now!"

"We are not going anywhere", *HeShT* replied, "This is *What is Always Happening*, Here and Now – Stay in communion." Then I was engulfed by an enormous, loving, peopled Vastness, before plunging down a long, dark tunnel into black unconsciousness...

The next thing I became aware of was the sound of clanking metal objects and a distant voice saying, "Dr. Boddy's coming round." I wondered confusedly where on earth I was: it didn't feel or sound much like my bedroom. Then a voice said "Enni, Enni, wake up. Don't worry we have everything under control."

Another voice said, "I wonder what all that 'My Lord and my God' stuff was about."

I opened my eyes, and there I was, still in the operating theatre, with gowned figures, scurrying about. I tried to speak but the surgeon stopped me. "Don't try to talk yet. You gave us a bit of a fright there. We had just started putting you under when you had a small heart attack. I hope you won't make a habit of this sort of thing. We have had to put off your op until you have recovered." I managed to blurt out, "Sorry to have wasted so much of your time." She replied, "Oh, it was only a few seconds, don't worry. We will have you back in your prime in a week or two – God willing!" A ripple of laughter went around the theatre.

The next thing I remember was being wheeled back along the corridors again by the indifferent nurses, with the dubious lights passing overhead. Then I thought I heard a snatch of music and it all came back to me: all that I had been experiencing in those few seconds when I was out. I thought I saw again briefly, HeShT's beautiful, determined and compassionate faces, and I cried out, "Thank you, thank you, thank you!" One of the nurses said, "Don't thank us, thank the doctors." I replied, "If you only knew–if you only knew..." The other nurse said,

"We have a right one here, to be sure."

As we trundled back to the ward, it occurred to me to wonder if all this had just been me talking to myself whilst in an anaesthetic stupor: that none of it, in fact, had come from *Beyond*. I resolved to write it down before I forgot it all, so that others could judge for themselves.

[What do *you* think?]

We arrived back in the ward, the sun was shining through the open windows and the other patients seemed to be glowing with its fire. I was put gently back to bed with its welcoming touch of cool, clean sheets. A busy nurse passed and gave me a beautiful, caring smile, and I thought I caught a snatch of that music again. So I fell into a blissful, proper sleep.

Consider:

Prayer and Evolution in the New Testament

For all who are led by the Spirit of God are children of God... When we cry, "*Abba! Father!*" it is that very Spirit bearing witness with our spirit that we are children of God, and if children, then heirs, heirs of God and joint heirs with Christ–if, in fact, we suffer with him so that we may be glorified with him.

I consider that the sufferings of this present time are not worth comparing with the glory yet to be revealed to us. For the Creation waits with eager longing for the revealing of the children of God; for the creation was subjected to futility, not of its own will but by the will of the one who subjected it, in hope that the creation itself will be set free from the bondage to decay and will obtain the freedom of the glory of the children of God.

We know that the whole creation has been groaning in labour pains until now; and not only the creation, but we ourselves, who have the first fruits of the Spirit, groan inwardly while we wait for adoption, the redemption of our bodies. For in hope we were saved. Now hope that is seen is not hope. For who hopes for what is seen? But we hope for what we do not see, we wait for it with patience.

From the 8th chapter of St. Paul's Letter to the Christians in Rome.

The Cosmic Christ

He is the image of the invisible God, the firstborn of all creation; for in him all things in heaven and on earth were created, things visible and invisible, whether thrones or dominions or rulers or powers-all things have been created through him and for him.

He himself is before all things, and in him all things hold together.

He is the head of the body; he is the beginning, the firstborn from the dead, so that he might come to have first place in everything.

For in him all the fullness of God was pleased to dwell, and through him God was pleased to reconcile to himself all things, whether on earth or in heaven, by making peace through the blood of his cross.

And you who were once estranged and hostile in mind, doing evil deeds, he has now reconciled in his fleshly body through death, so as to present you holy and blameless and irreproachable before God-provided that you continue securely established and steadfast in the faith, without shifting from the hope promised by the gospel that you heard, which has been proclaimed to every creature under heaven.

From the first chapter of the Letter to the Christians at Colossae.

Now may the faith of God 'the Father'
> **the love of God 'the Son' and**
> **the hope of God 'the Holy Spirit'**
> **be with us all NOW and for ever. Amen.**

Select Annotated Bibliography

The following is a sample of some of the books which I have read over many years and which I have found useful and inspiring in devising my dialogues. It is not complete–nor could it be, not least because I have forgotten many of my sources. I append it, partly by way of acknowledging the contributions of many of my teachers; partly to show anyone who is interested where I am coming from; and lastly, perhaps to suggest some follow-up reading for anyone who may want it. (Lent 2000)

Popular Science

There is a huge number of books currently under this category. I have listed just some of those which I have found particularly helpful. All of us–even the most knowledgeable–are only amateurs the moment we step outside the bounds of any expertise we may have, and popular introductions are perhaps the only way we can realistically broaden our knowledge.

The New World of Mr. Tompkins. George Gamow & Russell Stannard. Cambridge Univ. Press. 1999.

New edition of a justly popular book that introduces relativity and quantum theory to the non-scientist.

QED. The Strange Theory of Light and Matter. Richard P. Feynman. Princeton. 1985.

A rather more difficult popular introduction to particle physics, centred upon light.

The Mystery of the Quantum World. Euan Squires. Adam Hilger. 1986.

A good account of the queerness of things quantal for the layperson.

God and the New Physics. P.C.W. Davies. Dent. 1983

> A popular book, remarkable for the way the author is sensitive to the possible religious implications of modern physics.

The Mind of God. P.C.W. Davies. Simon & Schuster. 1992

> The author considers science a truer way to the mind of God than religion!

The Quantum Self. Danah Zohar. Flamingo, HarperCollins. 1991.
The Quantum Society. Danah Zohar & Ian Marshall. Flamingo, HarperCollins. 1993.

> These two books attempt to apply some of the strange behaviours of quantal entities to our understanding of consciousness, the Self and Society.

Chaos. J. Gleick. Heinemann. 1988

> A good popular introduction to the subject of mathematical chaos - the 'butterfly effect' etc.

The Elegant Universe. Brian Greene. Jonathan Cape. 1999.

> A remarkable attempt to convey the excitement of String Theorists as they think they may be closing in on 'A Theory of Everything'.

Lucifer's Legacy. Frank Close. OUP. 2000.

> An examination of the role of broken symmetries in the evolution of the cosmos.

The Emperor's New Mind. R. Penrose. OUP. 1989.
The Shadows of the Mind. R. Penrose. OUP. 1994

> Two substantial books by a mathematical physicist, in which he examines, among other things, the possibility that new developments in quantum

mechanics may throw scientific light on the mind and consciousness.

Mind, Matter, and Quantum Mechanics. H.P. Stapp. Springer Verlag. 1993.

> A very illuminating study of the possible relevance of quantum theory to consciousness using Heisenberg's interpretation of quantum mechanics and William James' psychology. This author later went on to make interesting connections with the Process Philosophy of Whitehead and his followers. I have found this approach particularly useful in articulating my 'myth'.

Journal of Consciousness Studies. Vols 1-7. Imprint Academic. 1994ff.

> A new and innovative Journal that brings together thoughts, beliefs, experiments, and speculations about consciousness from a very wide range of sources: psychology, physics, artificial intelligence, philosophy (ancient and modern, Eastern and Western), mysticisms of many kinds, and religions. It is a veritable mine of ideas for the would-be myth-maker.

The Descent of Woman. Elaine Morgan. Souvenir Press. 1972.

> One of several books by this author which, by exploring the 'aquatic ape' hypothesis of the evolution of humanity of Sir Alister Hardy, and laying much emphasis upon the possible positive contribution to the process by human females, manages both to support the evolutionary theory of human origins and to show how speculative much of it must still be.

Philosophy of Science

This is clearly an area of human endeavour which is relevant to anyone trying to formulate a personal 'myth'. These are some of the books I have found stimulating in this regard.

Adventures of Ideas. A.N. Whitehead. Penguin Books. 1948.

The classic 'popular' statement of Process Philosophy by its modern exponent. Much more accessible than his 'Process and Reality' it can serve as an introduction to that much more demanding work.

Philosophic Problems of Nuclear Science. Werner Heisenberg. 1934. (Trans. F.C. Hayes,) Faber & Faber.

Philosophical reflections on quantum physics by one of the founding fathers of the discipline.

Physics and Philosophy. Werner Heisenberg. Penguin Books. 1989.

As above. It is always illuminating to read the philosophical reflections of genuinely creative persons, especially since they are often more open-minded than their followers who try to tidy things up.

Greek Science. B. Farrington. Penguin Books. 1944.

Western thought, religious as well as scientific, owes much to classical Greek thought as it broke with the ancient mythological systems of the time. It also serves as a positive model for being ready to think things out afresh.

The Origins of Modern Science. H. Butterfield. G. Bell & Sons. 1950.

A remarkable account of the origins of modern Western science by an historian who managed to convey something of the excitement and freshness of the time, even to non-scientists. Although many scientist also: those without any historical perspective on their subject, have benefited from reading this 'classical' work.

Pierce and Pragmatism. W.B. Gallie. Penguin Books. 1952.

This American philosopher can perhaps be thought of as the inventor of pragmatism, a down-to-earth type of philosophy which appeals to many scientists and politicians alike.

The Transformation of the Scientific World View. Karl Heim. SCM Press. 1953.

This, and other books by this German philosopher-theologian, were important to me as the first major introduction to how modern physics and the Christian faith could be reconciled. I 'discovered' him as a student, although it was many years before I was able to follow up his approach.

Personal Knowledge. M. Polanyi. Routledge & Kegan Paul 1958

An important work which draws attention to the importance of 'tacit' knowledge–that unconscious component of all skills, of which even its best practitioners may not be aware.

The Structure of Scientific Revolutions. T. Kuhn. Chicago (2nd Edn.) 1970.

A very widely influential work which introduced the idea of the 'paradigm' as a complex of ideas, 'facts', beliefs, theories and practices, which characterise the approach to a subject at any particular time in history. The 'revolutions' occur when some fatal flaw is detected in the paradigm and the whole body of facts, theories etc. has to be re-contextualised. The paradigm idea is applicable in other fields too, including religion (See Küng below).

The Tao of Physics. Fritjof Capra. Fontana Paperbacks. 1976.

> An example of the so-called 'New Age' approach to religion, philosophy and science. Now rather out-of-date in its understanding of quantum physics, it is none-the-less interesting in drawing attention to the resemblances between quantum-physical ideas of reality and those of Far-Eastern Religions, particularly Zen.

The Life of the Cosmos. Lee Smolin. Phoenix Paperback. 1997.

> An exciting presentation of contemporary cosmological ideas with a passionate plea for a better appreciation of the relevance of the holistic ideas of Leibnitz. It contains also an account of the author's hypothesis about the possible evolution of universes, and of ways of 'verifying' this possibility. An exciting read.

Problems of Life. L. von Bertalanffy. Watts and Co. 1952. *General System Theory.* L. von Bertalanffy. Penguin Press. 1971.

> These two books were important to me for introducing me to early twentieth century forms of 'holistic' thought, before the advent of chaos theory and an appreciation of non-locality in quantum mechanics.

The Creative Cosmos. Ervin Laszlo. Floris Books. 1993.

> An example of controlled scientific speculation, well-beyond the horizon of 'established' science. The writer does not recognise either myth or wish to entail religion and has a different approach to

time from the one developed in this book. Highly stimulating, all the same.

Science and Religion

The Twentieth Century saw many authors attempting to find an acceptable way of reconciling notions of truth derived from religions and science. The following brief selection includes some innovative personal contributions which I have found helpful, and some very useful summaries. There are many more.

Christian Faith and Natural Science. Karl Heim. SCM Press. 1953.

This was an important book in my personal pilgrimage as I wrestled with how to reconcile my Christian beliefs with my newly acquired scientific knowledge.

Nature and God. L. Charles Birch. SCM Press 1965

For me, one of the most useful introductions to Process Theology–the attempt to use the Process Philosophy of Whitehead and Hartshorne in the service of Christian Theology. As the author was a biologist I suppose he must also have 'spoken my language'.

Issues in Science and Religion. I.G. Barbour. SCM Press 1966.
Religion in an Age of Science. (Gifford Lectures.) I.G. Barbour. SCM Press. 1990.

Two books by one of the most respected expounders of the thoughts of many others on this subject, whose own leanings are towards Process thought–very illuminating.

Science and Christian Belief. John Polkinghorne. SPCK 1994

Science and Theology, An Introduction. John Polkinghorne. SPCK/Fortress Press. 1998

> Two books by a retired mathematical physicist who is also an ordained minister in the Church of England. He writes very thoughtfully and clearly about the relationships between science and Christian faith, and considers them complementary.

Jesus

> No person in recorded history has been so influential as the Jew from Nazareth–especially in the West, but now increasingly all over the world. The Christian theological assessment of him is, of course, controversial and, in some respects, hard to understand, except with the eye of faith. Recent times have seen many attempts to recover the historical person, using historical and sociological procedures. In these hands he tends to disappear altogether (which is perhaps theologically significant), leaving only the conundrum of how and why it was that some first-century Jews felt moved to write the New Testament about him, in which he is portrayed as divine–a very curious things for any Jew to do!

The History of the Jewish People in the Age of Jesus Christ. Emil Schürer (Revised by G. Vermes, F. Millar & M. Black.) Vols I - IIIb. T&T Clark 1973-1987.

> This is a major update of a classical nineteenth century work. It is a very thorough treatment of the Jewish background in the time of Jesus by both Christian and Jewish scholars,

The Prayers of Jesus. Joachim Jeremias. SCM Press. 1967.

> The work which introduced many of us to the

idea that the Aramaic word 'Abba' was the primary prayer of Jesus. It spoke of his passionate and intimate sense of Sonship before God, and he gave his followers permission to use the word too, It was probably a central datum in the development of Christology, especially in New Testament times.

Jesus the Jew. Geza Vermes. William Collins Sons & Co. 1973. Fontana. 1976.

A fascinating treatment of Jesus the Jew from a Jewish scholar, well-versed in ancient Judaism and the significance, for instance, of the Dead-Sea Scrolls. Although he often throws new light on the Jewishness of Jesus, he is not without his own Jewish prejudices!

Jesus before Christianity. Albert Nolan O.P. Darton, Longman & Todd. 1977.

A portrait of the 'historical Jesus' from the perspective of South African Liberation Theology during the time of aparteit. A good book for loosening the chains of a too narrowly 'theological' view of Jesus.

The Resurrection Narratives. Norman Perrin. SCM Press. 1977.

A good run-down on the Synoptic narratives of the resurrection of Jesus, without attempting to offer any solution to what 'really' happened.

The Formation of the Resurrection Narratives. Reginal H. Fuller. SPCK. 1980.

Another scholarly account of the origins of the New Testament narratives.

The Birth of Christianity. John Dominic Crossan. T&T Clark. 1998.

Jesus, A Revolutionary Biography. J. Dominic Crossan. HarperSanFrancisco. 1994.

> This author is a founder member of the 'Jesus Seminar', a mostly American group of scholars who have a profoundly sceptical view of the historicity of the Gospels, both with regard to the sayings and the deeds of Jesus. They remain, however, fascinated by this figure and are still evolving their thoughts.

Christ

> This is the main early title used to encapsulate the theological assessment of the significance of Jesus of Nazareth. It was the Greek translation of the Hebrew word 'Messiah', that is the One Anointed by God for a very special task–even the Final Great Task of completing Creation. There is a huge literature on this subject: here are a few I found helpful.

Early Christian Creeds. J.N.D. Kelly. Longmans. 1960.

> A good, 'classic' account of the history of the development of early christian thought about God, Jesus Christ and the Holy Spirit.

Christology in the Making. J.G. Dunn. SCM Press. 1980.

> A 'sound', scholarly treatment of the development of thought specifically about Jesus Christ, beginning in the New Testament Period and into the following centuries.

The Gnostic Gospels. Elaine Pagels. Penguin Books. 1979.
Adam, Eve, and the Serpent. Elaine Pagels. Penguin Books. 1988.

Two books which explore the question of whether there may be useful things to be learnt about Jesus and the development of theological thought about him, from what the early church regarded as 'heretical' writings.

Jesus Christ in Modern Thought. John Macquarrie. SCM Press. 1990.

I have learned more theology from this author than anyone else, though he may not approve of where I have got to! This is a splendid tracing of a particular style of Christology, which the author calls 'dialectical theism', stretching from the New Testament to modern times.

Bible

The Christian Bible consists of the Old Testament (which is the Jewish Bible written by many authors over many centuries) and the New Testament which is a short collection of mainly Jewish writings, centred upon Jesus and the early church, all written within a century of Jesus' death. There is a wide variety of styles of interpretation of these Scriptures by christians. My 'bias' is indicated by the collection below.

The Interpreter's Bible. Vols. 1-12. Abingdon Press. 1957.

This is an encyclopaedic collection of historical, exegetical and expositional articles on all the books of the Bible written mainly by American scholars who were at least sympathetic to what might be called the 'Albright School'.

A History of Israel. John Bright. 2nd Edition. 1972.

A standard work on the history of the of the Jewish and Christian faiths set against the background of Near and Middle Eastern history. Again from

271

the Albright School, it has formed the basis of my understanding of the history of the biblical period.

The Bible in the Modern World. James Barr. SCM Press. 1977.

Fundamentalism. James Barr. SCM Press. 1977.

Two books by a respected biblical scholar who outlines the modern 'liberal' method of interpreting the Bible and contrasts it with certain, timid, conservative attempts to accommodate to modern thought - inappropriately.

The Jerusalem Bible. Darton, Longman & Todd Ltd. First Edition 1966.

Basically an English translation (with reference to the originals) of a modern French translation of the Old and New Testaments (with the Apocrypha) made by Roman Catholic scholars of a liberal persuasion. It is remarkable for its format, the use of invented heading to sections, and copious notes, some of which betray a 'Roman' catholic stance. I have used it much, though not exclusively.

Theology

Theology is the attempt to think rationally and coherently about one's religious faith, with due respect for the truths of other disciplines.

Principles of Christian Theology. John Macquarrie. Revised Edition. 1977.

This book has been my theological 'bible' and I am much indebted to the author. He tries to show how the existential philosophy of Heidegger and others can illuminate the meaning of Christian theology. This approach is perhaps too 'unBritish' to have caught on widely in Britain, but it captured my colonial-British attention.

Christianity. The Religious Situation of Our Time. Hans Küng. SCM PRess. 1995.

> One of a series of investigations of religion in our time by a Roman Catholic maverick. He manages to survey the religious scene of the last 3000 years or so by using Thomas Kuhn's device of paradigms and paradigm shifts. (See above.)

The Shaking of the Foundations. Paul Tillich. SCM Press. 1949.

> A striking selection of sermons by a remarkable theologian who attempted Systematic Theology– from an existential point of view–at a time when it had become unfashionable.

The Christian Hope. J.E. Fison. Longmans. 1954.

> A 'liberal evangelical' eschatological writing which is remarkable for its passion.

Love's Endeavour, Love's Expense. W.H. Vanstone. Darton, Longman & Todd. 1977.

> A justly loved exposition of the theme of the loving, vulnerable God.

Christianity Rediscovered. Vincent J. Donovan. SCM Press. 1978.

> An account of a Roman Catholic experiment to let God the Holy Spirit guide the development of the Christian faith amongst the Maasai tribe in Kenya. It is contrasted with the more usual missionary tactic of imposing a Western pattern, lock-stock-and -barrel.

God Incarnate: Story and Belief. Ed. A.E. Harvey. SPCK.
1981

> A collection of articles by 'liberal' theologians
> expressing scepticism about the relevance for
> today of the Doctrine that in Jesus Christ God
> became human. Useful for causing the 'believer'
> to try to think clearly about this fundamental
> matter.

Sexism and God-Talk. Rosemary Radford Ruether. SCM Press.
1983.

> Provoking thoughts about Christianity from a
> feminist perspective.

Eternal Life? Hans Küng. William Collins & Son. 1984.

> A wide-ranging examination of the Christian doc-
> trine of eternal life which does not shrink from
> asking many of the difficult questions which occur
> to modern, western people. Unlike me however,
> he is not willing to consider the possibility that
> 'reincarnation', in some form, could be a part of
> Christian doctrine.

The Way of Paradox. Cyprian Smith. Darton, Longman &
Todd. 1987.

> A good exposition of the thought of Meister
> Eckhart.

The Divine Risk. Richard Holloway (Ed.). Darton, Longman
& Todd. 1990.
Dancing on the Edge. Richard Holloway. Fount Paperback,
HarperCollins. 1997.

> Two of many books by the retired Bishop of
> Edinburgh, whose writing is always colourful
> and provoking, although loathed by the more
> conservative brethren and sisters. Themes include

the necessary imperfection of our knowledge of
the divine and the need to be free to 'improvise'
theology and ethics.

Religious Philosophy

The highly technical, main-line Anglo-Saxon
philosophy of the Twentieth century had all but
rejected any philosophical relevance of religion.
That did not stop all philosophical thought on
the subject, however. Here are some that I found
helpful in keeping the subject alive for me.

Twentieth Century Religious Thought. John Macquarrie. 4th
Edition. SCM Press. 1988.

I have never ceased to be amazed at this author's
capacity for entering into the thought-forms of
others and then summarizing them succinctly
and critically. This is a splendid 'crib' for all students of religion, philosophy and science who are
interested in the development of the subject in
the last century.

On Selfhood and Godhood. C.A. Campbell. Allen and Unwin.
1957.

Campbell was Macquarrie's tutor, and this work
was a set-book for one of my own formal religions
courses. It is a good exercise for the mind.

Religious Language. I.T. Ramsey. SCM Press. 1957.

In the heyday of logical positivism, this book tried
to show that there are valid, empirical, religious
experiences which the author called 'moments
of disclosure'.

The Self as Agent. (Gifford Lectures.) John MacMurray. Faber
& Faber. 1957.

Philosophers in the West have generally discussed

275

the Self in terms of some sort of 'substance'–
however rarefied. MacMurray saw the Self rather
as Agent, which is more dynamic.

I and Thou. Martin Buber. T. & T. Clark. 1959

This Jewish philosopher is famous for distinguish-
ing between *I-It* relationships which we have with
things; and *I-Thou* relationships which we have
with other persons and with God.

God-Talk. John Macquarrie. SCM Press 1967.

It is important to recognise that human language
about God is quite different from our language
about the things and persons we encounter in life.
Failure to recognise this is a source of much of
the confusion in religious controversy.

Thinking about God. John Macquarrie. SCM Press. 1975.

The language of Being is especially useful for
expressing the ontological significance of the God
of the Bible where images are primarily used.

In Search of Humanity. John Macquarrie. SCM Press. 1982.
In Search of Deity. John Macquarrie. 1984.

These two books, together with *Jesus Christ in
Modern Thought* (see above) form a trilogy, cul-
minating in the author's Gifford Lectures. In
them he examines the Christian Doctrines of
God, of Humanity and then finally, the God-Man,
Jesus Christ.

God's World, God's Body. G.M. Jantzen. Darton, Longman &
Todd. 1984.

An exploration of the possibility that the Cosmos
could be regarded as 'The Body of God' by one
of Macquarrie's distinguished pupils.

276

Theology for the Third Millennium. Hans Küng. Harper Collins. 1991.

> Always worth reading, this remarkable Roman Catholic writer wrestles here with the question of how Christian Theology might have to develop in this new millennium. Big changes are needed: paradigm shifts, in fact.

The Life Divine. Sri Aurobindo. Shri Aurobindo Ashram, Pondicherry. 1955.
Recovery of Faith. Radhakrishnan. George Allen and Unwin. 1956.

> Two books by Western-educated but thoroughly Indian Hindus, whose writings were useful to me for stretching the mind and drawing attention to philosophical and religious systems other than our own.

Doctrine and Argument in Indian Philosophy. Ninian Smart. George Allen and Unwin. 1964.

> A detailed exposition of Indian philosophy by a western expert which helped me appreciate better works such as those above.

The Shroud

> Ever since I first encountered this remarkable object in a Readers' Digest article, I have had a 'gut feeling' that it must be significant for faith. This has sometimes been hard to hold onto in the teeth of the common dismissal of it as 'obviously' just another superstitious mediaeval relic like the innumerable pieces of the true cross, or the thumb of John the Baptist etc.

The Turin Shroud. Ian Wilson. Victor Gollancz Ltd. 1978.
The Blood and the Shroud. Ian Wilson. Weidenfeld & Nicholson.
1998.

Much partisan nonsense (both for and against) has
been written about this object, with both 'believers'
and 'detractors' being equally guilty of foul play
and much special pleading. This author, however,
who is a Roman Catholic historian, has always
seemed to me to be a level-headed presenter of
the issues. Although he (like me) would, I suspect,
<u>like</u> the Shroud to be found to be authentic, he
would be quite willing to abandon this wish, were
it shown to be impossible. Many suppose that
the recent dating of the cloth to the Fourteenth
Century has closed the matter permanently. But
there are genuine doubts about the validity of the
tests (without impugning the testers) and Wilson
describes these fairly. I consider the matter still to
be open, and the kind of historical reconstruction
which Wilson offers (and which I use and extend
in this myth in Cycles 21 & 22) remains entirely
conceivable and interesting.

Mythology

The word 'myth' has many technical meanings in
different disciplines. I use it to mean the biggest
story that a person or culture can tell about the
meaning of this mysterious 'existence' which we
find ourselves embarked upon. It wil be composed
of 'facts'. 'truths', supposed truths, speculations
and numinous images, Stories etc., whose truth
status is only verisimilitudinous, though possibly
false, or even obviously products of the imagination only.

Before Philosophy. H. & H.A. Frankfort, J.A. Wilson, Thorkild Jacobsen. Penguin Books. 1949.

> An insightful account of the transition from Near Eastern mythopoeic thought of the Babylonians and Egyptians, and the non- or less-mythopoeic philosophical and religious thought of the Greeks and Hebrews.

Myth and Ritual in Christianity. A.W. Watts. Thames & Hudson. 1954.

> This was the first book to acquaint me with the notion that myths are indispensable to any living religion–even an 'historical' one like Christianity. This is because all religions, by definition, are trying to understand and relate to that which is necessarily beyond human understanding. This was my 'California' period, with yoga and all that.

The Phenomenon of Man. Pierre Teilhard de Chardin. Collins. 1959.

> This Jesuit palaeontologist is well-known for his attempt to make positive use of the theory of evolution to express a Christian view of nature and humanity. Although not entirely successful, he was certainly very influential and many of us are indebted to him for his vision.

The Scope of Demythologizing. John Macquarrie. SCM Press. 1960.

> Early in the Twentieth Century there was a revolt in main-line German theology, led by Bultmann, against the mythological elements still to be found in Scripture. They considered these to be the main obstacle in the way of moderns appropriating the faith. So a programme of 'demythologising' was undertaken. Macquarrie does

his usual, clear, insightful and critical analysis of this programme. Perhaps we are now due for some 're-mythologizing'!

Myth and Mankind. Time-Life Books. 2000.

There are many compilations of the Classical Myths of Mankind. I have found this one to be good and useful.

Modern 'Mythological' Writings

Few modern writers would own up to writing mythopoeically. However, I believe that many do do without recognising the fact, or at least, have mythological elements in their works.

A Study of History. Vols 1-13. Arnold J. Toynbee. Oxford University Press. 1954ff.

This is a very impressive attempt to see the whole of human history synoptically. It is a remarkable fact that the author started out intending the treat religions incidentally, but found instead that they are the very heart and soul of civilization.

Christianity as Mystical Fact. Rudolf Steiner. Rudolf Steiner Press. (Revised) 1972.
Rudolf Steiner - Scientist of the Invisible. A.P. Shepherd. Floris Reprint 1991.

Anthroposophy is, in my opinion, an example of a modern myth, written around the turn of the nineteenth and twentieth centuries. Rudolf Steiner himself was a fine, good and clever man who attempted a synthesis of Christianity (he was originally a Roman Catholic), the scientific world-view of his time, and that tail-end of ancient mythology–theosophy. His followers, so far as I can see, have mostly not been capable of updating his thought, which has none-the-less produced some remarkable educational systems.

The Beginnings of Christianity. Andrew Welburn. Floris Books. 1991.

This is an example of an anthroposophical thinker attempting to show how Rudolf Steiner's system (see above) can be applied to the study of the historical Jesus and the rise of the church. He lays special emphasis on the contribution of Gnostic and similar ancient writings. It could doubtless supply a mythological schema for some people: for me it is only an example, with some fascinating angles.

The Cosmic Trilogy. C.S. Lewis. Pan Books. 1989. (Originally, Bodley Head.1938-1945)

This collection of three space-travel stories, while now out-of-date with respect to their technology, are excellent examples of what I would regard as a mythological work. It is possible that Lewis was partly influenced by Rudolf Steiner through his great friend Owen Barfield, though I know of no-one who has seriously explored this possibility.

The Divine Comedy. Dante. (Trans. Dorothy L. Sayers) Penguin Classics. 1955

While not 'modern' in normal usage, Dante's great work is a magnificent example of a personal myth as I understand the word. It is interesting that the main framework of this work was an already out-of-date astronomy, though many of his original readers would not perhaps have realised it.

The Lord of the Rings. J.R.R. Tolkien. Guild Publishing London. 1981.

> Tolkein was a close friend of C.S. Lewis, and like him had a gift for writing mythologically.

The Aquarian Conspiracy. Marilyn Ferguson. Routladge Kegan & Paul. 1981

> Mythological thought is alive and operating in the writings of the so-called 'New Age' move-ment. This book gives a clear outline of the phenomenon.

Dune Series. Frank Herbert. New English Library. Paperback. 1972-1984

> Mythological thought is also to be found in much science-fiction. This is a good example, being a large-scale imagining of a possible future for the human race, with remarkable technical, ecological, genetic and political shinanigans.

Four Quartets. T.S. Eliot. Faber and Faber. 1954.

> This American poet recognised the reality of the 'mythical method', and this, his greatest (though not perhaps most influential) poem is rich in mythological themes.

On the Four Quartets of T.S. Eliot. Anon. (Foreword by Roy Campbell). Vincent Stuart. 1953.

> The book most responsible for me recognising the mythological aspects in the above poem.

Religions

> It is no-longer intellectually respectable either to ignore the contributions which the major world-religions have, and are still making towards civi-lization, or to claim one of them to be the sole

possessor of ultimate religious truth. This does not mean that they are all equal 'in the eyes of God', or that they can simply be combined into some super-religion–only that they are here to stay, and will continue to grow and develop – especially in dialogue with each other.

The Varieties of Religious Experience. W. James. Collins. Fontana Books. 1960.

A 'classical' treatment of religious experiences by a great psychologist.

The Idea of the Holy. R. Otto. Penguin Books. 1959.

A phenomenological analysis of the human encounter with the divine as a *'mysterium tremendum et fascinans'*

World Religions: A Dialogue. Ninian Smart. SCM Press. 1960.

A good introduction to the thought of some major World Religions by one of the best known western scholars of the subject; using a dialogical method.

Doctrine and Argument in Indian Philosophy. Ninian Smart. George Allen & Unwin. 1964.

If one doubts that any culture other than the Greeks arrived at sophisticated philosophies, then this book would dispel that illusion.

The Religious Experience of Mankind. Ninian Smart. Fontana. 1969.

This is a good scholarly introduction to the subject. It is worth remembering though, that religion is not simply a matter 'facts' to be believed and actions to be performed: religion can only be appreciated *from within*, and any particular instance of it takes a long time to appropriate personally. Only then can they be 'judged'.

The Mediators. John Macquarrie. SCM Press. 1995.

My favourite religious author again! This time he gives a useful, short run-down of some of the major religious of the world by outlining what can be known about their founders.

The Battle for God, Karen Armstrong. Harper Collins. 2000.

An extremely well-informed and thoughtful exposition of the rise of that panic-reaction to modernism which we call 'fundamentalism'. This book is a strong antidote to all attempts to absolutize our sectional views of reality.

Psychology

In modern times, psychology has become a major contributor to our view of what it is to be a human being. As such, it will have a place in any contemporary myth. Although Freud is perhaps the best known psychologist, my preference has been for Carl Jung whose remit has a much wider mythological scope.

Experiment in Depth. P.W. Martin. Routledge & Kegan Paul. 1956.

What immediately attracted me to this book, when I originally found it, was its recognition that three of my favourite authors, T.S. Eliot, Arnold Toynbee and Carl Jung had all appreciated the place of myth in human life. The book offered a 'method' for personally finding a myth for oneself–which I seem to have done!

The Self and its Brain. Karl R. Popper & John C. Eccles. Springer International. 1977

> This is one example of a work (not very widely favoured) by a famous brain physiologist and an equally famous philosopher, that attempts to come up with an explanation of the relationship between the brain and the mind. Their approach is dualist, i.e. there are two distinct entities that interact in some way. Whether this way of seeing the matter is relevant depends upon whether dualism is really and truly dead at last, or whether it is ultimately inescapable.

Religion and the Cure of Souls in Jung's Psychology. Hans Schaer. (Trns. R.F.C. Hull) Routledge & Kegan Paul. 1951.

> Jung's unorthodox treatment of Christianity from the perspective of his clinical psychiatric experiences is very interesting and mind-bending. This book covers the ground well from a Lutheran angle.

Memories, Dreams, Reflections. C.G. Jung. Collins and Routledge & Kegan Paul. 1963.

> Jung's own autobiography allows one to assess something of his importance–although some significant (and not always creditable) aspects of his life and thought are omitted.

Psychological Types. C.G. Jung. Routledge & Kegan Paul. 1971.

> Part of Jung's psychology was a typology of styles of consciousness (of which the 'extravert' and 'introvert' types are the best known). This, along with his notion of inherited mental 'archetypes', is his most important contribution to our self-understanding.

Personality Types. Jung's Model of Typology. Daryl Sharp. Inner City Books. 1987.

> Jung's own writings are often large and rather difficult to read. This is an example of a useful explication of the above book. There are many more.

Please Understand Me: Character and Temperament Type. D. Keirsey and M. Bates. Prometheus Nemesis Book Co. 1978

> This book uses the Myers-Briggs Typology (based upn Jung's analysis of consciousness) to suggest a modern formulation of the four classical temperaments attributed mainly to Galen. I consider this a useful way of classifying people, and it is the basis of Cycle 11 in this work.

Prayer and Temperament. C. Michael and M. Norrisey. Open Door Inc. 1984.

> This is an illustration of the application of the above work on the four temperaments to the matter of styles of spiritual life and their development. Some classical styles of spirituality are best suited to one temperament and not to others; or rather, some of them are easier to use by a particular temperament *to begin with.* Then later, as one matures spiritually, the other styles should be used stretch one's underdeveloped sides and provide a road to what Jung called 'individuation'–the full rounding-out of the personality, and therefore the maturing of one's service to God.